MW00812953

THE RISE OF THE FALSE PROPHET

THE RISE OF THE FALSE PROPHET

By Jeremy Reis

Book 2 of the Final Revelation Series

DISCLAIMER

This is a work of fiction. Names, characters, businesses, places, events, locales, and incidents are either the products of the author's imagination or used in a fictitious manner. Any resemblance to actual persons, living or dead, or actual events is purely coincidental.

The views and opinions expressed in this book are those of the author and do not necessarily reflect the official policy or position of any agency or organization. Readers should not take any content or characters as literal or as a representation of reality.

The publisher and the author make no representations or warranties with respect to the accuracy or completeness of the contents of this work and specifically disclaim all warranties, including without limitation warranties of fitness for a particular purpose. No warranty may be created or extended by sales or promotional materials.

To my wife Jennica and nine beautiful children

Chapter 1

T his wasn't the first time David Mitchell felt the cold, hardened steel of a 9mm gun pressed to the back of his head.

Inside the dimly lit apartment, the smell of stale tobacco smoke hung heavy in the air.

The apartment was tiny, and the walls were cracking and peeling from the damp. The only furniture was a bed propped up against one wall, a dresser was tipped over on its side and leaning against a wall, and a recliner in the center of the room, a girl sitting on it.

"Hey, man!" a menacing voice barked from behind him. "Who the hell are you?"

"Uh, I'm here to fix the internet," David said, trying to hide the concern in his voice. "The landlord sent me."

"You're not a maintenance guy," the drug dealer snarled. "You look like a cop!"

"Listen," David replied calmly, "I promise you, I'm

just here to fix the internet. I don't want any trouble."

"Prove it!" the drug dealer demanded, keeping the gun firmly against David's skull.

"Look, man," David began, taking a deep breath. "If I was a cop, would I be here alone? Wouldn't I have backup or something?"

"Maybe you're just stupid," the drug dealer retorted, obviously unsure.

"Or maybe," David continued, his voice steady and composed, "I'm just some guy trying to do his job and get home to my family at the end of the day."

The drug dealer hesitated for a moment, weighing the truth of David's words. Finally, he lowered the gun and stepped back. "Fine," he grumbled. "Fix it."

With his back turned to the drug dealer, David worked on untangling wires. He could sense the young man's growing impatience and paranoia.

"Understood," David said, breathing a sigh of relief. He quickly finished up with the wires, all the while mentally preparing for the next phase of his plan: getting the girl out of this dangerous situation.

The drug dealer's cell phone rang, the shrill sound cutting through the tense atmosphere. He glanced at the screen and scowled. "I've got to take this," he muttered, keeping his eyes locked on David as he backed out of the room.

As soon as the door clicked shut behind him, David seized the opportunity. He turned to the hedge fund manager's daughter, Sarah, sitting on a worn-out recliner in the center of the room. Her eyes were red from crying, and she looked small and vulnerable amidst the chaos of the drug den.

"Sarah, I'm here to get you out of here," David whispered urgently, crouching down beside her.

"Who are you?" she asked, her voice trembling.

"Your father hired me to bring you home," he explained, his gaze never leaving the door. "We need to go now before your boyfriend comes back."

"No!" Sarah protested, her eyes widening with fear. "I love him! He'll be so angry if I leave!"

"Sarah, listen to me," David said firmly, his voice tinged with desperation. "You're 17 years old, and this is not the life you want. If you don't come with me right now, I'll have no choice but to call the police and have them remove you. And trust me, that won't end well for anyone involved."

She hesitated, torn between her feelings for her boyfriend and the reality of the situation she found herself in. Finally, she nodded, tears streaming down her face as she took David's outstretched hand. They crept through the apartment, David's senses on high alert as they made their way towards the exit.

As they exited the building, the drug dealer emerged from the building's side door, his eyes wild with fury as he spotted David and Sarah. Without hesitation, he raised his gun and fired several shots in their direction.

"Get down!" David shouted, pushing Sarah behind the cover of a nearby dumpster. Bullets ricocheted off the metal, and David knew they needed to move quickly if they were going to escape. He grabbed Sarah's hand and sprinted towards his car, praying they could make it without getting hit.

As they dove into the vehicle, David slammed on the gas, tires squealing as they sped away from the scene. The drug dealer's enraged shouts and gunfire faded into the distance, and Sarah buried her face in her hands, sobbing with relief.

"Thank you," she choked out between sobs. "I was so stupid to leave my dad's house. I'm so sorry."

"Hey, it's okay," David reassured her, keeping his eyes on the road as he navigated through the city streets. "You're safe now, and that's what matters."

In that moment, despite the chaos surrounding them, David was grateful for the opportunity to help someone in need – a small glimmer of hope amid the darkness that had consumed his life since his days at The Circle. And as he glanced over at Sarah, he knew he would continue fighting for those who couldn't fight for themselves, no matter the cost.

"Are you with the NYPD or the FBI?" Sarah asked, her voice shaky as she tried to process the whirlwind of events that had just occurred.

David glanced at her briefly before returning his attention to the road. "Neither," he replied. "I'm a private detective."

Sarah let out a breath she didn't know she'd been holding. "Well, thank you... for saving me."

As they drove through the city, it was impossible not to notice the stark contrast between the world as it had been only a year prior and its current state. The once-bustling metropolis was now a shell of its former self – a grim testament to the aftermath of the rapture. Abandoned cars littered the streets, their owners having died during that fateful day. Graffiti-covered walls bore messages of despair and pleas for answers, while the remaining citizens navigated their daily lives with a heavy air of uncertainty.

"Hard to believe it's already been a year since everything changed," David mused, his thoughts echoing the somber atmosphere around them.

"Sometimes it feels like a lifetime ago," Sarah agreed, staring out the window at the desolate cityscape. "So many people dead... immediately. My mom died that day. I think I did too."

"Yep," David said quietly, his memories threatening to consume him. He shook off the weight of those thoughts, focusing on the young woman beside him who still had a chance to rebuild her life. "But there are still people left, trying to make sense of everything. People like you and me – we have to keep going, and try to make the best of what's left."

Sarah nodded, wiping away tears that threatened to fall. "You're right. I can't change the past, but I can learn from it. And maybe help others along the way."

Sarah broke the silence with a small voice, "Thank you for saving me."

David just nodded, focusing on the road ahead. The day had just begun, and it was already turning out to be a really bad one.

Chapter 2

D avid Mitchell stood in front of the mirror, staring back at himself with a mix of frustration and resignation. He was no longer the respected FBI agent he once was, nor the Director of International Security at The Circle. It was 3 months since The Circle fell apart and now he was David Mitchell, private detective – an occupation he never thought he'd find himself in.

Almost one year had passed since the rapture, leaving a world in chaos and confusion. As a former employee of The Circle, David's reputation was tarnished, making it impossible to find work in law enforcement. His days were spent answering calls from desperate people pleading for help – a far cry from his previous life of taking down powerful criminals.

"Another day, another case," David muttered to himself as he buttoned up his shirt and straightened his tie. He glanced at his watch, noting the time with a sigh. "Time to get going."

Stepping outside his small apartment, the desolation that blanketed the city greeted him. Abandoned cars littered the streets and buildings showed signs of decay, a constant reminder of the lives lost and families torn apart. David's heart ached at the sight, but he pushed forward, determined to bring hope back into this broken world.

As he walked to his office, he couldn't help but reflect on the events that led to The Circle's downfall – his own role in exposing their nefarious agenda, and the price he paid for standing up against such a powerful organization.

Sometimes, late at night, he wondered if it had all been worth it.

"Morning, Mr. Mitchell," a voice called out, snapping David back to reality. It was Mrs. Jenkins, the elderly woman who owned the building where his office was located. Despite her age and frailty, she always greeted him with a smile.

"Morning, Mrs. Jenkins," David replied, offering a warm smile in return. The exchange may have been brief, but it was one of the few human connections he still had in this post-rapture world. With a slight nod, he continued up the stairs to his office.

The day's work consisted of managing a handful of cases – tracking down missing persons and gathering evidence for suspicious spouses. It was monotonous and far from the high-stakes work he had once thrived on, but it paid the bills and kept him occupied.

As the sun dipped below the horizon, David leaned back in his chair, rubbing his eyes. The isolation weighed heavily on him, and he longed for the camaraderie he had once shared with his colleagues at the FBI. But he knew that those days were gone, replaced by a new reality where trust was a luxury and hope was in short supply.

"Another day down," he whispered to himself, turning off the lights in his office before locking the door behind him. As he descended the stairs, he couldn't help but feel a pang of loneliness, accompanied by an overwhelming sense of loss.

But despite it all, David Mitchell refused to give up. He knew that there was still good left in the world, and as long as he could help even one person find hope amidst the darkness, he would continue to fight – one case at a time.

David's thoughts drifted to Lucien Morreau, the man whose rise to power had been nothing short of meteoric. Once a charismatic Prime Minister of Belgium, Morreau had become the head of The Circle, and it was under his guidance that they negotiated a historic peace treaty with Israel. David remembered when he first met Morreau – the charm, the confidence, the air of authority that surrounded him.

As David walked through the dimly lit streets in the cool evening air, deep in his reflections, he recalled the unease that had crept into him as Morreau's true nature began to reveal itself. The whispers of his colleagues, the inexplicable events, and the horrors that unfolded at the UN – all pieces of a puzzle that pointed to an unthinkable truth: Lucien Morreau was none other than the Antichrist.

"Hey, Mitchell!" a gruff voice called out from behind, snapping David out of his reverie.

"Detective Rollins," David replied, turning to face the familiar figure of a burly, middle-aged man in a worn leather jacket. He was a disheveled man with a bushy mustache and bags under his eyes, and he had a habit of casually rubbing his chin as he spoke. "What brings you to this side of town?"

"Thought I'd grab a drink after work. You know how it is." Rollins shrugged, rubbing the back of his neck. "But honestly, I wanted to talk to you. Heard you're struggling to find steady work."

"Word travels fast," David muttered, trying to mask the bitterness in his voice.

"Look, we all know what happened with The Circle wasn't your fault," Rollins said, sympathy evident in his eyes. "You were just doing your job, like the rest of us. But people are scared. They don't want to take chances on someone who's been associated with... well, you know."

"An organization that tried to take over the world?" David finished for him, his jaw clenched. "Yeah, I've heard that one before."

Rollins cleared his throat, "Actually, I came across something that might interest you. A friend of mine at a security penetration testing firm, Twilight Technologies, mentioned they're looking for someone to do some physical security testing. I don't have all the details, but they pay well. Interested?"

David raised an eyebrow, "Physical security testing? Sounds intriguing. I'm always willing to talk to someone."

"Good," Rollins nodded, "I'll set it up. Might be the break you're looking for."

"Thanks, Rollins," David said, managing a weak smile. "I appreciate it."

"Anytime," Rollins replied, clapping David on the back. "Now come on – let's go get that drink. My treat."

As they headed towards a nearby bar, David felt a renewed sense of purpose. The world might have changed, but opportunities still existed for those willing to seize them. And David Mitchell was more than ready to take on whatever challenges lay ahead.

Chapter 3

D avid sat at the edge of his bed, cradling his head in his hands. Every morning brought a new wave of anxiety and uncertainty, as he struggled to find a way to reclaim his life. He thought about the people he had left behind when The Circle fell, the friends and colleagues who were now scattered to the wind.

He thought about Becca.

How long had it been since he last talked to her? Three weeks now?

Feeling the weight of his thoughts, David reached for the TV remote on his nightstand, hoping to distract himself for a moment. He turned on the TV and began flipping through the channels, the images flashing by in a blur of colors and sounds.

Suddenly, he landed on a channel broadcasting a live event. The camera panned over a massive auditorium filled with thousands of people, all focused on the charismatic figure on stage. The banner behind him read, "The Power of You."

"Remember, you hold the power to your own future!" the man, Gabriel Vale, proclaimed with fervor. His voice echoed through the auditorium, amplified by the speakers. "You are the master of your destiny! Don't let anyone or anything hold you back from achieving greatness!"

David watched for a moment, taking in the scene. There was something about Gabriel's demeanor, the way he spoke, that sent a shiver down David's spine. It wasn't the message itself, but the energy behind it. There was an underlying negativity, a force that David couldn't quite put his finger on, but it made him uncomfortable.

With a grimace, David quickly turned off the TV, the screen going black. The brief distraction had done little to ease his mind, and he was once again consumed by his thoughts.

It seemed like everyone was suffering, and David couldn't shake the feeling that it was his fault.

The sound of his phone ringing snapped him out of his thoughts. Picking it up, he saw Chaz's name on the screen. David hesitated for a moment before answering.

"Hello?" he said cautiously.

"Hey David, it's Chaz," came the warm, familiar voice of his pastor. "I just wanted to check in with you, see how you're doing."

"Thanks, Chaz. I'm... I'm hanging in there," he replied, trying to sound more confident than he felt.

"Good to hear," Chaz said, though he could sense the strain in David's voice. "We've really missed you at church, you know. Things haven't been the same since you left."

David felt a pang of guilt. "Yeah, I miss it too. But right now, I need to focus on finding a job and getting my life back on track."

"Of course," Chaz agreed. "But don't forget that you have a community here who cares about you and wants to help. You don't have to face this alone."

David looked around his small apartment, the walls closing in around him, and the weight of his past pressing down on his chest. It was hard to feel anything but isolation.

"Sometimes it feels like I am alone, Chaz," he admitted, his voice cracking. "I've been turned away from so many jobs because of my association with The Circle. People are afraid of me, or they think I'm some kind of monster. It's... it's hard."

"David," Chaz said softly, concern evident in his tone, "you're not a monster. You're a good man who took down evil. And the people who truly know you – we're not afraid of you. We believe in you."

"Thanks, Chaz," David whispered, the tears gathering in his eyes. "I just wish I could find a way to make everyone else see that too."

"Give it time," Chaz advised. "Keep doing the right thing, and eventually, people will come around. Trust in God, and trust in yourself."

"Trust," David mused, letting the word roll around his mind. It had been a long time since he'd allowed himself to do that.

"Stay strong, David," Chaz encouraged. "You've overcome so much already, and I have faith that you'll rise above this too. Just remember – you're never alone."

"Thank you, Chaz," David said, wiping away his tears as they ended the call. As he sat there, he felt a small spark ignite within him – a flicker of hope that perhaps things would get better.

Suddenly, his phone buzzed with a new message. It was from Detective Rollins. "Twilight Technologies wants to speak with you about a security testing assignment. Mid five-figure deal. Interested?"

David's heart raced. This could be the opportunity he was waiting for. He quickly typed back, "Absolutely. Always willing to talk."

As he set his phone down, the weight on his shoulders felt a little lighter. Maybe, just maybe, things were starting to turn around.

Chapter 4

Amidst the bustling CIA headquarters, Becca Lawrence sat at her desk, her eyes darting between the multiple screens before her. Each displayed a different piece of the ever-changing global puzzle, from grainy surveillance footage to encrypted intelligence reports. The hum of activity around her was constant, like the buzz of bees in a hive, but Becca's focus never wavered.

"New data coming in," she muttered to herself, furiously typing as her mind raced to keep up with the flood of information. It had been months since the disintegration of The Circle, and the world was still reeling from the power vacuum it left behind. Nations vied for dominance while the new US Presidential administration struggled to assert its control.

Becca knew that the stakes were higher than ever, and her responsibility to protect her country and her daughter weighed heavily on her shoulders. Her fingers flew across the keyboard as she analyzed the data, piecing together threads of potential threats and calculating their impact on global security.

She squinted at one of the screens, pausing for a moment to process the significance of a particular report. "Has this been verified?" she asked, her voice barely audible above the din of her colleagues' conversations.

"Working on it," came a reply from a few desks away.

"Keep me updated," Becca said, her tone firm yet professional.

As she continued her analysis, her thoughts briefly drifted to Leila, her ten-year-old daughter. How would she explain the complexities of this world to her? How could she ensure a stable, secure life for her child amidst such chaos? With a silent sigh, Becca pushed those thoughts aside. Now was not the time for distraction.

"Analysis complete," she finally murmured to herself, the lines of code on her screen painting a picture that was all too familiar – instability, fear, and conflict. She leaned back in her chair, her eyes focused and her mind sharp, knowing that the real work was just beginning. The world needed her expertise now more than ever, and Becca Lawrence was determined not to let it down.

She turned to her colleague, a seasoned agent named Jack, who was hunched over his own workstation.

"Jack, have you seen this?" Becca asked, gesturing to one of her screens. "There's unusual activity in Europe, specifically threats about possible terrorist attacks."

"We're always getting reports of 'possible terrorist attacks' in Europe," Jack replied, his voice gruff but focused. He strode over to Becca's desk, his brow furrowed as he examined the data on the screen. "Could be related to that arms shipment last week. We need to analyze this further."

"Agreed, maybe less sarcasm in your voice next time," Becca said, her mind already racing with possibilities as they dove into the data together. They exchanged theories and information, their conversation a rapid-fire volley of intelligence and strategy.

"Could be the remnants of The Circle trying to regroup," Jack mused, rubbing the stubble on his chin thoughtfully. He gave Becca a half smile.

"Or a new threat entirely," Becca countered, her gaze never leaving the screen. "We can't afford to underestimate them." Her thoughts were fully absorbed in the task at hand, the weight of global security resting on her capable shoulders.

Just then, her phone rang, the shrill tone piercing through the loudness of the office. She glanced at the caller

ID, seeing the name of Leila's school flash across the screen. Becca hesitated for a moment, her focus momentarily divided, before answering the call.

"Hello?" she said, her voice betraying a hint of concern.

"Ms. Lawrence, this is Principal Martin. I'm calling to let you know that Leila isn't feeling well. She has a fever, and we think it's best if she goes home."

"Of course, I'll be right there," Becca replied, her heart clenching with worry for her daughter. She knew it was probably just a cold, but that didn't ease the instinctual concern of a mother.

"Jack, I need to step out for a bit," Becca said, her voice tense as she collected her things. "Leila's sick and needs to be picked up from school."

"Go ahead, we've got this covered," Jack reassured her, his eyes understanding and supportive. "Family comes first."

"Don't let the director hear you say that," Becca joked, her professionalism momentarily giving way to humor as she rushed out of the office, her thoughts now consumed by her daughter's well-being.

Becca sprinted through the sterile halls of the CIA headquarters, her shoes clicking urgently against the tile floor. Her mind raced with thoughts of Leila's flushed cheeks and feverish eyes, and she pushed aside the nagging worry that she was abandoning her post at a critical time.

The world could wait; right now, her daughter needed her.

"Lord, help me," she prayed silently as she threw open the exit doors, blinking against the harsh sunlight before climbing into her car. She started the engine and pulled away from the curb, her hands gripping the steering wheel tightly.

Chapter 5

M ommy!" Leila exclaimed when Becca entered the nurse's office at her school. The little girl's face was pale, her eyes glazed with discomfort.

"Hey, sweetheart," Becca murmured, pulling Leila into her arms and feeling her forehead. It was hot to the touch, confirming the principal's assessment. "Let's get you home and into bed, okay?"

"Okay," Leila sniffled, burying her face in her mother's shoulder. As Becca carried her out to the car, she couldn't help but think about how different their lives would be if not for her career – if she had never become involved in the dangerous world of intelligence and global security.

"Mom?" Leila asked softly as Becca pulled onto the highway, her voice small and weak. "Am I gonna be okay?"

"Of course you will, sweetie," Becca reassured her, reaching over to squeeze her hand. "It's just a cold. You'll feel better in no time." But even as she spoke, her mind flickered back to the office, to the conversations about Europe and the potential threats looming on the horizon. How could she protect her daughter from something so vast and unknown?

"Promise?" Leila whispered, her eyes heavy and tearful.

"I promise," Becca said firmly, her resolve crystallizing. She would do whatever it took to keep Leila safe, both from the distant dangers of the world and from the simple, everyday trials of life. With a silent prayer for strength and guidance, she drove on, determined to be the mother her daughter needed her to be.

Leila's shallow breaths filled the small bedroom as Becca tucked the blanket snugly around her daughter's shivering body. The feverish sheen on the girl's forehead sent a pang of worry through Becca, but she knew she had to stay strong for her child.

"Get some rest, sweetheart," Becca said softly, brushing damp strands of hair away from Leila's face. "I'll be right here if you need anything."

"Thanks, Mom." Leila's voice was barely a whisper, her eyes fluttering closed.

Becca watched Leila drift off to sleep before pulling out her encrypted phone. While one hand remained protectively on her daughter's arm, the other scrolled through intelligence reports and surveillance footage that she had missed while attending to Leila. Her mind raced to connect the dots, analyzing potential threats and formulating strategies to counter them.

"Europe...what are they planning?" Becca muttered under her breath, her eyes narrowing at the data streaming across the screen. The Biblical prophecies echoed in her mind, reminding her of the Tribulation and the dwindling time they had left. The weight of the world's fate pressed down on her, but she wouldn't let it break her spirit. She had Leila to think about. What kind of world was her daughter going to inherit?

The sound of Leila's slow, steady breathing filled the dimly lit room as Becca sat by her daughter's bedside. She watched the rise and fall of Leila's chest. A tinge of worry lingered in Becca's heart.

Her phone vibrated on the nightstand, startling her from her silent vigil. She glanced at the screen, her brow furrowing when she saw it was a call from one of her colleagues at the CIA.

"Go ahead," she whispered, careful not to wake Leila.

"Becca, there's been an attack in downtown Berlin," her coworker's voice came through the speaker, urgent and strained. "Multiple bombs. We think it's connected to the chatter you saw earlier today."

Her heart skipped a beat, but she kept her voice steady. "How bad is it?"

"Very. Casualties are in the dozens, and they're still counting. The bombing was concentrated in the business district, and it was still early morning there. Not a lot of people around." The raw emotion in his voice betrayed the gravity of the situation. "We need you back at the office, now."

"Understood." Her mind raced, calculating the minutes it would take to get to headquarters. "Give me an hour."

"See you soon," he replied before hanging up.

Setting the phone down, Becca looked at Leila's peaceful face and felt the familiar tug between duty and motherhood. With a deep breath, she dialed her mother's number.

"Mom?" she whispered into the phone, glancing again at Leila. "I know it's short notice, but I need you to come watch Leila. Something's happened at work."

"Is everything alright?" Her mother's concerned voice echoed through the line.

"Leila has a fever, but I think she'll be okay. I just can't leave her alone right now," Becca explained, her voice wavering for a moment.

"Of course, dear. I'll be there as soon as I can."

"Thank you, Mom." The relief in Becca's voice was palpable.

As she hung up, Becca gazed at her daughter one more time, brushing a strand of hair from her forehead. A silent prayer crossed her lips, asking for strength and protection for both Leila and the countless lives affected by the attacks.

Becca heard the front door open, announcing her mother's arrival. Becca turned, her eyes shiny with unshed tears, as her mother entered the room. The lines of worry etched across her mother's face mirrored Becca's own turmoil.

"Go," her mother urged softly, placing a reassuring hand on Becca's shoulder. "I'll take good care of her."

"Thank you, Mom." Becca managed a weak smile, though her heart ached with the choice before her. She hesitated at the doorway, torn between the fierce need to protect her daughter and the urgent call to serve her country.

"Lord, give me strength," she prayed silently, steeling herself for what was to come.

With a final glance back, Becca stepped out of the room, her footsteps echoing down the hallway as she hurried towards the door. As she stepped into the chilly night air, the wind whipped around her, as if urging her forward.

As the city lights blurred past her, Becca's mind raced with thoughts of Leila, of the terrorists wreaking havoc on innocent lives, and of the delicate balance she walked every day between motherhood and duty. But she knew in her heart that, with God's help, she would find the strength to do what was necessary – for her daughter, for her country, and for herself.

Chapter 6

The CIA headquarters was buzzing with activity when Becca arrived. Agents and analysts were huddled in groups, their faces grim, their voices a low murmur of shared information and theories. The large screens on the walls displayed news footage of the aftermath in Berlin, with smoke rising from the bombed sites and emergency services rushing to help.

Jack was waiting for her at her workstation, his face lined with fatigue. He looked up as she approached, his eyes searching hers for a moment before he began to speak.

"Becca," he began, his voice low and urgent, "the situation's a mess. The bombing was executed using a rental truck. It targeted an office building, a local café, and a data center."

Becca's eyes sharpened. "How bad is the damage?"

"The office building took a hit, but it's still standing. Most of the damage was to the exterior. The café, a popular French spot, was almost entirely destroyed. The data center suffered partial damage, but it's significant enough to disrupt their operations," Jack explained, pointing to the images on the screen.

Becca hunched over her desk, her eyes intense. A pen dangled from her right hand, and her fingers tapped its rhythm on the desk top. Becca leaned in, studying the images. "Any leads on who's behind this?"

Jack shook his head. "No group has claimed responsibility yet. It could be anyone from the Red Army Faction to Al Qaeda. We're still gathering intel."

Becca frowned, her mind racing. "What's the significance of the office building?"

Jack glanced at his notes. "It appears to be an insurance company. Nothing that stands out as a typical target."

"And the café?"

"Just a local French café. No known affiliations or controversies," Jack replied.

Becca's gaze lingered on the image of the damaged data center. "Tell me more about this data center."

Jack adjusted his glasses. "It's a cloud hosting firm. They have a variety of clients, ranging from small businesses to larger corporations. We're still digging into their client list to see if there's any connection."

Two thoughts struck Becca. "The insurance company is an intriguing target. Maybe someone screwed out of a claim gets revenge? In that case, localized terrorism is not the CIA's mandate. Alternate theory: could the bombing be related to someone using the hosting center? Maybe it's not about the physical location but the data it holds."

The leather chair squeaked as Jack leaned back, settling in. "Your second theory is interesting. It's a possibility. If someone wanted to disrupt or access specific data, targeting the data center would make sense."

Becca nodded, her mind working overtime. "We need to get a list of all the clients using that data center, especially any recent additions. There might be a connection there."

Jack agreed. "I'll get the team on it. We'll comb through every piece of data and see if anything stands out."

Becca took a deep breath, steeling herself for the task ahead. "We need to get to the bottom of this, Jack. Find out who's behind it and why," she said firmly.

Jack nodded. "I'll get the team working on it right away."

Becca tapped her pen against her desk, considering their options. She paused, then added, "We should also look into the source notes from the chatter earlier today. This might not be the last attack in Europe. Let's look at the rental truck company records."

Jack raised an eyebrow. "You think there may be connections between this attack and other threats?"

"It's possible," Becca replied. "If we can find a pattern or common thread, we might be able to trace back to the source."

Alone in her office, Becca began piecing together what she knew so far.

The targets seemed random and weren't major hubs of activity. It suggested someone was going after specific information or data rather than just causing chaos for its own sake. The data center seemed to be the key; if they could identify who had been using its services recently then they might have a lead on whoever was responsible for the bombing. With that thought in mind, Becca set off to start tracking down leads and gathering evidence for what she was certain would be a long and complicated investigation.

Chapter 7

The elevator doors slid open, revealing a dimly lit hallway adorned with cheap, framed art that seemed to be chosen more for their nondescript nature than any aesthetic appeal. David Mitchell stepped out, glancing around the bland space. The carpet beneath his feet was a dull shade of gray, matching the walls that seemed to absorb the already limited light. The air was stagnant, carrying the faint scent of stale coffee.

Following the room numbers, David found himself outside a door with a simple plaque reading "Twilight Technologies." He took a deep breath and knocked.

The door opened to reveal an equally uninspiring office. The furniture was basic, the kind one might find in a budget catalog, and the walls were barren save for a whiteboard with a few scribbled notes. David couldn't help but comment, "Quite the... minimalist setup you have here."

A woman with sharp features and a no-nonsense demeanor extended her hand. "Clara Napier, Vice President of Operations. And yes, the barrenness is intentional. In our line of work, it's best not to draw attention."

David shook her hand, noting the firm grip. "David Mitchell. I was expecting something... different."

Before Clara could reply, a door at the far end of the room opened, and a tall man with salt-and-pepper hair stepped out. "Ah, good, you waited for me," he said, adjusting his tie. "Apologies for the delay. Just wrapped up a conference call with our client, Horizon Holdings."

David nodded, recognizing the name. "Julian Knight, I presume?"

Julian smiled, extending his hand. "The one and only. Pleasure to finally meet you, David."

"The feeling's mutual," David replied, taking a seat as Julian motioned for him to do so.

Julian leaned forward, his blue eyes sharp and assessing. "So, David, Horizon Holdings has contracted us to perform security penetration testing on their systems. They want to ensure their defenses are robust and can withstand any potential threats. Are you familiar with penetration testing?"

David raised an eyebrow, intrigued. "I've had some experience, yes. It's essentially testing a system by simulating an attack, correct?"

Julian nodded, clearly pleased. "Exactly. We're looking for vulnerabilities, weak points that could be exploited. And we believe you have the unique skill set to help us with this."

David leaned back, processing the information. "Horizon Holdings is a major player. This won't be a walk in the park."

Clara interjected, "Which is precisely why we need someone of your caliber. Your background, your experience with the FBI, even with The Circle... it's invaluable."

David's eyes momentarily darkened at the mention of The Circle, a shadow passing over his face. He had hoped that part of his life was behind him, but it seemed to follow him like a persistent ghost.

Clara, noticing the slight wince, continued, "I understand your past with The Circle might be... sensitive. But it's precisely that experience we value. While we at Twilight Technologies are adept at digital penetration testing, we need someone with a unique set of skills to test the physical barriers."

Julian leaned in, his gaze intense. "Horizon Holdings isn't just another tech company, David. They're at the forefront of next-generation payment technologies. Imagine a world where transactions are instantaneous, where currency barriers are non-existent. That's the future Horizon is building. And their source code? It's the blueprint."

David nodded, absorbing the information. "So, you want me to break into a facility and download this blueprint?"

"In essence, yes," Clara replied. "But remember, the source code is likely encrypted. Even if you get it, it'll be gibberish without the decryption key. Our goal isn't to steal their work but to prove it can be done. If you can deliver that encrypted code to us, you'll have proven their physical security measures are lacking."

David leaned back, processing the enormity of the task. "You're asking me to break into one of the most advanced tech companies in the world, bypass their security, and download their crown jewel?"

Julian smiled, "When you put it that way, it does sound quite thrilling, doesn't it?"

David smirked, "Thrilling or insane. But I'm intrigued. What's the plan?"

Clara pulled out a tablet, tapping a few times before turning it to face David. A blueprint of a large facility appeared on the screen. "This is Horizon's main R&D center. The source code is stored here."

David studied the layout, noting the security checkpoints, camera placements, and potential entry and exit points. "This won't be easy."

"That's why we called you," Julian said with a hint of amusement. "We'll provide you with all the intel we have, but the execution? That's all you."

David raised an eyebrow, his gaze shifting between Clara and Julian. "So, what's the compensation for a job of this magnitude?"

Clara leaned forward, her fingers interlacing on the table. "We're offering $50,000 for this assignment. $35,000 will be provided upfront, and the remaining $15,000 upon completion."

David's eyes widened slightly. It was a substantial amount, but given the risk involved, he wasn't entirely surprised. "And if I find a vulnerability?"

Julian grinned, "If you crack their security and expose a vulnerability, our client has agreed to a $10,000 bonus. But even if you don't, you keep the initial $50,000."

David considered the offer, his mind calculating the risks and rewards. "And if things go south? If I get caught?"

Julian's grin faded, replaced by a serious expression. "If you get caught, you call me immediately. I'll have a 'get out of jail free' card ready for you. But David, let's be clear: you're testing their security systems. Getting caught would be considered a failure. We don't want to fail with this project."

David nodded, understanding the implications. "And the timeframe?"

"You have 60 days," Clara replied. "Horizon Holdings has asked us to move quickly."

David took a deep breath, feeling the weight of the decision before him. The money was tempting, and the challenge even more so.

He looked up, meeting Julian's gaze. "Alright. I'm in. But I'll need complete access to all the intel you have on Horizon. And I'll operate on my terms."

Julian extended his hand, a satisfied smile playing on his lips. "Agreed. Welcome aboard, David."

As they shook hands, David couldn't help but feel a mix of excitement and trepidation. He was about to embark on one of the most challenging assignments of his career.

As he left Twilight's offices, he pulled out his cell phone and texted Nadia, "I need your help with something."

Chapter 8

T he quaint coffee shop on the corner of 7th Street was a favorite of locals, known for its rich brews and artisan pastries. David had chosen it for its quiet ambiance, a place where he could discuss business without the usual city din. He was early, securing a corner table with a view of the entrance. He nervously tapped his fingers on the table, waiting for Nadia.

His head snapped up when the bell above the door jingled. Nadia walked in, her dark hair pulled back in a loose ponytail, but she wasn't alone. Right behind her was Becca, her blue eyes scanning the room until they landed on David. A rush of emotions flooded him: surprise, happiness, and a twinge of guilt.

"David," Nadia greeted, her voice light, "I hope you don't mind. I brought Becca along."

David stood up, trying to mask his surprise. "Of course not. It's good to see you, Becca."

Becca gave a small smile, her gaze searching his. "You too, David. It's been a while."

The trio settled into their seats, the initial awkwardness palpable. David cleared his throat, "I didn't expect to see you here, Becca."

She tilted her head, her expression thoughtful. "Nadia mentioned she was meeting someone for coffee. When she said it was you, I thought it might be a good time to catch up."

David nodded, taking a sip of his coffee to buy himself a moment. He cared deeply for Becca, but the complexities of their respective worlds had created a chasm he wasn't sure how to bridge. "I've been meaning to reach out," he began, "but things have been... complicated."

Becca's eyes softened. "I've missed you, David. I wish you'd talked to me instead of pulling away."

David sighed, running a hand through his hair. "I didn't want to be a liability for you, especially with your position at the CIA. I thought I was protecting you."

Becca reached across the table, her fingers brushing against his. "You don't get to make that decision for me."

Nadia, sensing the tension, interjected, "So, David, you mentioned needing some help?"

Grateful for the change in topic, David nodded. "Yes, I've taken on a security penetration gig for a company called Horizon Holdings. I could use some expertise, especially on the digital front."

Nadia raised an eyebrow, intrigued. "Sounds challenging. What's the objective?"

David explained the details of the assignment, emphasizing the importance of the physical and digital aspects of the operation.

Becca listened intently, her analytical mind already processing the information. "Horizon Holdings is a major player in the tech world. This won't be easy."

David met her gaze, a hint of a smile playing on his lips. "That's why I need the best."

Nadia chuckled, "Well, you've come to the right place. Count me in."

Becca hesitated for a moment, then nodded. "I can't be involved in the operation, but giving you some hypothetical advice may be fun."

David's heart swelled with gratitude. "Thank you, both of you."

David leaned forward, his eyes alight with the spark of a plan. "I've got a couple of ideas on how to break their security," he began, his voice low and conspiratorial.

"First, we'll need some USB drives—ones that we can load with a payload to exploit their network."

Nadia nodded, her fingers already tapping away at her laptop. "I can handle that. A bit of coding, and we can create a backdoor as soon as someone plugs them in."

"Next, we'll need some smart personal-sized coffee makers. This will take a little coding, but I think it will be worth it."

Becca replied, "You're thinking you could use them as a trojan horse?"

David shook his head, "Sort of, I have a different idea in mind."

After an hour of brainstorming, Nadia shut her laptop with a decisive click, breaking the intense concentration that had settled over the table. "I've got to head out," she announced, gathering her belongings. "There's a lot of code to write for these exploits, and I need to get started."

Becca's gaze shifted to Nadia, her eyes silently asking if she was expected to leave as well. Nadia caught the look and, with a knowing smile, said, "Why don't you two spend some time hashing out the operational details? I think you've got some catching up to do."

With a wink, Nadia stood up, slinging her bag over her shoulder. "Good luck, you two," she called out as she made her way to the exit, leaving David and Becca alone at the table.

David shifted in his seat, a mix of excitement and nervousness evident in his eyes. The ambient noise of the coffee shop seemed to fade as the weight of the moment settled between them.

Becca took a deep breath, her gaze steady on David. "I know you think you were protecting me by keeping your distance," she began, her voice soft but firm. "But David, we're living in the end times. I don't need protection from you. I need you in my life, standing by my side, protecting me. We've been through too much together for you to just disappear on me."

David looked down, guilt evident on his face. "I'm sorry, Becca," he murmured. "I thought I was doing the right thing, but I realize now how wrong I was. I've missed you... and Leila. Every day."

Becca's eyes softened, the hurt and confusion giving way to understanding. "A good start would be seeing you at church again this Sunday," she suggested gently. "The whole crew misses you, David. We're a family, and it hasn't been the same without you."

David nodded, a small smile playing on his lips. "I'll be there," he promised. "And thank you, Becca. For understanding, for forgiving, and for being there."

The two of them sat in comfortable silence for a moment, the weight of the past few weeks lifting as they reconnected. The challenges ahead were daunting, but with each other's support, they felt ready to face whatever came their way.

Chapter 9

The sun was setting, casting a golden hue over the city as David parked his car a block away from the Horizon Holdings building. From his vantage point, he could see the impressive structure, its sleek glass facade reflecting the city lights. He took out his binoculars and began observing the entrance.

David had been staking out the building for days, trying to find a weak point in their security. But so far, Horizon Holdings seemed to be a fortress. He had tried the old trick of calling in food deliveries to see if he could get a sense of the building's inner workings. But each delivery person was stopped right at the lobby. If security didn't have a record of someone placing an order, the delivery person wouldn't get past the first set of doors. And if they did have a record, the delivery person was held at the security desk until the employee came down to pick up the order. No one was allowed past the lobby without proper clearance.

David sighed, frustrated. He had hoped to use the food delivery angle to get a better look inside, maybe even plant a bug or two. But that plan was now off the table.

He tried scattering the USB drives that Nadia had prepared. They were loaded with custom code that, when plugged into a computer, would give them remote access. David had discreetly dropped a few in the parking lot, hoping an employee would pick one up and plug it into their system out of curiosity. But Horizon Holdings seemed to be one step ahead. As employees entered the building, they passed through a scanner in the lobby. Any USB drives were immediately detected and confiscated by security.

David leaned back in his seat, rubbing his temples. This was going to be harder than he thought. He needed a new plan, and fast.

He took out his phone and dialed Nadia. "Hey, it's me," he said when she picked up. "The USB plan didn't work. They've got scanners in the lobby. Looks like we need to move to plan B."

Nadia sighed on the other end. "I was afraid of that," she said. "Horizon Holdings is known for their tight security. But I'm not sure plan B will work."

David was engrossed in his surveillance, his focus solely on the Horizon Holdings building. So engrossed, in fact, that he didn't notice the first security guard approaching his car. It was only when he saw the second one out of the corner of his eye that he realized he was no longer alone.

The security guard closest to David's car had a stern expression, his hand resting on the holster of his gun. "Sir, I'm going to need you to step out of your vehicle," he said in a commanding tone.

David's heart raced, but he kept his composure. He glanced to his left and saw the other guard, positioned behind a pillar, gun drawn and pointed at a 45-degree angle, ready to take action if needed.

Putting on his best southern accent, David replied, "No problem, sir. How can I help you?" He slowly opened the car door and stepped out, making sure to keep his hands visible.

The security guard took a step closer, his eyes scanning David from head to toe. "Sir, you've been sitting in your car for some time and acting suspiciously. I need to see some ID, sir."

David nodded, his mind racing. "No problem, son. I've got it right here." He reached into his pocket and pulled out a fake ID he had kept from his days at the Bureau. The ID read 'Randy Johnson' from Memphis, Tennessee.

The security guard took the ID and examined it closely. David continued, "You see, I own a window washing business. I was told that if I came down here, I might be able to get a meeting with the building owner. But no one would let me in the building. So, I've just been waiting out here, hoping the building manager might have some time for me."

The security guard looked skeptical but seemed to relax a bit. "You should have checked in with the front desk," he said, handing back the ID.

David nodded, feigning embarrassment. "I tried, but they wouldn't let me past the lobby. I figured I'd wait out here a bit longer, see if I could catch someone on their way out."

The security guard sighed. "Alright, Mr. Johnson. But I'm going to have to ask you to move along. Can't have people loitering around the building."

David nodded, his southern accent still in place. "Of course, sir. I apologize for any inconvenience. I'll be on my way."

The security guards watched as David got back into his car and drove off. Once he was a safe distance away, David let out a sigh of relief. That had been close.

Chapter 10

The room was stark, with plain gray walls and a long wooden table surrounded by chairs. The overhead lights cast a harsh glow, making the atmosphere feel even more tense. At one end of the table sat Julian and Clara from Twilight Technologies, their expressions unreadable. Next to them was Richard Allen, the VP from Horizon Holdings, looking confident and slightly smug.

Richard wore a black suit, white shirt and red tie with a thin black strip lined with small gold fleur-de-lis. He had short, neatly trimmed hair and a neatly trimmed beard. He was mid-forties but could easily pass for a man in his thirties.

David Mitchell stood at the other end, a projector screen behind him displaying the title: "Horizon Holdings Security Assessment."

The weight of the presentation pressed heavily on his shoulders, but it was a weight he welcomed. The excitement bubbled up inside him, a feeling he hadn't experienced in months. This was his chance to truly impress both Twilight and Horizon, to showcase his skills and expertise. He had meticulously prepared for this presentation, pouring over every detail, ensuring that every slide was perfect, every point was concise. He knew the stakes were high, but the potential rewards were even higher.

The possibility of a future with Twilight was tantalizing. David could see himself working alongside their team, delving into the intricate world of cybersecurity, and making a real difference. The thought of potentially joining them as a contractor or even an employee was exhilarating. It had been months since he felt this good about his work, this proud of what he had accomplished. The dark cloud that had been hanging over him seemed to lift slightly, replaced by a glimmer of hope and optimism. This presentation was more than just a job to David; it was a chance at a new beginning, a brighter future. He took a deep breath, squared his shoulders, and stepped into the room, ready to seize the opportunity before him.

David cleared his throat, adjusting his tie slightly. "Thank you all for being here today. As you know, I was tasked with testing the physical security measures of

Horizon Holdings." He clicked a remote, and the screen changed to show a list of his attempts.

"First, we tried the direct approach," David began, detailing the various delivery services he had sent in. "Each one was turned away at the lobby. No exceptions." The screen showed images of delivery personnel being stopped by security.

"Next, we sent in repair technicians, from various service providers. None of these individuals knew what we were doing, we called in a service request to see how the security team would react. Again, none made it past the security checkpoint." The screen shifted to show images of technicians being questioned and then escorted out.

"We also dropped USB drives in the parking lot, hoping an employee might pick one up and plug it into a company computer." David clicked again, and the screen showed CCTV footage of security personnel collecting the drives. "From what we could tell, all of them were confiscated."

Richard leaned back in his chair, a smirk playing on his lips. "Impressive security measures, wouldn't you say?"

David nodded, "Absolutely. Your team has done an excellent job in training and implementing security protocols." He paused for effect. "However, that's not the end of the story."

Richard raised an eyebrow, his smirk fading slightly. "Go on."

David continued, "We also tried a more indirect approach. We impersonated IT personnel and made calls to several employees, trying to gain remote access." He clicked the remote, and the screen played recordings of the calls, each one ending with the employee refusing to give out any information.

Richard's smirk returned. "So, as I said, you failed."

David smiled, a hint of mischief in his eyes. "Not quite. Let's get to the interesting part of the report."

The room was filled with a palpable tension as David Mitchell continued his presentation. The stark gray walls of the conference room seemed to close in on the attendees, the only splash of color coming from the three small, sleek coffee makers placed neatly on the table in front of Julian, Clara, and Richard.

"Once our initial attempts failed," David began, his voice steady, "we decided to think outside the box." He gestured towards the coffee makers. "These are not just any coffee makers. They're Bluetooth-enabled personal devices that we purchased from a Chinese wholesaling site. They come with both the device and the source code for a mobile app, allowing them to be white-labeled."

Richard's brow furrowed in confusion, but David continued, "I altered the code of the app to display a login screen during setup." He paused, letting the implication sink in. "The recipient could falsely believe the app needed the credentials to install, but in reality, it needed them to connect to the network."

Richard interrupted, his voice edged with disbelief, "But we have MAC address filtering on our network. No unauthorized devices can connect."

David nodded, "Yes, you do have MAC filtering. That's why I didn't rely on the device connecting to the network. Instead, I did it through the app. The cell phone, being an authorized device on the network, was our way in."

He clicked a button, and the projector displayed a mock-up of the app's login screen. "We shipped 22 of these coffee makers to your development staff," David continued. "Each one came with a letter from Horizon, congratulating the employee on their outstanding performance in the past quarter."

Richard's face paled as the realization hit him. David pressed on, "Out of the 22 recipients, 12 took the coffee makers home. Eight either didn't install the app or didn't provide their credentials. But two of them did. One of them was a manager."

The room was silent, the weight of David's words hanging heavily in the air. "With the app installed," David said, "it downloaded everything from your internal source code repository and uploaded it to a file-sharing website. Of course, the source code is encrypted, so it isn't immediately usable. But the mere fact that we could access it is concerning."

He handed Richard a folder. "You'll find the address to the zip file in your final report."

Richard took the folder, his hands trembling slightly. The room was silent for a moment, the gravity of the situation sinking in. David had not only exposed the vulnerabilities in Horizon's security but had also shown them just how easily they could be exploited.

Julian finally broke the silence, "Thank you, David. This has been an eye-opening presentation. We clearly have some work to do."

David nodded, "That's the goal. To find the vulnerabilities before someone with malicious intent does."

The meeting concluded shortly after, but the impact of David's findings would be felt for a long time to come.

The conference room was quiet now, the tension that had filled the air just moments ago dissipating with the presentation's completion. Julian's gaze lingered on David, an unreadable expression on his face. David relied on his FBI training and experience to read Julian's emotions, but it was like trying to decipher hieroglyphics. Julian's face gave nothing away; it was almost as if he had no emotions at all.

"David, could you stay back for a minute?" Julian's voice was calm, but there was an undercurrent of seriousness that wasn't lost on David.

Clara, sensing the shift in atmosphere, escorted Richard out with a polite smile. "Thank you for your hard work, David," Richard said, offering a firm handshake. "Your contribution has been invaluable."

Once the door clicked shut, Julian motioned for David to sit. "You've done an excellent job, David. Twilight will definitely keep you in mind for future projects." The hard lines of Julian's face fell away. He smiled, a broad smile that pushed up the corners of his mouth and crinkled his eyes to show a row of teeth.

David nodded, a sense of relief washing over him. "Thank you, Julian. I appreciate the opportunity."

But as Julian leaned forward, the weight of the situation pressed down on David once more. Julian's piercing blue eyes seemed to see right through him. "We value secrecy at Twilight. It's paramount. Did you bring anyone else into this project?"

David's mind raced, images of Nadia and Becca flashing before him. They had been instrumental, their expertise invaluable. But the instinct to protect, to shield them from any potential fallout, was overpowering. "No," he responded, the lie slipping out smoothly, "I used no-code programming tools to alter the app's source code."

Julian's gaze was unwavering, his eyes searching David's for any hint of deception. After what felt like an eternity, Julian nodded. "Good, that's good. We value our clients' privacy above all."

He slid an envelope across the table. "The full amount and the bonus are in there. All the work you did is now the property of Twilight. Do you have any USB drives or coffee makers left?"

David reached into his bag, pulling out the remaining devices. "I brought everything with me today."

Julian's expression softened slightly. "Thank you, David. Your help has been invaluable."

David was curious about the intensity in Julian's eyes. It was a look that spoke volumes, one that hinted at layers of complexity beneath the surface. As they wrapped up their conversation, David felt a mix of excitement and trepidation. The prospect of working with Twilight was enticing, but Julian's demeanor gave him pause. There was something about the man that David couldn't quite put his finger on, an enigmatic quality that both intrigued and unnerved him.

As Clara re-entered the room, Julian stood up, signaling the end of their meeting. "Clara will see you out."

Chapter 11

Becca Lawrence sat in the semi-darkness of her office at the CIA, the glow from her computer screens casting a pale light across her focused face. The constant churn of her mind was like a relentless engine, always pushing forward, dissecting every shred of data that came her way. She had been waiting for this list of clients from the bombed Berlin data center for what felt like an eternity. Each passing hour without it gnawed at her, a stark reminder of how every second could mean the difference between safety and catastrophe.

As she sat there, her fingers tapping a staccato rhythm on the cold, hard desk, Becca felt the familiar knot of tension winding tighter in her stomach. It was the same feeling that gnawed at her in the quiet hours of the night, the same feeling that whispered of danger lurking just beyond the horizon. The weight of responsibility pressed down on her, a constant reminder of the delicate balance she maintained between national security and the safety of her own family.

When Jack finally arrived, the relief that should have flooded her was instead replaced by a surge of frustration. Why did it take the BND so long to provide something as simple as a client list? She knew they were overwhelmed, but time was a luxury they couldn't afford. Each moment wasted was a moment that the perpetrators remained shrouded in the shadows, plotting their next move.

"Here's the list of clients from the Berlin data center," Jack said, handing over the documents. His face was drawn, the lines around his eyes deepened from too many hours spent poring over intelligence reports.

Becca raised an eyebrow, flipping through the pages. "Took long enough. What's the hold-up?"

"BND's been swamped," Jack replied, referring to the German Federal Intelligence Service. "The past few months have been a mess. They're stretched thin."

She nodded, understanding the strain all too well. Her eyes scanned the list, a litany of company names and details that blurred into a monotonous stream. But then, a name jumped out at her, snapping the world into sharp focus: Horizon Holdings.

Becca's breath hitched slightly. "Horizon Holdings," she murmured, her voice barely above a whisper. "This can't be a coincidence."

Her heart skipped a beat, not out of excitement, but a deep-seated fear that clawed at her insides. This was no mere happenstance; it was a calculated move in a game that they were all unwittingly playing. Becca's mind raced, piecing together past briefings, reports, and the nagging feeling that had been her constant companion since the bombing. Her mind went to David. What was Twilight Technologies up to? Is he an unwitting accomplice to something bigger and more deadly?

Jack leaned in, his interest piqued. "What's up?"

She tapped the name on the paper, her mind racing. "There's a lot of businesses and government agencies hosted in this data center. This might take awhile. Thanks for getting it. Do you have analysts on it?"

"Yeah, I have Julianna tasked with background research on each name. I'll let you know if we find anything."

Becca's eyes darted across the screen, her gaze intense and focused as she sifted through the digital mountain of evidence collected from the Berlin bombing. The room around her faded into a blur, the distant conversations of her colleagues becoming a mere background hum to the symphony of her thoughts. Each piece of evidence was a thread, and she was convinced that if she pulled the right one, the whole nefarious tapestry would unravel.

She pulled up surveillance footage, witness statements, and forensic reports, her mind a whirlwind of analysis and deduction. The data center, now a charred husk in the heart of Berlin, had housed the servers of countless entities, but Horizon Holdings stood out like a sore thumb. It was too prominent, too entwined with her own world of espionage and shadow games to be a mere casualty of circumstance.

Her fingers flew over the keyboard, commands and queries flowing from her like an extension of her own investigative will. She cross-referenced the list of clients with recent financial transactions, communications intercepts, and travel logs of known operatives. Becca was looking for patterns, anomalies, anything that would suggest a connection deeper than mere coincidence.

She leaned back in her chair, rubbing her temples as she tried to massage away the onset of a headache. The connections were there, subtle and complex, but undeniable. Becca knew she was onto something significant, something that could potentially expose a network of activities far more insidious than a simple bombing. She needed to speak with David *now*.

Becca's heart skipped a beat as the sharp knock echoed through her office, a sound that seemed to resonate with a foreboding she couldn't quite place. She looked up to see two stern-faced officers from the CIA's internal investigative services framed in her doorway. Their presence alone was enough to tighten the muscles in her neck, a physical manifestation of the sudden anxiety gripping her.

"Ms. Lawrence?" the taller of the two inquired, his voice carrying an authoritative edge that left no room for ambiguity.

"Yes," Becca replied, her voice steady despite the flutter of nerves in her stomach.

"We're here investigating a shooting that took place approximately four months ago," the agent continued, his eyes scanning her office as if looking for clues in the mundane details of her workspace.

A shooting? She tried to mask her surprise with a calm exterior, but her mind was racing, flipping through the mental calendar pages of the past four months. What incident could they possibly be referring to?

She couldn't recall any personal involvement in such an event, but the fact that these agents were standing in her office suggested a connection she couldn't immediately see.

"Ok? Did I get shot at four months ago? I don't recall," she responded with a hint of sarcasm, trying to buy time as she sifted through her memories. Her attempt at humor fell flat in the heavy air between them.

"No, this is a shooting at a suite that contained then-Majority Leader and now-President Felix Hayes," the second agent clarified, his tone suggesting the gravity of the situation.

The mention of Felix Hayes sent a jolt through Becca's system. She knew this wasn't going to be good. The implications were massive, and the fact that they were bringing this to her now, couldn't be a coincidence. Her mind whirred with the potential connections, the political ramifications, and the personal danger that such an inquiry could unearth.

She wanted to protest and tell them how she *saved* the life of President Hayes, but she knew her words would fall deaf on these two.

"We need to talk to you *now* about the incident," the first agent insisted, his gaze locking onto hers with an intensity that seemed to probe her very thoughts.

Becca felt a cold sweat forming at the base of her skull. Her hands felt clammy as she clasped them together to stop them from shaking. This was serious, potentially career-ending, or worse, life-threatening. She had to tread carefully, to navigate the minefield of this interrogation with precision and caution.

"Of course," Becca said, her voice a controlled calm that belied the turmoil inside her. "Let's talk." She got up from her desk to follow the two agents to an interrogation room, her mind already racing through every possible angle of this unexpected and unwelcome development.

Chapter 12

T he interrogation room was sterile and cold, the kind
of place designed to make a person feel exposed and
vulnerable. Becca sat rigidly in the metal chair, her hands
resting uneasily on the table before her. Across from her,
Martin's presence was a silent accusation, a reminder of
the assignment that had spiraled out of her control. He
was the one who had thrust her into the political quagmire
surrounding Felix Hayes, and then abruptly pulled her
out when she had started to see the strings being pulled
behind the curtain.

The interrogator's voice was matter-of-fact, but the
words hit Becca like a physical blow. No lawyer. No shield
against the barrage of questions that would come. She
understood the rules – this was a matter of national
security, after all – but the absence of legal counsel made
her feel like she was walking a tightrope without a net.

As they explained the need for a polygraph, Becca's
mind raced. She knew the machine was not infallible, but

the very request felt like an insinuation that she was already guilty of something. Her heart rate picked up, a silent drumbeat against her ribs, and she fought to maintain an outward appearance of calm. "Yes," she agreed, her voice steady despite the turmoil inside. She couldn't afford to show fear or hesitation; either could be interpreted as guilt.

The cold touch of the monitoring devices against her skin was a stark reminder of the gravity of the situation. Becca felt a bead of sweat trail down her spine as the straps were adjusted around her chest, the sensors adhered to her fingertips. She focused on her breathing, trying to slow the rapid pace of her heart, aware that every spike in her physiological responses would be scrutinized and potentially used against her.

In her mind, Becca replayed the events of that night, the standoff, the shattering glass, the escape. She had acted to prevent a potential assassination, to protect an elected official, but now she was the one under the microscope. The feeling of being railroaded was palpable, a narrative being constructed where she was a rogue element rather than a dedicated agent.

As the interrogator began the questioning, Becca steeled herself. She would tell the truth, the whole truth, as she had lived it. But in the pit of her stomach, a knot of anxiety tightened with the understanding that sometimes, the truth wasn't enough to set you free.

The interrogator, a man with a face as unreadable as the blank walls of the room, began methodically flipping through the pages of Becca's After Action Report. His fingers, clad in latex gloves, made a soft shuffling sound that seemed unnaturally loud in the silence of the room.

"Agent Lawrence," he started, his voice devoid of inflection, "your AAR states that you fired your weapon to prevent an imminent threat to Representative Hayes. Can you elaborate on what led you to that conclusion?"

Becca's eyes locked onto the interrogator's, her gaze unwavering. "Yes. The two unknown agents in the room were assembling a high-powered rifle. Given the context and their refusal to stand down, I assessed that there was a direct threat to Representative Hayes' life."

"And what made you decide to fire at the window, specifically?" the interrogator pressed on.

"I needed a diversion," Becca replied, her voice firm. "Breaking the window created confusion, which allowed Hayes and the other individual to escape the room. It was a split-second decision to disrupt the sightline of the potential sniper and prevent loss of life."

The interrogator made a note before looking up again. "You mentioned two unknown agents. Did you identify them or their agency?"

Becca shook her head slightly. "No. They claimed to be from a different agency but provided no identification. Their behavior and equipment suggested they were not standard CIA or FBI."

The interrogator leaned forward slightly. "Your report doesn't mention any attempts to apprehend these individuals. Why is that?"

"The immediate priority was to ensure the safety of Representative Hayes," Becca explained, her voice steady despite the tension coiling inside her. "Once the immediate threat was neutralized, my next concern was to extract myself and my team from a potentially volatile situation."

"And you had no prior knowledge of the planned assassination attempt on Representative Hayes?" the question came like a sharp jab.

"None whatsoever," Becca asserted, feeling the weight of the monitoring devices on her body. "My role was surveillance based on intel suggesting Hayes was meeting with a foreign agent. The events that transpired were beyond the scope of my assignment."

The interrogator paused, his eyes scanning her face for any sign of deception. Becca met his gaze squarely, her resolve as clear as the truth she spoke. She knew her actions that night had been the only thing standing between life and death, and no amount of questioning could shake her confidence in that fact.

The interrogator continued, his tone remaining even, "Agent Lawrence, you fired into the suite across the street where Representative Hayes was meeting the unidentified individual. Was this action sanctioned by your superiors?"

Becca's posture remained upright, her hands folded on the table. "No, it was not sanctioned. It was a judgment call made in the moment to prevent a greater harm."

The interrogator's pen paused over his notepad. "And who authorized you to make such judgment calls?"

"I was the senior officer on site. The decision was mine," Becca stated, her voice betraying no hint of doubt. "In situations where immediate action is required to save lives, protocol allows for autonomous decision-making."

The interrogator's gaze lingered on her for a moment longer before he continued. "In your report, you mentioned a 'stand down' order received by Agent Carla Haskins. Did you receive the same order?"

Becca inhaled slowly, recalling the tension of that moment. "I did not receive any such order. My actions were based on the information available to me at the time."

"And yet you chose to defy the order given to your colleague. Why is that?"

Becca leaned forward, her eyes narrowing slightly. "Because the order did not align with the unfolding situation. It would have resulted in the loss of life. My duty is to protect, and that's what I did."

The interrogator nodded, jotting down her response. "Let's talk about the aftermath. You left after the two unknown agents. Why didn't you apprehend them?"

"The priority was to ensure the safety of the team and the target. The unknown agents left the scene immediately after the disruption. Pursuing them without backup would have been reckless and against protocol."

The questions continued, each one probing deeper into the events of that night. Becca answered each with the same level of confidence and detail, her training keeping her focused despite the growing fatigue. She knew that every word, every inflection, was being analyzed for veracity. But the truth was her ally, and she clung to it like a shield against the barrage of suspicion.

The interrogator shifted in his seat, his eyes briefly flicking towards Martin before returning to Becca. "Agent Lawrence, describe your relationship with Case Officer Martin Wilson. Was there ever any disagreement on how to handle the Hayes surveillance?"

Becca's gaze hardened as she glanced at Martin, the man who had once been her mentor. "We had professional disagreements, yes. I believed the surveillance on Representative Hayes was becoming a witch hunt, and I voiced my concerns."

"And how did Case Officer Wilson respond to your concerns?" the interrogator pressed, observing the dynamic between the two.

"He removed me from the assignment," Becca replied, her voice steady but laced with a tinge of bitterness. "I was pulled out before I could see it through."

The interrogator made a note before continuing. "Did you ever act on your own initiative, against direct orders or without the knowledge of your superiors?"

Becca met the question with a level stare. "I have always acted within the bounds of my authority and the ethical guidelines of this agency. My initiative has always been in the interest of the mission and national security."

Martin remained silent, his eyes downcast, avoiding Becca's accusatory looks. She could feel the tension emanating from him, a stark contrast to the confident leader he once was. It was clear to her that Martin's role in this was more than just a passive observer. His lack of support in this room spoke volumes, and she wondered when he had lost the conviction that once made him a great case officer.

The interrogator leaned back, his demeanor suggesting that he was nearing the end of his questioning. "One final question, Agent Lawrence. Do you believe your actions on the night of the incident with Representative Hayes were justified?"

Without hesitation, Becca responded, "Absolutely. I took the necessary steps to prevent a potential assassination. I stand by my actions."

The door closed with a soft click behind the departing interrogators, leaving Becca and Martin in a silence that was almost deafening. Martin finally looked up, his eyes meeting Becca's, but whatever he was searching for in her gaze, he seemed not to find. He opened his mouth as if to speak, then closed it again, the words unspoken.

A moment later, the door reopened, and one of the internal investigators stepped back into the room. His face was impassive, giving nothing away as he addressed Becca.

"Agent Lawrence, effective immediately, you are being placed on administrative leave," he stated in a matter-of-fact tone. "You will retain your pay and benefits during this time, but you are not to engage in any active duty or agency-related activities."

Becca's jaw tightened, but she nodded once, sharply. She had expected this, yet the reality of it stung—a forced step back from the life and career that defined her.

"Furthermore," the investigator continued, "you are instructed not to discuss this investigation with anyone outside of these proceedings. You are also required to remain available and within the local area until the conclusion of this investigation. Do you understand these conditions?"

"I understand," Becca replied, her voice betraying none of the turmoil that churned inside her. She was a professional, and she would handle this with the same composure she brought to her fieldwork.

The investigator gave a curt nod. "You will be contacted with further instructions. Please ensure that your contact information with the agency is up to date."

With that, he turned and left the room, his footsteps receding down the hallway. Becca stood slowly, her mind racing through the implications of her enforced leave. She felt the weight of the scrutiny, the invisible eyes that would be watching her every move from now on.

Martin finally broke the silence. "Becca, I—" he started, but Becca held up a hand to stop him.

"Save it, Martin," she said, her voice cold. "Whatever you were going to say, it's too late now."

She gathered her things, her movements deliberate and controlled. As she passed Martin, she paused, looking down at the man who had once been a pillar of strength and guidance.

"I don't know when you lost your way, Martin, but I won't let your decisions drag me down. I did what was right, and I'll continue to do so, with or without the agency's approval."

Without waiting for a response, Becca walked out of the interrogation room, her head held high.

Chapter 13

D avid's hand froze over the workbench, the buzz of his phone slicing through the silence like a siren's call. He glanced down, his eyes quickly scanning the message that flashed across the screen. "Great car insurance rates! 202-777-9000." To anyone else, it would have seemed like just another piece of spam, an annoyance to be swiped away. But to David, those words were a beacon, a silent alarm that set his heart racing.

He didn't hesitate. The tools he'd been working with—a soldering iron, a half-assembled circuit board, wires splayed out like mechanical entrails—were left abandoned as he grabbed his jacket, sidearm, and keys. His mind was a whirlwind of scenarios, each more dire than the last. Becca was in trouble; that much was clear. The Greek cafe, once a place of laughter and the clinking of coffee cups, now stood as their clandestine meeting point—a shadow of its former self, much like they were.

As he drove, the streets blurred past him, the traffic lights bleeding into streaks of red and green. His grip on the steering wheel tightened with each mile, the worry for Becca gnawing at him. She was tough, one of the toughest people he knew, but the message meant she was in a situation she couldn't handle alone. And that scared him more than he cared to admit.

The cafe loomed ahead, its windows dark, the 'Closed' sign hanging crookedly as if in defeat. He parked in the back, away from prying eyes, and made his way to the back entrance they always used. His hand hesitated on the door handle, his breath catching in his throat. What was he about to walk into? What had happened to Becca?

He pushed the door open, the familiar creak of its hinges a stark contrast to the pounding of his heart. The cafe's interior was shrouded in shadows, the once vibrant murals on the walls now just specters in the dim light that filtered through the dusty blinds.

"Becca?" he called out softly, his voice steady despite the turmoil inside him. There was a shuffle, a soft sound of movement, and then she stepped out from the back room, her face a mask of tension and resolve.

David's worry morphed into relief, then back into a coil of apprehension. She was here, she was safe, but the very fact that she had summoned him like this meant that they were far from being out of the woods.

As David stepped into the dimly lit back room, Becca rose from the table, her movements betraying a vulnerability he had seldom seen in her. She crossed the room swiftly, and without a word, wrapped her arms around him in a tight embrace. David, taken aback by the intensity of the moment, returned the hug, his arms encircling her with a protective strength. He could feel the tension in her body, the tremors of stress that she so rarely displayed.

"Thank you for coming," she murmured, her voice muffled against his shoulder. As she stepped back, he could see the gratitude in her eyes, mingled with the strain of her current ordeal. "I'm under investigation."

David's brow furrowed with concern as he took in her appearance—she looked worn, the usual spark in her eyes dimmed by the weight of her troubles. "Talk to me, Becca. What's this investigation about?" he asked, his voice low and serious.

She sighed, a long and weary exhalation, as she returned to her seat. "It's about the Hayes incident," she began, her fingers absently tracing the edge of the table.

David's concern deepened, his mind racing with the implications. "Why now? Why are they digging this up?" he asked, his thoughts already turning to ways he could help her.

Becca shook her head, her gaze fixed on some unseen point as she pieced together her thoughts. "I'm not entirely sure," she admitted, "but I have a theory. President Hayes... he's been cleaning house, trying to rid the agency of the corruption that festered under the previous administration. It seems I've been swept up in the purge."

David's hands clenched into fists at his sides. The idea of Becca, one of the most honorable agents he knew, being caught in the crossfire of political games was infuriating. "But you've done nothing wrong," he said, his voice firm with conviction. "You were just doing your job."

"I know," Becca replied, her eyes meeting his with a mixture of resolve and resignation. "But in their eyes, I was at the center of it all. I was there, David. And now, I'm a loose end that needs tying up."

David moved closer, his protective instincts in full force. "We'll figure this out, Becca. You're not alone in this," he assured her, his voice a steady anchor in the storm that was brewing around them. "We'll clear your name, no matter what it takes."

Becca's expression softened as she offered a simple "thanks" to David, but her eyes remained troubled, hinting at the gravity of what she was about to disclose. "There's a bigger issue at hand," she said, her voice steady despite the weight of her words. "I've been investigating the Berlin bombing. It targeted a data center, and one of the clients was Horizon Holdings."

David's reaction was immediate, his surprise evident. He had seen the news, the images of destruction that had been broadcast around the world, but this connection brought a personal dimension that was unexpected. His mind raced, thoughts tumbling over each other as he tried to make sense of the situation. 'Could the bombing have been a message? A warning?' he wondered. 'Or perhaps a diversion for something bigger?'

He looked at Becca, his eyes narrowing as he considered the implications. "It can't be a coincidence that I was hired for security testing," he said, his voice tinged with a growing realization. "Maybe Horizon Holdings wanted to test their security in response to the bombing. They might have seen a vulnerability and wanted to address it."

But Becca shook her head, her gaze intense. "No, David, it's more serious than that. Twilight Technologies... it doesn't exist. The parent company is just a shell corporation in the Bahamas. The company that hired you has a digital footprint, but it's all a facade."

David felt a chill run down his spine. The pieces of the puzzle were falling into place, but they formed an image he hadn't expected. His work with Twilight, the security testing, the bombing—it was all connected, but how? 'Was I used as a pawn in a larger scheme?' he questioned internally. 'And if Twilight is a ghost, who's really pulling the strings?'

He looked back at Becca, his eyes reflecting the turmoil inside him. "This is big, Becca. If Twilight is a sham, then someone went to great lengths to set this up. They've covered their tracks with a sophistication that's... it's chilling."

David's mind was reeling, the gravity of the situation pressing down on him like a physical weight. He had been meticulous, professional, and thorough, but now he was gripped by the chilling realization that he might have unwittingly played a role in a plot with potentially catastrophic implications. "I gave them the encrypted source code," he muttered, his voice barely above a whisper, the words tasting like ash in his mouth. "I thought I was testing their security, not handing them the keys to the kingdom."

Becca's face was a mirror of his concern, her eyes dark pools reflecting a storm of implications. "We don't know exactly what was on those servers in Berlin," she said, her voice steady despite the undercurrent of urgency. "But if it was the encryption key, then the people who bombed that data center might be in league with whoever is behind Twilight. And if that's the case, they could now have full access to the software code for the most significant payment technology breakthrough we've ever seen."

David's hands clenched into fists, the frustration and fear battling for dominance within him. "This could change everything," he said, his voice hardening. "If they can break the encryption, they could manipulate financial transactions on a global scale. We're talking about the potential for unprecedented economic chaos."

Becca nodded grimly. "Exactly. And it's not just about money. This kind of power could shift the balance of geopolitical power. It could destabilize governments, undermine democratic processes. It's a weapon."

The silence that followed was heavy with the weight of unsaid words. David's mind was a whirlwind of scenarios, each more dire than the last. He had seen the dark side of technology, the way it could be twisted and turned against the very people it was meant to serve. And now, he was potentially at the center of a maelstrom that could engulf the world's financial systems.

"We need to act," Becca said, breaking the silence. "We need to find out who's really behind Twilight, who bombed that data center, and what they're planning to do with the code. Time isn't on our side, David."

Chapter 14

The green room was a sanctuary of calm, a stark contrast to the bustling energy of the studio outside. Gabriel Vale stood before a full-length mirror, adjusting the collar of his crisp white shirt. He was the epitome of modern success: a tech mogul turned spiritual leader, with a billionaire's bank account and the adoration of millions.

Gabriel's rise to fame had been meteoric. His invention had revolutionized communication—a sleek, cutting-edge device that connected users to a lightning-fast mesh network. It wasn't just a phone; it was a portal to a world of instant gratification, where entire movies could be downloaded in the blink of an eye and no call was ever dropped. His full head of lustrous brown hair, chiseled features, and an ever-present tan made him as physically appealing as the devices he created.

But Gabriel's ambitions extended beyond the realm of technology. He had a vision of himself as a guide for the spiritually adrift, a beacon of light in a world he saw as increasingly disconnected from the divine. His daily TV show, broadcasted not only on the proprietary ValeVision devices but also on cable and satellite, reached into homes across the globe, his words instantly translated into dozens of languages.

Today, Gabriel was poised on the cusp of unveiling his latest innovation—a virtual AI avatar of himself. This digital doppelgänger would offer personalized spiritual advice 24/7 to anyone with a ValeVision device. It was more than a technological marvel; it was his way of embedding himself into the very fabric of his followers' lives.

As he prepared to step onto the set, Gabriel paused, taking a deep breath. The air was scented with the subtle fragrance of sandalwood, a touch that grounded him. He looked at his reflection, not just at the man but at the empire he had built, the influence he wielded. There was a glint in his eye, the spark of someone who knew they were about to change the game once again.

"Mr. Vale, it's time," his assistant said, her voice a gentle interruption.

Gabriel turned, his expression shifting from contemplation to the charismatic, confident persona the world knew. "Let's enlighten the world," he said with a smile, striding towards the stage where his audience awaited, ready to hang on his every word.

The stage was set with an air of serene simplicity, bathed in warm, inviting light that seemed to embrace the audience as Gabriel Vale stepped into view. The crowd hushed, their anticipation palpable in the silence that followed. Gabriel's presence was magnetic, his confidence unshakable as he surveyed the sea of faces before him.

"Ladies and gentlemen," Gabriel began, his voice resonating with a calm authority that demanded attention. "In this post-3/16 world, we find ourselves at a crossroads. The institutions we once relied upon have shown their fragility. The beliefs we held dear have been tested. And in this time of uncertainty, there is but one truth that remains unchallenged—that the power to shape our destiny lies within each of us."

He paced the stage, his movements fluid and purposeful. "We have been conditioned to seek guidance from external sources, to look beyond ourselves for salvation. But I tell you this—the only salvation that exists is the kind that we forge from our own will, our own strength."

Gabriel paused, letting his words sink in, his gaze connecting with individuals in the crowd, making each feel seen, understood. "The world has changed," he continued. "The old ways, the old gods, and the old leaders have failed us. It's time to turn inward, to the divine spark that resides in each of our hearts. It's time to awaken the god within."

The audience was rapt, hanging on his every word, a collective breath held in anticipation. "You are the architects of your future. You hold the chisel and the hammer needed to sculpt your destiny. In the post-3/16 world, we must rise like the phoenix from the ashes of the old, and it begins with a simple belief—a belief in oneself."

Gabriel's voice rose, infused with passion. "Embrace the power you possess! Cast aside the chains of doubt and fear, and step into the light of self-reliance and self-empowerment. This is the path to enlightenment. This is the way to a future that we will not only endure but one in which we will thrive!"

The crowd erupted into applause, a standing ovation that filled the auditorium with a thunderous roar. Gabriel stood at the center of it all, a solitary figure who had ignited a fire in the hearts of many, a preacher of self-reliance in a world desperate for a message of hope.

The applause still echoed in the auditorium as Gabriel's expression softened, reflecting a more personal touch. "These times have been challenging since the tragedy of 3/16," he acknowledged, his voice a gentle timbre that seemed to cradle the collective grief of the audience. "Millions of lives were extinguished in an instant, and the world as we knew it was irrevocably altered."

He paused, a moment of silence for the lost, his head bowed in reverence. "I, too, struggled to find my footing in the aftermath of that fateful day. The path was dark, and the future uncertain. But it was through seeking enlightenment, through embracing the power within, that I emerged not just unscathed, but reborn—a better man, one who understands his fate and role in this vast, interconnected universe."

Gabriel raised his head, his eyes scanning the crowd, his gaze imbued with an intensity that seemed to reach out and touch each person there. "You must find that strength within yourselves," he urged. "In these trying times, the only surety is the resolve that resides in your heart, the unyielding spirit that defines who you are."

The mood in the room shifted as Gabriel's message of self-reliance transitioned to one of celebration. "And now," he said, his voice rising with excitement, "to remind us of the beauty that life still holds, to inspire us with the power of dreams, I am thrilled to introduce a shining star whose voice has been a beacon of hope to many."

The stage lights dimmed, and a single spotlight illuminated the figure stepping into view. Elara Blaze, the pop sensation known for her ethereal voice and captivating presence, approached the microphone with a graceful confidence.

"Please welcome the incredible Elara Blaze, here to perform her hit song, 'Dreamscape,'" Gabriel announced, stepping aside to allow the artist the stage.

The opening chords of "Dreamscape" filled the auditorium, a haunting melody that seemed to suspend time. Elara's voice soared, pure and clear, weaving a tapestry of sound that enveloped the audience in a collective dream. The song spoke of hope, of reaching beyond the pain and loss, of building a world borne of our deepest desires—a dreamscape of our own making.

As Elara sang, the crowd was transported, lifted from the weight of their reality, if only for a moment, by the power of her music. Gabriel watched from the wings, a knowing smile on his lips.

The applause for Elara's performance lingered like a sweet echo as Gabriel stepped back onto the stage, his presence commanding yet warm. He approached Elara, who was basking in the adoration of the crowd, her cheeks flushed with the thrill of her performance.

"Elara, that was truly moving," Gabriel said, turning to face her, his voice carrying over the crowd. "Tell us, what was the inspiration behind 'Dreamscape'?"

Elara's eyes sparkled with a mix of excitement and humility as she addressed the audience. "Honestly, I've been so inspired by Gabriel and the vision he shares with all of us," she confessed, her gaze flitting to Gabriel with admiration. "The idea of creating our own reality, our own dreamscape, it resonated with me deeply."

She laughed lightly, a hand brushing a stray lock of hair from her face. "I'm still pinching myself that I'm here on stage with you," she said to Gabriel, her voice tinged with disbelief. "I've been following your journey, and to be here, it's a bit surreal."

Gabriel chuckled, the sound rich and genuine. "Kind words from such a talented artist," he replied, his eyes meeting hers. "But I must admit, I'm a bit starstruck myself. Your music has touched the lives of so many, including my own."

Elara's smile widened, and she shook her head slightly, as if to dismiss the compliment. "Your teachings have been deeply meaningful to me," she said earnestly.

"They've helped me navigate through my own challenges and find a sense of peace and purpose. 'Dreamscape' is a reflection of that journey, of the hope you've helped instill in me and my listeners."

The audience watched the exchange, a palpable sense of warmth and mutual respect emanating from the stage. Gabriel's teachings had bridged the gap between guru and pop star, between spiritual enlightenment and musical expression, creating a moment of unity that transcended the ordinary, much like the dreamscape Elara sang about.

The stage lights dimmed to a soft glow, casting an intimate ambiance over the auditorium as Gabriel turned to the audience, his voice a blend of excitement and solemnity.

"I've always believed in sharing the journey of enlightenment with as many souls as possible," he began, his eyes sweeping over the sea of faces hanging on his every word. "I created ValeVision and this network to spread a message of self-reliance and inner strength."

A hush fell over the crowd, every person leaning in, as if trying to catch a whisper of what was to come.

"If I could," Gabriel continued, "I would be with each of you, every hour of every day, guiding and supporting your path to enlightenment. But since I can't physically do that," he paused, a knowing smile playing on his lips, "I've been working on something very special."

The anticipation in the room was palpable, a collective breath held in suspense.

"This breakthrough," Gabriel said, his voice rising with enthusiasm, "will allow me to be a part of your lives in a way that has never been done before."

He stepped back, his arms opening wide as if to embrace the crowd. "Would you like a sneak peek of what the future holds? Would you like to see how we can connect more deeply, more personally, than ever before?"

The audience erupted in cheers and applause, a resounding "Yes!" filling the auditorium. Gabriel nodded, his smile reflecting the excitement of the crowd, as he prepared to unveil his revolutionary creation that promised to change the way they interacted with their spiritual guide forever.

Chapter 15

In the dimly lit room, the only sound was the soft hum of electronics until the distinctive chime of a CALEB notification broke the silence. David and Becca exchanged a glance, each recognizing the urgency that a message from Nadia carried. They reached for their phones in unison, the glow from the screens illuminating their faces with a bluish tint.

Nadia's message was terse, a stark contrast to her usually verbose texts: "Turn on ValeVision. Now."

Without a word, David grabbed the remote and flicked on the television, the screen coming to life just as Gabriel Vale stood center stage, his presence commanding even through the digital divide. The audience's anticipation was almost tangible, their faces a mosaic of eagerness and curiosity.

Gabriel's voice filled the room, smooth and confident. "We stand on the brink of a new dawn, my friends," he proclaimed. "A dawn where distance and time no longer separate us. Where my guidance can be a constant presence in your lives."

Becca leaned forward, her instincts as an analyst telling her that whatever was about to be revealed was more than just another tech gadget.

"Do you want to be the first to see the future?" Gabriel asked, his arms outstretched as if to welcome the world into his embrace.

The crowd's response was a resounding affirmation, their cheers reverberating through the speakers. David and Becca watched intently, knowing that Nadia's alert meant this was more than just a spectacle—it could very well be a significant development.

David and Becca sat transfixed as the massive screen on stage was suddenly dominated by the towering figure of a digital Gabriel Vale. The avatar was a perfect replica, down to the charismatic smile and the meticulously styled hair. It turned to face the audience, its movements fluid and eerily human.

"Hello, Gabriel," the avatar spoke with a voice that was a mirror image of the real Vale's, resonating with the same authoritative timbre that had captivated millions.

"Hello, Virtual Gabriel," the flesh-and-blood Gabriel responded, turning to address the audience with a showman's flair. "Tell us, what can you do?"

Virtual Gabriel's digital eyes seemed to sparkle with intelligence. "I am here to be the spiritual companion you've always desired," it began. "I can answer your questions, provide guidance, inspire you, and help you navigate the complexities of life."

David's brow furrowed, sensing the implications of such technology. Becca, too, was visibly concerned, her analytical mind racing through the potential uses—and abuses—of a system so intimately woven into the fabric of people's lives.

"And the best part," Virtual Gabriel continued, "is that I am integrated into your ValeVision phones. I will learn about you, grow with you, and be able to offer proactive help whenever you need it."

The audience erupted into applause, but David and Becca were not swayed by the spectacle. They knew that anything with the power to learn and adapt so personally carried risks far beyond what the cheering crowd could imagine. They exchanged a look that said as much, both understanding that this development could change the game entirely.

The audience watched in awe as Gabriel Vale, with his characteristic zeal, proclaimed the virtues of his latest creation. "Virtual Gabriel isn't just a program; it's a revolution in spiritual companionship," he declared, his voice swelling with pride. "This is a guru who knows you more intimately than you could imagine, always there, always ready to guide you."

He gestured grandly towards Elara Blaze, who was already engrossed in conversation with her own Virtual Gabriel. Her eyes were wide with wonder, her voice filled with excitement as she shared her experience with the crowd. "It's like having a wise friend in your pocket," she enthused. "Someone who understands you and is there for you during those quiet moments when you need guidance the most."

The crowd was visibly moved, many reaching for their own phones, eager to experience this personal spiritual guide for themselves. Gabriel watched, a satisfied smile playing on his lips as he witnessed the immediate impact of his words.

Chapter 16

D avid's heart was pounding as he navigated the familiar streets, the urgency of the situation pressing down on him like a weight. He had known Rollins for years, but the detective's tone on the phone had been strained, almost fearful, which was out of character for the usually unflappable man.

The baseball field was deserted, a stark contrast to the vibrant, cheering crowds it usually hosted. David's gaze immediately locked onto Rollins' car, isolated under the harsh glow of a solitary streetlamp. The engine's soft purr was the only sound in the chilling silence of the night.

As he parked his car, David's instincts screamed that something was terribly wrong. Rollins' body was slumped unnaturally over the wheel, the driver's side window splattered with a dark substance that David's gut told him was blood. He bolted from his car, his training taking over as he approached the vehicle with caution, his eyes scanning the surroundings for any sign of the perpetrator or an ambush.

Reaching the car, David's worst fears were confirmed. Rollins was motionless, his skin ashen, a small stream of blood trickling from a wound hidden by his disheveled hair. David's hands shook as he checked for a pulse, finding only the stillness of death.

Fumbling with his phone, David's voice was steady as he reported the situation to the emergency operator. "Officer down at Westfield Baseball Park. Gunshot wound, I need an ambulance and backup immediately." He rattled off the address with mechanical precision, his mind racing with the implications of Rollins' death.

As he waited for the sirens that would soon pierce the night, David stood guard over Rollins, a sentinel in the darkness, his mind swirling with questions and the chilling realization that he was now deeply entangled in something far more dangerous than he had anticipated.

The scene was a hive of activity as the police arrived, their presence swiftly followed by the arrival of homicide detectives and the stern-faced members of internal affairs. Among the detectives was a familiar figure, Detective Fiona Grey. David's history with her stretched back to his days in the FBI, a time when their paths had crossed more than once on cases that required a joint task force. She was as he remembered: all business, her sharp mind hidden behind a stoic facade.

As she approached, David felt a twinge of the old camaraderie, but it was quickly overshadowed by the gravity of the situation. Her gaze was piercing, and he knew she would remember him as the agent who always had a knack for finding himself in the middle of trouble.

"David Mitchell," she said, her voice carrying the authority he remembered well. "I didn't expect to see you here. What's your involvement?"

He could feel the weight of her scrutiny as he explained his presence, the familiar itch of being back in the investigative spotlight. "I'm working as a PI these days," David said, his voice steady despite the adrenaline still coursing through his veins. "Rollins reached out for a meet. Said he had a job for me."

Grey's eyes flicked to her notepad as she scribbled a few words. "He give you any details?"

David hesitated, a part of him longing for the simplicity of his FBI days when he could share information with a colleague and trust in the system. But those days were gone, and now he was entangled in something that could reach much higher than a local police matter. "No," he lied, "he wanted to discuss it in person."

She regarded him for a moment longer, her expression unreadable. "Alright, we'll be in touch if we need anything further. Stay available."

David lingered for a moment, watching the meticulous dance of the crime scene investigators, before turning back to Grey. "One last question, Detective, if I may?" His tone held a hint of the professional courtesy that had always underpinned their interactions.

Grey paused, her pen hovering above the notepad. "Sure, shoot."

He glanced over at the cluster of Internal Affairs officers, their presence like a dark cloud over the scene. "Why is Internal Affairs involved?" he asked, his voice low, hinting at the gravity he placed on the question.

Grey leaned in slightly, her voice dropping to a conspiratorial whisper that belied the professional distance she maintained. "Off the record? We've got reason to believe Rollins might've been caught up in some unsavory dealings. There's talk of bribes linked to a local sports betting ring. And, well, the guy had a reputation for playing the odds a bit too much, if you catch my drift."

Her eyes searched his face for a reaction. "You wouldn't happen to know anything about that, would you?"

David met her gaze squarely, his own expression a carefully crafted mask of neutrality. "No," he replied, his response measured and deliberate. "As I mentioned, Rollins hadn't given me any specifics. We were supposed to discuss the job today." His words hung between them, an unspoken acknowledgment of the complexities that lay beneath the surface of every investigation.

As she walked away to confer with her colleagues, David's mind was a whirlwind of emotion. Guilt for lying to an old ally, fear for what Rollins' death might mean for his own safety, and a deep-seated concern for Becca and the tangled web they were all caught in. He knew he was walking a fine line, but until he could piece together the puzzle of Twilight Technologies, the facts of this situation would need to stay in the shadows.

Chapter 17

Lucien Morreau's fists pounded rhythmically against the plush fibers of the exotic animal rug, each thud echoing off the opulent walls of his Dubai high-rise apartment. His face, usually a mask of composed malevolence, was now twisted in a snarl of unbridled fury. The air around him was thick with his rage, almost palpable in its intensity.

"Why? Why must I endure this?" he seethed, his voice a guttural growl that seemed to emanate from the very depths of his being. "The Circle was perfection, the key to utopia, and yet it crumbled... thwarted by the ignorance of the masses!"

He slammed his fists down harder, the force of his anger leaving his knuckles white and his skin reddening against the coarse fur beneath him. His breath came in ragged gasps, each one laden with the weight of his indignation and the sting of betrayal.

"How can they not see? How can they be so blind to the paradise I offer?" he raged, his voice rising to a crescendo that filled the room and reverberated against the floor-to-ceiling windows. "I am the harbinger of their salvation, the architect of their deepest desires!"

Lucien's body shook with the force of his emotions, his entire being consumed by the fervor of his convictions. He was the chosen one, the one who would lead humanity into a new era of hedonistic splendor, and yet he was being rejected, his grand vision unfulfilled.

"Why do they resist me? Why do they not flock to my side?" His questions were a litany of frustration, the words of a man who could not fathom why his grandiose vision of indulgence was not universally embraced.

The rage within him boiled over, a tempest that could not be contained. Lucien Morreau, the man who saw himself as a god among men, was now reduced to a primal display of fury, his vision for the future denied, his purpose questioned, his very essence seemingly under siege.

The sharp rap at the door jolted Lucien from his tumultuous reverie, his head snapping up, eyes blazing with the remnants of his earlier tempest. "I gave explicit instructions not to be disturbed!" he barked, his voice laced with venom.

From the other side of the door, the unflappable voice of Oliver Lancaster, his long-time butler, permeated the thick wood with practiced calm. "Apologies, Mr. Morreau, but Mr. Gabriel Vale has just arrived in the lobby. He insists on meeting with you."

Lucien's scowl deepened, the interruption unwelcome, yet the mention of Gabriel Vale's name seemed to douse the flames of his anger with a flicker of intrigue. He pushed himself off the rug, his movements now deliberate, the chaotic energy that had possessed him moments ago receding like the tide.

"Show him up," Lucien commanded, his tone now cool and collected, the storm within him caged once more. "Inform Mr. Vale I shall be with him in fifteen minutes."

He could hear Oliver's retreating footsteps, the soft affirmation of his compliance. Lucien straightened his attire, smoothing out the wrinkles that his outburst had wrought upon his expensive clothing. He glanced at his reflection in the mirror, the visage of a man who wielded power and demanded respect staring back at him.

With a deep, steadying breath, he began to compose himself, the mask of the composed, charismatic leader returning to its rightful place. Lucien Morreau, the man who envisioned himself as the savior of mankind's carnal pleasures, was ready to face Gabriel Vale, another titan of industry and influence. Whatever the reason for this impromptu visit, Lucien was determined to ensure that it played into his grand design.

Lucien emerged from the seclusion of his bedroom, the remnants of his fury now cloaked beneath a veneer of gracious hospitality. As Gabriel entered the expansive living space, Lucien approached with open arms, the warmth in his greeting belying the turmoil that had so recently consumed him.

"Gabriel, my friend, your presence is a balm," Lucien declared, enveloping the tech mogul in a firm embrace that spoke of shared understandings and unspoken alliances. "I am truly grateful for your visit."

Gabriel returned the embrace, a knowing look in his eyes as he stepped back to hold Lucien at arm's length, his gaze penetrating. "Lucien, there's no need for thanks. I can see the struggle within you," Gabriel said, his voice a soothing timbre. "Pain and heartbreak are transient, yet they carve the path to enlightenment."

He placed a hand on Lucien's shoulder, a gesture of solidarity and support. "Remember, individuals can indeed be caring and compassionate. They will recognize the sincerity of your intentions," Gabriel continued, his words weaving a spell of reassurance. "But the masses... they are indeed a tempestuous sea, fickle and capricious in their affections."

Lucien felt the tightness in his chest ease, the storm within quelled by Gabriel's affirmations. It was a rare moment, one where the master of manipulation found himself susceptible to the influence of another. Gabriel's presence, his words, they were a lifeline thrown into the turbulent waters of Lucien's discontent, and he clung to them, allowing a feeling of peace to wash over him.

"Your insight is invaluable, Gabriel," Lucien said, a genuine note of appreciation threading through his voice. "In times like these, it's easy to forget the power of individual connections amidst the crowing of the crowd."

They shared a moment of understanding, two titans in their respective realms, finding common ground in the complexities of influence and the human condition. Lucien, bolstered by Gabriel's visit, felt a renewed sense of purpose.

Lucien paced the length of the room, his steps measured, the soft thud of his footsteps mingling with the distant hum of the city below. He paused by the floor-to-ceiling windows, gazing out at the sprawling metropolis that twinkled like a constellation grounded on earth. "I appreciate your words, Gabriel, but appreciation alone won't quell the storm. I need to act, to step out of the shadows. The world... it needs what I have to offer," he said, his voice a mix of determination and a plea for direction.

Gabriel watched him, his expression thoughtful, the gears of strategy turning behind his calm exterior. "Lucien, the sidelines are no place for a man of your caliber. The world does indeed need you," he affirmed, stepping beside Lucien to share the view. "That's precisely why I'm here. I want to help you reclaim your place, to emerge not just as a figure returned from exile, but as the prodigal son whose homecoming is celebrated."

Lucien turned to face him, a spark of interest igniting in his eyes. "A return to the world's stage, you say? A prodigal son..." he mused, the biblical reference not lost on him. "And how do you propose we orchestrate this feast, this grand return?"

Gabriel placed a hand on Lucien's shoulder, a gesture that bridged the gap between mentor and ally. "Together, we'll craft a narrative that resonates with the hearts and minds of the people. We'll use every tool at our disposal—

media, technology, and the allure of redemption. Your story will be one of transformation, a journey that turns past transgressions into lessons of growth and enlightenment."

Lucien's stance softened, the tension ebbing away as he considered Gabriel's words. "A feast for the world, you say... A celebration of change and new beginnings," he whispered, almost to himself. The idea was appealing, intoxicating even. It was a chance to reshape his legacy, to turn the tide of public opinion.

"Yes, Lucien," Gabriel said, his voice firm with conviction. "Your return will be the feast the world didn't know it was starving for. And I will be there to ensure it's a feast that will be remembered for ages to come."

Chapter 18

The air in the abandoned Greek cafe was thick with tension, the scent of old coffee grounds and dust mingling with the gravity of the conversation. David leaned against the counter, his arms crossed as he recounted the recent events to his friends. The weight of the world seemed to press down on his shoulders, but as he spoke, his gaze drifted to Mark and Nadia. Mark's hand rested gently on Nadia's back, a small but significant gesture of support and affection. David couldn't help but feel a warmth spread through him at the sight. In the midst of chaos, there was still room for tenderness, for human connection. It was a silent reminder of what they were all fighting for.

Nadia's eyes were wide with concern, and Mark's jaw was sct, a clear sign of his shock and determination to help. David appreciated their presence, their solidarity. It was moments like this that reminded him of the importance of their bond, of not facing the darkness alone.

Chaz, ever the voice of reason and camaraderie, chimed in with a firm tone. "David, listen to me," he said, locking eyes with him. "You're not an island, man. You can't just vanish when things get hot. We're in this together, you got that? No more lone-wolf heroics. We need you, and you need us. We're a team, and we stick together, no matter what."

David met Chaz's gaze, a mix of gratitude and humility in his eyes. He nodded, acknowledging the truth in Chaz's words. "I know, Chaz. I'm sorry. It won't happen again," he promised. The group, this makeshift family, was his anchor, and he realized now more than ever how much he relied on their strength and support.

Nadia's fingers danced across her phone as she accessed CALEB, her eyes scanning the encrypted messages that flowed like a digital river of whispers. "There's talk that Gabriel Vale is gearing up for something... monumental, beyond the AI avatar," she said, her voice tinged with a mix of curiosity and concern.

Becca leaned in, her brow furrowed. "What could possibly be bigger than having a virtual copy of yourself in everyone's pocket?" she mused aloud, the question hanging in the air like a challenge.

David rubbed his chin thoughtfully, his mind racing with the implications of their conversation. "I'm struggling to piece this all together," he admitted. "If we're in the end times, and Lucien Morreau was taken down with The Circle, was he really the antichrist? And where does Gabriel fit into all this?"

Chaz, who had been listening intently, spoke up, his voice steady and sure. "Remember, God's still sovereign. He allowed 3/16 to happen, and He's allowing all this to unfold. It's all to bring glory to His name, to fulfill His divine plan." He paused, looking each of them in the eye. "We're in the Tribulation, no doubt. But it's not for us to understand every move on the chessboard. Our job is to stay faithful, to be the light in an ever-darkening world."

The group fell silent, considering Chaz's words. There was a certain comfort in the idea that a higher power was at play, that they were not alone in their struggle against the encroaching darkness.

David nodded slowly, a sense of resolve settling over him. "Then we'll stand firm," he declared. "We'll be the resistance, the truth-seekers. No matter how bad it gets, we'll hold the line."

The group's eyes met, a silent vow passing between them. They were more than survivors; they were warriors in a battle that spanned beyond the physical realm.

"Well, I'm starving." Mark's casual remark about hunger cut through the tension like a knife, and he ambled toward the back door, oblivious to the forgotten phone on the table. "And there isn't a gyro coming out of this kitchen. I'm going out to grab some food," he said with a half-smile.

Nadia's voice lifted in a shout after him, "Mark, your phone!" But her words were lost in the distance as he stepped out. Becca, ever the quick responder, grabbed the device and followed, calling out to him.

As she swung the door open, her eyes caught a sinister glint from above—a reflection that didn't belong. Time seemed to slow as her instincts kicked in. She reached out, her hand clamping down on Mark's arm with an urgency that brooked no argument, yanking him back just as the sniper's bullet sang its deadly song, slamming into the door where moments before she had stood.

The door crashed shut behind them, Becca's training taking over as she covered the entrance with her gun, her body a shield between the unseen threat and the safety of the cafe.

David's heart thundered in his chest, the sound of the shot echoing in his ears like a starting pistol. Adrenaline surged as he drew his Glock 17, the familiar weight a cold comfort in his hand. "Get down!" he barked at Chaz and Nadia, his voice a command born of too many similar situations.

He sprinted toward the back door, every sense heightened, ready for a fight. His mind raced — calculating, anticipating. The cafe, once a haven, now felt like a trap, every shadow a potential threat, every silence a prelude to chaos.

Becca and Mark reappeared, moving with the precision of those who knew that hesitation could mean death. Becca's gun was steady, her eyes scanning for the next threat, her posture one of controlled aggression. David fell in step beside her, his own weapon raised, a silent promise to protect his friends against whatever was coming for them.

The gravity of the situation settled on David like a lead cloak. They were targets, and someone had just tried to take them out. The realization was a cold splash of reality, sharpening his focus.

David's voice was firm, the authority of his former FBI days resurfacing as he assessed the situation. "You okay?

What do you got back there?" he called out to Becca, his eyes darting to the front, ensuring no threats would catch them off guard.

"Sniper, at least one. Caught a reflection—wrong place, wrong time," Becca's voice was calm, but the undercurrent of urgency was unmistakable.

"Keep focused on the back," David instructed, his mind racing through their options. "We're sitting ducks here. We need to move, now!"

He turned to the group, his commands clipped and clear. "Grab what you need, and only what you need. We're not safe here, and we won't be for long."

Chaz, his usual jovial demeanor gone, replaced by the seriousness of the situation, nodded towards the street. "I'm parked at the end of the block, usual spot."

"That's our exit. Front door," David said, already moving towards the window. "We can't come back here. We need to cover our tracks, leave nothing behind."

The plan was desperate, but it was all they had. "Becca, Chaz, you're on point. We smash the front window, move fast and stay low. I'll cover our six and torch the place."

The group moved with a practiced efficiency born of necessity. David could feel the weight of every second passing, a silent drumbeat urging them to haste.

Becca and Chaz took positions by the window, ready to break through. David took one last look around the cafe that had been their sanctuary, their war room, and now, their pyre.

With a swift, decisive motion, he ignited the accelerant they'd prepared for just such an emergency. Flames began to lick at the edges of the room, a growing inferno ready to consume all they'd left behind.

"Go!" he shouted, and the window shattered, the sound of breaking glass a clarion call to action. Becca and Chaz burst through the opening, their figures silhouetted against the chaos.

David followed, the heat of the fire at his back, the uncertainty of survival ahead. He spared a glance behind him, the flames reflecting in his eyes—a beacon of their resolve to escape, to survive, to fight another day.

Chaz's hands were steady on the wheel as the SUV roared to life, the engine's growl a stark contrast to the chaos they'd just fled. The tires screeched against the asphalt as they made their getaway, the cafe now a blazing beacon in the rearview mirror.

Nadia's chest heaved with rapid, shallow breaths, her eyes wide with the shock of their narrow escape. The questions poured out of her in a torrent, her voice tinged with the sharp edge of panic.

"Who was that? Why are they—"

"Hey, hey, Nadia, look at me," Becca's voice cut through the panic, firm yet soothing. "You need to slow your breathing. In, then out. Slow and deep."

Nadia's breaths were ragged, but at Becca's prompting, they began to even out, the rhythm becoming more deliberate, more controlled.

Becca reached for a water bottle in the jumble of their hastily grabbed supplies, unscrewing the cap and handing it to Nadia. "Drink this. Small sips. It'll help."

Nadia took the bottle with trembling hands, the cool liquid a small comfort in the midst of the adrenaline that threatened to overwhelm her senses. She took a sip, then another, the act of drinking helping to ground her, to anchor her back to the present moment.

Becca kept a watchful eye on her, her own breathing measured and calm, a counterpoint to Nadia's distress. She knew the importance of staying level-headed; panic was a luxury they couldn't afford, not when every second mattered.

Chaz maneuvered the SUV into the dimly lit 4th avenue parking garage, the concrete structure echoing with the sound of their arrival. David scanned the area with a practiced eye before pointing out an old Chevy Blazer parked in the corner. Without hesitation, he was out of the SUV, his movements swift and precise as he broke into the Blazer and hot-wired the engine, the vehicle rumbling to life under his deft touch.

They transferred their gear and themselves into the Blazer, the change of vehicles a necessary step to throw off anyone who might be tracking them. Becca, however, stood apart, her expression resolute.

"I need to split off here," she said, her voice carrying a weight that drew David's attention immediately.

"What happened to sticking together?" David's concern was evident, his brow furrowed in a mix of frustration and worry.

Becca met his gaze, her own eyes steady. "You need to get everyone to safety. That's your priority. Mine is to find out who was behind that sniper. It's the only way we'll know what we're up against."

David wanted to argue, to insist she stay with them, but he knew Becca was right. She had the skills and the contacts to track down the assassin, to unearth the motives behind the attack.

They embraced, a tight hug that conveyed more than words ever could. "Stay safe," he whispered, his voice low.

"I will. And you make sure they're safe too," Becca whispered back.

David pulled back, his hand lingering on her arm. "What about Leila?"

"She's with my mom at my aunt's place. They're safe," Becca assured him, a flicker of tenderness crossing her features at the mention of her daughter.

"Alright. We'll head to Chaz's place in Virginia. Meet us there when you have something," David said, the plan set, their course of action clear.

Becca nodded, a silent promise passing between them. Then, with one last look, she turned and disappeared into the shadows of the parking garage, leaving David to shepherd the rest of the group to safety.

Chapter 19

The stage was set with a serene backdrop, hues of soft blues and gentle greens creating an atmosphere of tranquility. Gabriel Vale stood center stage, his presence commanding yet comforting, a beacon of calm in the storm of daily life. The audience was hushed, hanging on his every word, seeking solace in his message.

"Forgiveness," Gabriel began, his voice a soothing balm, "is not just an act we extend to others. It is a gift we must first bestow upon ourselves. For how can we offer to others what we have not accepted within?"

He paced slowly, hands clasped behind his back, his gaze sweeping over the sea of faces before him.

"To forgive oneself is to acknowledge that we are more than our mistakes. It is to recognize that each error is a step on the path of growth, a lesson learned, a strength gained."

Gabriel stopped and faced the audience directly, his eyes earnest and intense.

"Consider the weight you carry, the burdens of past regrets and missteps. Feel them as a physical presence upon your shoulders. Now, imagine releasing that weight, not with a sense of loss, but with the understanding that you are freeing yourself to move forward."

He raised his hands, palms up, as if physically lifting the weight from his audience.

"True forgiveness does not excuse the wrong. It does not forget the pain. But it acknowledges that holding onto resentment binds us to the past. Forgiving yourself is the first step towards healing, towards freedom."

Gabriel's voice rose, not in volume, but in passion.

"When you forgive yourself, you open the door to receive forgiveness from others. You signal to the world that you are ready to begin anew, to embrace the lessons learned and to step into a future unshackled by the chains of past grievances."

He paused, allowing his words to resonate, to settle like leaves upon a still pond.

"Forgive yourself, my friends. Do it sincerely and do it often. For in forgiveness, we find the truest form of love—the love of oneself, which radiates outward and touches the lives of everyone around us."

The hush that had fallen over the audience was palpable as Lucien Morreau stepped onto the stage. His presence was a stark contrast to the peaceful aura Gabriel had cultivated. The audience's silence was a mix of shock and a curious, wary anticipation.

Gabriel, ever the gracious host, gestured to the chairs set before a backdrop of a serene landscape painting, inviting Lucien to sit. The two men, both powerful in their own right, settled into the comfortable armchairs that faced each other, an intimate setting that seemed to shrink the distance between them and the audience.

"Lucien," Gabriel began, his voice gentle, "you've been a shadow figure these past months in Dubai. Tell us, what have you been striving to achieve?"

Lucien's face, usually so composed, flickered with the strain of recent events. "I've been working tirelessly," he admitted, "to maintain the peace agreements that are so easily frayed in these turbulent times. It's a delicate balance, one that requires constant attention."

Gabriel nodded, his expression understanding. "And The Circle," he prodded softly, "what happened there? What went wrong?"

Lucien sighed, a sound that seemed to carry the weight of the world. "The Circle was meant to be a force for global unity, but it was undermined by the actions of a few who didn't share our vision. I disbanded it because I didn't want those actions to tarnish the potential for real peace."

"Yes," Gabriel leaned forward, his eyes locked on Lucien's, "but there's more to it, isn't there? Do you have any regrets?"

For a moment, Lucien looked vulnerable, his usual confidence waning. "Yes," he said, his voice cracking slightly, "I regret that we couldn't achieve the good we set out to do. That I couldn't... prevent the harm that was done."

Gabriel's voice was soft but insistent. "Before you can seek forgiveness from the world, Lucien, you must find a way to forgive yourself. Can you do that?"

Lucien's struggle was visible, his internal battle playing out before the audience. It was then that a voice pierced the silence, full of hope and support. "You can do it, Lucien! We still believe in you!"

The audience, moved by the display of vulnerability and the show of support, erupted into applause, a wave of encouragement washing over the stage.

Gabriel seized the moment, the crescendo of clapping bolstering his words. "Lucien, let the support of these people guide you. Forgive yourself. It's the only way to move forward."

Tears glistened in Lucien's eyes as he looked out over the crowd, their applause a tangible force. With a shaky breath, he spoke, his voice barely above a whisper, "I... I forgive myself." The words seemed to lift a burden from his shoulders, his posture subtly shifting as if a chain had been broken.

The applause swelled, a chorus of humanity offering redemption. Gabriel reached out, placing a supportive hand on Lucien's shoulder. "And that, my friends," he said, turning to the audience with a smile, "is the first step towards true healing."

Gabriel's voice rose with a fervor that matched the renewed energy in the room. "If Lucien can stand before us, before the world, and forgive himself, then why," he spread his arms wide, encompassing the entire studio, "why can't we extend that same grace to him?"

The audience was silent, hanging on his every word. Gabriel paced the stage, his movements as compelling as his speech. "Lucien has done much good in the world, and yes, he has made mistakes—just as each and every one of us has. Should we not then, as fellow travelers on this journey of life, offer him the hand of forgiveness?"

He stopped center stage, turning to face the audience directly, his gaze sweeping across the faces before him. "It's all too easy to hold onto the errors of the past, to let them define us—or others—forever. But that's not who we are, that's not what we are capable of as human beings."

Gabriel's voice softened, but the intensity in his eyes did not wane. "We have this incredible capacity for forgiveness, a gift that elevates us, that separates us from the beasts of the field. It is what binds us together in our shared humanity."

He walked back to where Lucien sat, placing a hand on his shoulder once more. "Let us come together, as one human family, and forgive. Let us allow this man, Lucien Morreau, to continue his work, to unleash the potential for good that I know— that we all know—still resides within him."

The studio, once filled with the tension of Lucien's arrival, now resonated with a sense of unity and purpose. Gabriel's call to forgiveness wasn't just for Lucien; it was a call to each person in the audience, to the viewers at home, to embrace a higher calling of compassion and understanding.

"And so, I ask you," Gabriel's voice reached a crescendo, "will we not forgive? Will we not accept Lucien back into the fold for all the good he can still do?"

The response was immediate and overwhelming. The audience stood, their applause and cheers a resounding affirmation of Gabriel's plea. The sound was like a wave, washing over any remaining doubt, carrying with it the promise of redemption and the power of collective forgiveness.

Lucien, visibly moved, stood as well, his eyes scanning the crowd, finding not judgment, but acceptance. Gabriel smiled, his mission accomplished, as he witnessed the barriers of the past crumble under the weight of human kindness and forgiveness.

Chapter 20

The coffee shop's ambient noise faded into the background as Becca's focus narrowed on Jack. She watched his every move, the casual way he ordered his coffee, the large size indicating a clear message to her trained eye. As he exited, she counted to three under her breath before standing up, her own movements casual but calculated.

She followed him out, keeping a safe distance, her senses heightened as she scanned the area. The street was bustling with the usual city life, nothing out of place, no one paying them any undue attention. She slipped into the passenger side of Jack's Land Rover with practiced ease as he pulled smoothly away from the curb.

The silence between them was comfortable, a mutual understanding of the gravity of their situation. Jack's eyes flicked to the rearview mirror as he made a seemingly random series of turns, a standard counter-surveillance route to ensure they weren't being followed.

Finally, when he was satisfied, he spoke without looking at her. "Thanks for your help," Becca said, her voice low.

Jack let out a soft chuckle, his eyes still on the road. "What help? You know I can't be here right now," he replied, the lightness of his tone belying the seriousness of their clandestine meeting.

He nodded toward the floor. "There's a file under your seat. You need to see it. It's about Henrik Falk."

Becca reached down without a word, her fingers finding the file exactly where Jack said it would be. She didn't need to open it to know it was important; anything that came from Jack had to be. She opened the file to the cover sheet.

CIA Profile: Henrik Falk

Codename: *The Northern Shadow*

Birthplace: *Gothenburg, Sweden*

Languages: *Swedish (native), Russian (fluent), German (fluent), English (fluent)*

Military Background:

- *Swedish Armed Forces*
- *Kustjägarna (Coastal Rangers) - Specialized in stealth, reconnaissance, and long-range elimination.*

Physical Description:

- *Height: 6'2"*
- *Weight: 185 lbs*
- *Hair Color: Blond*
- *Eye Color: Blue*
- *Distinguishing Marks: None known. Subject is meticulous in maintaining a low profile.*

Skills:

- *Expert marksman*
- *Trained in multiple forms of hand-to-hand combat*
- *Proficient in counter-surveillance measures*
- *Skilled in covert entry and escape tactics*

Psychological Profile:

- *Falk is disciplined, methodical, and exhibits signs of a classic loner.*
- *Displays a strong ethical code, with a history of avoiding contracts involving harm to children or non-combatants.*
- *Known to have a penchant for classical music and chess, suggesting a highly strategic mind and a possible avenue for psychological profiling and prediction of behavior.*

Known Associates:

- *None. Falk is a lone operator, known to occasionally collaborate with fixers and informants but maintains no consistent alliances.*

Operational History:

- *Suspected involvement in high-profile eliminations across Europe, particularly in Sweden, Germany, and Russia.*
- *No confirmed direct engagements with U.S. personnel, but the possibility of indirect impact on U.S. interests abroad.*
- *No known failed operations. Falk's success rate, as well as his ability to remain undetected, is of significant concern.*

Threat Assessment:

- *High. Falk's skills, combined with his disciplined approach to contract killings, make him a significant threat to personnel and operations.*
- *His ethical code may be leveraged in negotiations or engagements, but this should not be relied upon.*

Recommendations:

- *Immediate flagging of all travel documents matching Falk's description.*
- *Surveillance of known interests, including classical music venues and chess tournaments.*
- *Development of a psychological profile to predict potential targets and operational behavior.*

- *Recruitment of assets within European criminal networks to gather intelligence on Falk's movements and contracts.*

Status: *Active and dangerous. Engage with extreme caution.*

Her fingers brushed against the manila folder, a tangible symbol of the precarious path she was about to tread.

Her mind was a whirlwind of scenarios, each more complex and perilous than the last. Henrik Falk's name was a beacon in the fog of her current predicament, a lead on the man that took a shot at her.

Becca's heart rate ticked up a notch as she considered the implications of possessing the file. Jack's involvement was a risk in itself; his presence here was forbidden, a clear violation of protocol that could cost him everything. The gravity of his decision to help her wasn't lost on Becca, and it added a weighty sense of responsibility on her shoulders.

The silence in the car was a canvas for her thoughts, each one painting a stroke of what-ifs and maybes. She was acutely aware of the delicate dance of trust and treachery she was engaged in. The file represented a sliver of hope, a chance to gain the upper hand, but it also held the power to drag her deeper into the abyss.

As Jack navigated the streets with the ease of a man well-versed in the art of evasion, Becca's mind raced with the possibilities of what the file contained.

"Falk entered the country four days ago on a Canadian passport, using the alias Klaus Gerhardt," Jack explained, his eyes periodically scanning the rearview mirror for any signs of being followed. "The alias dropped off the map, so the NSA suspects he's switched to a new one while in the country."

Becca's mind raced. Falk's ability to vanish and reappear under different guises was a testament to his skill and the danger he posed. She interjected, her voice tinged with a mix of concern and certainty, "I think I might be the target."

Jack nodded, his expression grim. "It's possible. Falk doesn't usually rely on many local assets, but there might be a way to find them." He paused, as if weighing his next words carefully. "There was some intersection in college between Falk and someone who works at the Swedish Embassy. A woman named Giselle Blanc. Other than that, we don't have much."

Becca absorbed the information, her brain already formulating plans and contingencies. Giselle Blanc at the Swedish Embassy could be a crucial lead, a thread to pull in the tangled web that was Henrik Falk's operations.

"Thanks, Jack," Becca said, her tone sincere. She took the file, placing it carefully in her bag. The weight of the folder felt like a physical manifestation of the burden she carried.

Jack pulled over at a nondescript corner bustling with people. It was the perfect spot for Becca to blend in and disappear. As she opened the door, she took a moment to look back at Jack, an unspoken acknowledgment of the risk he had taken to help her.

Stepping out onto the sidewalk, Becca merged with the crowd, her senses heightened, her mind alert.

Chapter 21

The Swedish Embassy stood imposingly on the street, its facade a testament to diplomatic decorum and international relations. Becca, however, was not there for diplomatic reasons. She was tucked away in a nondescript car parked a discreet distance from the embassy, her eyes fixed on the entrance, a pair of binoculars and a camera within easy reach.

Surveillance work, especially patterns-of-life observation, was a task Becca was all too familiar with. She had spent countless hours in the Middle East, watching and waiting, recording the mundane activities of her subjects. It was a necessary part of the job, but one she found excruciatingly boring. The monotony of the task left her trapped with her own thoughts, a situation she found increasingly frustrating. She longed for action, for the opportunity to directly engage with the problem at hand, but surveillance required patience and stillness.

Over several days, Becca meticulously recorded Giselle Blanc's routine. The predictability of Giselle's life was almost clockwork – the early morning workouts, the return to her Georgetown apartment, the punctual arrival at the embassy by 8:30 am, and her departure at 6 pm. Becca noted every detail, no matter how insignificant it might seem. The routine nature of Giselle's life suggested she was not involved in clandestine services, but Becca knew appearances could be deceiving.

As she watched Giselle, Becca couldn't help but feel a sense of weariness. The hours dragged on, each minute stretching longer than the last. She hated the inactivity, the sense of being a passive observer rather than an active participant. Her mind wandered, replaying past missions, analyzing her current situation, planning hypothetical strategies. The mental gymnastics were exhausting, yet they were her only respite from the tedium of surveillance.

As Becca sat in her car, her gaze fixed on the Swedish Embassy, her mind kept circling back to Giselle Blanc. Giselle could be the key, the best lead she had in tracking down Henrik Falk. Becca knew the world of espionage was a tangled web of connections and relationships, often hidden beneath layers of mundane normalcy. Giselle's seemingly ordinary life, her routine that bordered on the robotic, was a gift to an intelligence officer. It would be easy to see something out of place in her routine.

Becca's focus sharpened as she watched Giselle Blanc leave the Swedish Embassy unexpectedly early. This deviation from her usual routine instantly piqued Becca's interest. She started her car and followed at a safe distance as Giselle hailed a ride-share car. Becca's mind raced with possibilities. Was this a routine change, or was it connected to Henrik Falk?

As they navigated through the city, Becca's experience in surveillance allowed her to blend seamlessly into the traffic, her eyes never leaving the car ahead. The Hathaway Hotel loomed into view, its upscale façade a stark contrast to the gritty streets they had just traversed. Giselle's destination was intriguing. The Hathaway was known for its discretion and privacy, a perfect place for clandestine meetings.

Becca parked her car a block away, her eyes fixed on the hotel's entrance. She pondered the significance of this location. Could Henrik Falk be staying here? It was a plausible hypothesis. The Hathaway offered the perfect cover for someone like Falk, who needed to stay hidden yet accessible. Becca's instincts told her this was more than a coincidence.

She watched as Giselle disappeared into the hotel, her mind racing with questions. Was Giselle meeting Falk? Or was she merely a courier, a go-between passing messages? The change in Giselle's pattern was too significant to ignore. Becca knew she needed to get closer, to find a way to observe without being seen.

She reached for her phone, considering her options. A direct approach was too risky; subtlety was key. Perhaps she could pose as a guest or find a vantage point to keep an eye on the hotel's comings and goings. Every fiber of her being was alert now, her training kicking in. This was the break she had been waiting for, and she wasn't going to let it slip through her fingers.

Becca weighed her options carefully. The Hathaway Hotel's lobby bar offered a strategic vantage point, but maintaining effective surveillance there would be challenging to do alone. She needed an extra pair of eyes, someone who could help her observe without drawing attention. However, her usual contacts within the CIA were off-limits due to her current situation.

She scrolled through her phone, considering her limited options. Then, a name came to mind – someone outside the usual channels but capable and trustworthy. She hesitated for a moment, knowing that involving this person could complicate things further. But the opportunity to uncover what Giselle was doing at the hotel was too crucial to pass up.

With a sense of resolve, Becca composed a text message, her fingers moving swiftly over the screen. She sent it, hoping for a quick response. The message was concise: "Need your help with surveillance. Can you meet at Hathaway Hotel ASAP?"

She locked her phone and slipped it back into her pocket, her eyes returning to the hotel's entrance. The minutes ticked by slowly as she waited for a reply, her mind racing with the possibilities of what could be unfolding inside the hotel. She knew that whoever she had contacted would understand the urgency and the need for discretion.

Finally, her phone vibrated with an incoming message. She quickly checked it, a sense of relief washing over her as she read the affirmative response. Help was on the way. She exited her car and made her way towards the hotel, blending in with the crowd. Her senses were heightened, her training taking over as she prepared to enter the lion's den.

As she approached the lobby bar, she scanned the area, looking for the best spot to settle in. She needed a place with a clear view of the hotel's entrance and the bar itself, somewhere she could observe without being too conspicuous. The game of cat and mouse was about to begin, and Becca was determined to uncover the truth behind Giselle Blanc's unexpected visit to the Hathaway Hotel.

Chapter 22

B ecca's face lit up with a mixture of relief and joy as she spotted Dr. Ephraim Goldman entering the hotel lobby. The sight of the end times prophecy expert, whom she had rescued from kidnappers in Nigeria shortly after the catastrophic events of 3/16, brought a sense of comfort and familiarity in the midst of her current turmoil.

As Dr. Goldman approached, Becca raised her hand to catch his attention. He recognized her immediately, his face breaking into a warm, welcoming smile. They embraced briefly, a hug that conveyed mutual respect and a shared history of challenging experiences.

"It's so good to see you, Ephraim," Becca said, her voice tinged with genuine happiness.

"The pleasure is all mine, Becca," Dr. Goldman replied, his eyes reflecting a deep sense of gratitude. "And how is David? I've been meaning to catch up with both of you."

Becca's expression sobered slightly. "David's... well, he's going through some things. It's a long story, and unfortunately, we don't have time for it today."

Dr. Goldman nodded understandingly, his eyes showing a hint of concern. "Of course, I understand. Time is of the essence. Tell me, how can I assist you today?"

Becca took a deep breath, gathering her thoughts. She quickly briefed Dr. Goldman on the situation – her surveillance of Giselle Blanc, the unexpected detour to the Hathaway Hotel, and her need for assistance in maintaining effective surveillance. She showed Dr. Goldman photos of Giselle and Henrik.

"We need to keep an eye on Giselle without drawing attention to ourselves," Becca explained. "I'll need you to watch the main entrance and keep an eye out for anyone who might be meeting with her. I'll focus on the lobby bar area. We need to figure out if she's meeting someone here, and if so, who that might be."

Dr. Goldman listened intently, his eyes scanning the lobby as he absorbed the details. "Understood," he said with a nod. "I'll take a position where I can observe the entrance without being too obvious. If I see anything unusual or if Giselle leaves, I'll let you know immediately."

"Thank you, Ephraim," Becca said, her tone filled with gratitude. "Your help means a lot."

With their roles defined, Dr. Goldman discreetly positioned himself near the entrance, blending in with the hotel's guests. Becca, meanwhile, settled into a strategic spot in the lobby bar, her eyes keenly observing the comings and goings of the hotel's patrons.

Together, they began their silent vigil, each acutely aware of the importance of their task and the potential implications of what they might uncover.

Becca's focus intensified as her phone vibrated softly, signaling a new message. She glanced down discreetly, reading the text from Dr. Goldman. Her eyes immediately shifted to the entrance of the bar, where she spotted Henrik and Giselle making their way inside. Her heart rate picked up slightly, a mix of adrenaline and caution coursing through her.

She observed Henrik's calculated movements, noting how he chose a table that offered a clear view of the bar's exits. His strategic positioning spoke volumes about his awareness and experience in such situations. Giselle, on the other hand, seemed more relaxed, casually moving a bowl of peanuts to another table as they settled in.

From her vantage point, Becca watched the pair engage in what appeared to be light conversation. They ordered Tapas and drinks, maintaining an air of casualness that belied the seriousness of their meeting. Becca remained vigilant, taking mental notes of their interactions, trying to decipher any hidden signals or coded communication.

After about an hour, Henrik and Giselle prepared to leave. Becca quickly sent a text to Dr. Goldman, instructing him to track which floor the elevator headed to but to avoid direct contact. She watched them exit the bar, her mind racing with possibilities and plans.

A few tense minutes passed before her phone buzzed again. "10," the message from Dr. Goldman read. Becca's mind immediately started formulating a plan. The tenth floor – that was their destination. She needed to find a way to get more information without blowing her cover or putting herself in unnecessary danger.

She quickly gathered her belongings, her mind already several steps ahead. She needed to get to the tenth floor, but she had to do it in a way that wouldn't draw attention. As she moved out of the bar, she sent a quick text to Dr. Goldman, thanking him for his assistance and letting him know she would take it from here.

Stepping into the elevator, Becca pressed the button for the tenth floor, her senses heightened. She knew that the next few minutes could be crucial in unraveling the mystery surrounding Henrik Falk and his connection to Giselle Blanc.

Becca's footsteps were measured and silent as she made her way along the corridor of the tenth floor. Her eyes scanned each door she passed, particularly noting those marked with "Do Not Disturb" signs. In her experience, individuals like Henrik Falk preferred to remain undisturbed, especially when involved in clandestine activities.

As she approached room 1009, her heart skipped a beat when the door suddenly swung open. Giselle Blanc stepped out, her presence catching Becca off guard. Without missing a beat, Becca continued walking, her pace steady, as if she were just another guest passing by. She resisted the urge to glance back, knowing that any sign of recognition or surprise could compromise her position.

Once she was a safe distance away, Becca allowed herself a moment to process what had just happened. A wave of frustration washed over her as she chastised herself for the lack of caution. She had been too eager, too rushed in her surveillance, and that moment of carelessness could have cost her dearly. Her cover could have been blown, or worse, she could have found herself in a dangerous confrontation.

Despite the close call, Becca couldn't help but feel a sense of relief mixed with her frustration. She now knew Henrik's exact location, a crucial piece of information. But the way she had obtained it left her feeling amateurish, a stark contrast to the seasoned field agent she knew herself to be.

She made her way to the stairwell, her mind racing with the next steps. She needed to regroup and plan her next move carefully. The information about Henrik's room was valuable, but it had come at the risk of exposing herself. She needed to be smarter, more calculated in her approach. As she descended the stairs, her thoughts were already formulating a new strategy, one that would allow her to gather the intelligence she needed without risking her cover or her safety.

Chapter 23

In the opulent office of Gabriel Vale, the two men sat across from each other, the air thick with anticipation and strategy. Lucien Morreau, once a pariah, now on the cusp of a grand resurgence, looked intently at Gabriel, his eyes reflecting a mix of gratitude and ambition.

Gabriel, ever the charismatic visionary, leaned forward, his hands clasped together on the desk. "Lucien, your episode on my show was nothing short of historic. Over one billion people tuned in to witness your moment of vulnerability and courage. It's unprecedented."

Lucien's lips curled into a smile, a sense of pride washing over him. "It's remarkable, Gabriel. I never imagined such a response."

Gabriel nodded, his expression turning more serious. "And it's just the beginning. Your book, 'Lucien Morreau: The Courage to Forgive Myself,' is perfectly timed. The world is ready to hear your story in your own words."

Lucien leaned back in his chair, his mind racing with the possibilities. "The timing does seem fortuitous. I believe this book could redefine my legacy."

Gabriel's eyes sparkled with excitement. "Absolutely. And there's more. The Virtual Gabriel tool has been a massive success. In its first week alone, we had over 500 million users. Now, we're looking at over a billion users this month. It's the fastest adoption of any digital tool in history."

Lucien's eyebrows raised in surprise. "A billion users? That's astounding."

"Yes, and it's a testament to the hunger for spiritual guidance in these trying times," Gabriel continued. "Your comeback tour, combined with the reach of Virtual Gabriel, will create a synergy like no other. We're not just talking about a book launch; we're talking about a movement."

Lucien nodded, his mind already envisioning the crowds, the interviews, the adulation. "A movement... Yes, I can see it now. My story, intertwined with the spiritual guidance of Virtual Gabriel, reaching billions."

Gabriel stood up, his presence commanding the room. "Lucien, together, we're going to change the world. Your redemption story will inspire millions, and with the technology we have, we'll be able to reach every corner of the globe. I'd like to talk to you about digital currency –"

Lucien's smile wavered slightly as Gabriel delved into the topic of digital currency, a realm that had been a cornerstone of The Circle's vision. He listened intently, his mind racing with memories of his own efforts and the complexities they had faced.

Gabriel, sensing Lucien's discomfort, raised a hand gently, signaling patience. "Lucien, I understand that The Circle had a monumental task at hand. You were dealing with the aftermath of 3/16, navigating peace deals, managing wars, and on top of that, trying to launch a new digital currency. It was a Herculean effort."

Lucien relaxed slightly, appreciating Gabriel's acknowledgment of the challenges he had faced. "Yes, it was a complex and ambitious endeavor. We believed in the transformative power of a unified digital currency."

Gabriel nodded, his expression one of understanding and respect. "And that vision was ahead of its time. But, coercion was a part of that strategy. It's a fragile foundation for any long-term plan."

Lucien leaned forward, intrigued. "So, what's different about your approach, Gabriel?"

Gabriel's eyes lit up with excitement. "We've developed a digital payment system that's not just an improvement over existing systems – it's a complete game-changer. It's user-friendly, secure, and most importantly, it's based on voluntary adoption, not coercion."

Lucien's interest was piqued. "Voluntary adoption? That's a bold strategy."

"Exactly," Gabriel continued. "People are wary of being forced into new systems, especially when it comes to their finances. Our system is designed to be so efficient and beneficial that users will naturally gravitate towards it. It's about offering a superior alternative, not imposing a new order."

Lucien nodded thoughtfully, the wheels in his mind turning. "That's a smart approach. People want control over their choices, especially in these uncertain times."

Gabriel leaned back, a confident smile playing on his lips. "And that's where we come in. With your comeback and the reach of Virtual Gabriel, we have the perfect platform to introduce this system to the world. Your story of redemption and our technological breakthrough will resonate with millions."

Lucien's smile returned, broader this time. "A new beginning, not just for me, but for the world's financial systems. It's ambitious, Gabriel, but if anyone can make it happen, it's you."

Gabriel stood up, extending his hand. "Together, Lucien, we'll not just change the financial landscape; we'll reshape the world."

Lucien Morreau stood up from his plush, leather chair, his posture rigid and commanding, a look of pride mixed with a hint of indignation in his eyes. The opulent room, adorned with modern art and sleek, high-end furniture, seemed to shrink under the intensity of his presence. "Gabriel, I appreciate your help renovating my image, I truly do," he began, his voice steady yet laced with a firm resolve. "But I must be clear—I am not here to play second fiddle to anyone. I am a natural leader, a visionary. I see myself as a world leader, not merely a co-host on a spiritual TV program."

Across from him, Gabriel Vale remained seated, his demeanor calm and composed, his eyes reflecting a deep understanding and patience. The soft lighting of the room cast a gentle glow on his face, accentuating his thoughtful expression. As Lucien finished speaking, Gabriel slowly stood up, his height and presence matching Lucien's. He met Lucien's gaze squarely, his voice firm yet imbued with a gentle persuasiveness. "Lucien, I think there's been a misunderstanding here," he said, his words carefully chosen. "I don't want you as my second fiddle. You possess a unique talent, a gift that sets you apart from others. You are born to lead, and not just on a small scale, or even a large scale, like on my TV network."

Lucien's expression softened slightly, his defensive posture easing as curiosity began to replace the initial skepticism in his eyes.

Gabriel's voice grew more animated, his eyes sparkling with enthusiasm and conviction. "You are meant to lead the world, Lucien. To save it. I don't envision you as my second fiddle; I see you as a savior to the world."

A flicker of surprise and intrigue crossed Lucien's face, his eyes widening as he processed Gabriel's words.

"This is our moment, Lucien. Our opportunity to guide the world into an age of enlightenment unlike anything ever experienced," Gabriel continued, his passion evident in his voice. "I want to use my platform, not to lead, but to elevate you. To assist you in leading mankind."

Lucien's posture relaxed, his expression turning contemplative. Gabriel's words resonated with him, stirring the grand ambitions that had always driven him.

"Your role is not to remain in the shadows, Lucien. It's to be at the forefront, guiding humanity towards its next great evolution. My role is to support you, to amplify your voice and vision. Together, we can achieve something truly extraordinary."

Lucien paused, letting the gravity of Gabriel's proposal sink in. The idea of leading the world, of being its savior, aligned perfectly with the grandiose vision he had always held for himself. Gabriel's offer was not just support; it was an affirmation of his destiny.

After a moment of reflection, Lucien extended his hand, determination shining in his eyes. "Gabriel, let's make history together."

As their hands clasped in a firm handshake, a powerful alliance was forged—one that promised to reshape the world's future, driven by two men who saw themselves as the architects of a new era of human history.

Chapter 24

D avid sat in the rustic living room of Chaz's childhood home, his body present but his mind miles away, lost in a whirlwind of thoughts and concerns. The tranquil Virginia countryside, with its gentle hills and serene landscapes, felt like a world apart from the chaos and danger they were entangled in. As Nadia delved into the intricacies of CALEB's security, her voice became a distant hum in David's ears. He admired her dedication and skill, but his own restlessness was growing, a gnawing sense of urgency that he couldn't shake off.

His thoughts kept drifting to Becca, out there on her own, navigating the perilous waters of their investigation. He knew her capabilities, her strength and resilience, but that knowledge did little to quell the worry that simmered beneath the surface. Images of her in dangerous situations flashed through his mind, each scenario more unsettling than the last. He trusted her, yet the thought of her facing unknown threats alone sent a shiver down his spine.

David's gaze was distant, his mind piecing together the puzzle of Twilight Technologies. An old contact, a key that might unlock some of the mysteries surrounding the shadowy organization, came to mind. He needed to act, to follow this lead back in Washington. The urge to contribute, to be actively involved in unraveling the web they were caught in, was overwhelming.

Standing up, he addressed Nadia with a sense of purpose, "Keep at it, Nadia. Your work is vital." His words were supportive, but his tone betrayed his inner turmoil.

Finding Chaz in the kitchen, the comforting smell of coffee in the air, David felt a brief respite from his worries. "Chaz, I have to head into the city," he said, his voice tinged with resolve. "There's a lead I can't ignore. Look after everyone here."

Chaz's understanding gaze met David's. "We've got this, David. Just be careful," he replied, his voice steady yet filled with concern.

David nodded, feeling the weight of their shared responsibility. He glanced around at the group—Mark, Nadia, Chaz—each engrossed in their tasks, each a crucial part of The Resistance. They had become more than just a team; they were a family, bound by a common cause.

Stepping outside, David took a deep breath, the fresh country air momentarily calming his racing thoughts. He couldn't help but worry about Becca, about the dangers she faced alone. But he also knew that action was necessary, that they had to keep moving forward, uncovering the truth hidden in the dark corners of power and conspiracy.

With a sense of determination, David walked to his car, his mind a mix of worry for Becca and resolve to pursue the lead in Washington.

David's fingers moved swiftly over his phone's screen, typing out a message to Liz Sinclair, his longtime contact at a hedge fund. He had always admired Liz's knack for uncovering the most elusive financial information, a skill that could prove invaluable in their current predicament. The message sent, he waited with a mix of anticipation and impatience, his gaze fixed on the phone.

Almost immediately, the screen lit up with a response. Liz was available for a late afternoon coffee. Relief washed over David. This meeting could be the breakthrough they needed. They quickly agreed on a quaint coffee shop in the heart of the city, a place known for its discretion and quiet corners, perfect for confidential conversations.

David started the car, the engine's familiar hum a comforting sound amidst the whirlwind of his thoughts. As he drove towards the city, the rural landscapes gradually gave way to the urban sprawl of Washington D.C. The familiar sights of the city brought back a flood of memories, both good and bad, from his time in the FBI.

His mind was a carousel of thoughts and strategies, planning his approach with Liz, pondering over what information she might uncover about Twilight Technologies. The importance of this meeting weighed heavily on him, a potential key to unraveling the complex web they found themselves entangled in.

Despite the task at hand, David couldn't shake off his concern for Becca. He hoped she was safe, that her skills and instincts would keep her out of harm's way. The thought of her alone in the field, possibly facing unknown dangers, gnawed at him. He made a mental note to check in with her as soon as he was done with Liz.

The city's skyline loomed ahead, a concrete jungle where secrets and power played a never-ending game of chess. David felt a surge of determination. They were close to something, he could feel it. The answers they sought were hidden somewhere in the intricate dance of shadowy corporations and covert operations.

Pulling into a parking spot near the coffee shop, David took a moment to gather his thoughts. He checked his reflection in the rearview mirror, straightening his jacket. This meeting with Liz Sinclair could be a turning point, and he was ready to play his part in uncovering the truth. With a deep breath, he stepped out of the car and made his way to the coffee shop, ready to delve into the depths of corporate intrigue.

Chapter 25

David sat in the quiet corner of the coffee shop, his mind a whirlwind of thoughts and emotions. He anxiously awaited Liz Sinclair, his old ally from his FBI days. As he scanned the crowd, memories of their past collaborations flooded his mind. Liz, with her unparalleled expertise in financial forensics, had been a crucial ally in unraveling complex financial crimes. Her ability to dissect the convoluted structures of shell corporations, especially in the Caribbean, had always impressed him.

For a time, the two had a romantic relationship.

When Liz finally appeared, her confident stride and professional attire cutting through the casual atmosphere, a wave of nostalgia washed over David. She reached out, touching his arm affectionately, a reminder of the deeper connection they once shared. "David, how have you been?" she asked, her voice laced with genuine concern.

David forced a smile, feeling a pang of melancholy. "I've been better, Liz. It's been a tough ride since 3/16," he admitted, the weight of recent events pressing down on him.

Their small talk was a dance of familiarity, a blend of comfort and a reminder of what once was. But David knew he couldn't dwell in the past. He had a purpose here, a mission that needed Liz's unique skills.

David shifted the topic, pulling out a folder thick with documents. "I need your help, Liz," he began, his tone serious. He laid out the information he had gathered on Twilight Technologies, explaining the potential dangers involved in digging deeper. Liz listened intently, her sharp mind already piecing together possible approaches.

"I'm glad to help, David," she said resolutely. "You know I've always enjoyed a good challenge."

The conversation took a more personal turn as Liz alluded to their past relationship. "Do you ever miss the old times?" she asked, a hint of nostalgia in her voice.

David paused, considering his answer. "Sometimes," he admitted. "But 3/16 changed a lot for me. Changed everything, really."

Liz nodded in understanding. "It's the same for me. The world isn't what it used to be."

As they wrapped up their meeting, Liz assured David she would get to work immediately. "I'll drop everything I find to your CALEB account," she promised. "It's the only way to communicate securely these days."

David watched as Liz stood up to leave, her farewell warm and friendly. As she disappeared into the crowd, David felt a mix of gratitude and nostalgia. He knew he could count on Liz, just as he always had. With her help, the mystery of Twilight Technologies might finally unravel.

David remained seated in the coffee shop, the bustle around him fading into a distant hum as he sank into deep contemplation. The past month had been a relentless torrent of events, each one more challenging than the last. He felt as if he were being swept along by a current too strong to fight against.

His thoughts turned to his faith, a cornerstone of his life that had been neglected amidst the chaos. He realized how distant he had become from Christ, how the turmoil of recent events had created a chasm between him and his spiritual anchor. A sense of longing, a yearning for that lost connection, welled up within him.

Quietly, almost instinctively, David bowed his head and whispered a prayer. He sought closeness with Christ, a return to the spiritual intimacy that had once been his guiding light. His words were a mix of confession, plea, and hope, a heartfelt request for guidance and strength.

After his prayer, David reached for his phone and opened his Bible app. The familiar words on the screen brought a sense of comfort, a reminder of the enduring presence of his faith in his life. He randomly selected a passage, trusting that whatever he read was meant for him at this moment.

The words of the scripture resonated within him, speaking to his current struggles and offering a sense of peace. He read slowly, absorbing each word, allowing the divine wisdom to fill the void that recent events had created. It was a moment of tranquility amidst the storm, a much-needed spiritual respite.

As he closed the app, David felt a renewed sense of purpose and clarity. With a deep breath, he stood up, ready to step back into the world.

Chapter 26

B ecca's fingers danced over her phone's keypad, sending a quick text to Dr. Ephraim Goldman. "Heading up now. Keep your eyes peeled," she typed, her heart pounding with a mix of adrenaline and caution.

She stepped into the elevator, her senses heightened. The device in her hand, a compact marvel of technology, was ready to unlock Henrik's room.

This device, resembling a small, handheld computer, was equipped with advanced algorithms capable of rapidly cycling through millions of potential combinations used in electronic locks. It interfaced seamlessly with the electronic locking mechanism of the hotel room door, connecting via a small port or wirelessly, depending on the lock's design. Once activated, the device employed a brute-force attack method, systematically trying every possible combination at an incredibly high speed. Despite the vast number of potential combinations, the device's powerful processor and optimized code allowed it to find the correct code in a matter of minutes, if not seconds. This capability made it an invaluable tool for intelligence operatives like Becca, who often needed to gain access to secure locations quickly and discreetly. The device's silent operation and small size made it easy to conceal and use without drawing attention, a crucial feature in the high-stakes world of espionage.

When she reached room 1009, she pulled out the device and it whirred softly as it cycled through millions of codes. Finally, with a soft beep, the door unlocked. Becca slipped inside, her movements silent and precise.

She began her search methodically, starting with the suitcase on the luggage rack. It was neatly packed with a few changes of clothes and basic toiletries, nothing that hinted at the man's true nature or intentions. She rifled through the pockets of his garments, checking for hidden compartments or sewn-in secrets, but found nothing.

Next, Becca moved to the nightstand, pulling out the drawer with a gentle tug. Inside, there were the usual hotel amenities – a notepad, a pen, a Bible. She flipped through the pages of the notepad, looking for indentations or scribbles, but it was untouched. The pen was just a pen, and the Bible hadn't been moved in what looked like ages.

Her attention then shifted to the room's small desk. She opened each drawer, her fingers probing the backs and undersides for any hidden catches or false bottoms. Papers, a hotel service menu, and a Gideon's Bible lay inside, but nothing that indicated Henrik's true purpose.

Becca moved to the closet next, sliding the door open. A few hangers clattered softly, but it was mostly empty, save for a lone coat. She patted down the coat, checking the lining and pockets, but it was just a regular piece of clothing.

The bathroom was her next target. She scanned the shelves and the area under the sink. The toiletries were standard hotel fare, and the small trash bin held nothing but a used tissue and a soap wrapper.

She checked inside the air vents and along the wall for any small hides for documents, but found nothing.

Finally, she checked under the bed, a classic hiding spot. But all she found was a layer of dust and the faint outline of shoe prints in the carpet – Henrik's, no doubt.

Her eyes fell on a receipt from a food delivery service, the only item that seemed out of place in the sterile room. She picked it up, her eyes scanning the details. A small, seemingly insignificant detail, but in the world of espionage and covert operations, such information could be gold.

She returned the receipt to the trash and exited the room as quietly as she had entered. Once safely in the elevator, she pulled out her phone and texted Dr. Goldman. "Came up empty. Heading out now."

As the elevator descended, Becca's mind raced. Henrik was a ghost, leaving barely a trace behind. But the note about the peanut allergy was a lead, however small. It was something she could use, a vulnerability in an otherwise impenetrable facade.

She stepped out of the elevator, her eyes scanning the lobby for any sign of danger. Seeing none, she made her way to the lobby bar and took her corner booth, her mind already working on the next move in this high-stakes game of cat and mouse.

Chapter 27

David stepped out of the coffee shop and started walking down the block. His instincts, honed by years in the field, kicked in as he noticed the tall blonde man in wrap-around sunglasses. The man's movements were too calculated, too synchronized with David's own steps. He was being tailed, and the realization sent a jolt of adrenaline through him.

He quickly assessed his options. Confrontation was risky, especially if this man was as dangerous as Becca's information suggested. Fleeing was the safer choice, but it would leave him with unanswered questions and possibly expose him to further surveillance.

Then, a third option emerged in his mind – a daring, tactical maneuver. He could attempt to turn the tables on his pursuer. It was a risky move, requiring precision and a bit of luck, but it appealed to David's strategic nature.

With a plan forming, David quickened his pace, taking a series of turns down side streets, trying to appear as if he were attempting to lose his tail. He needed to convince the man that he was genuinely fleeing. After a few minutes of this, he ducked into a busy department store, blending in with the crowd.

Inside, he made his way through the aisles, occasionally glancing out of the store windows to keep track of the blonde man. Once he was sure he had a good lead, David exited through a different door, circling back towards where he first spotted his tail.

His heart pounded as he retraced his steps, staying alert for any sign of the man. He moved with purpose, his senses heightened, every sound and movement catching his attention. This was a high-stakes game of cat and mouse, and David was determined to come out on top.

As he rounded a corner, he spotted the blonde man, now looking slightly disoriented, scanning the area for any sign of David. Keeping to the shadows, David followed him from a safe distance, his mind racing with possibilities. Who was this man? Who did he work for? What did he want with David?

The pursuit continued, with David maintaining a careful balance between staying hidden and keeping the man in sight. He knew he had to tread carefully; one wrong move could turn the hunter into the hunted. But

David was resolute, driven by a need to uncover the truth behind this mysterious figure.

David, with years of experience in surveillance and counter-surveillance, couldn't help but admire the skill with which the blonde man, Henrik, maneuvered through the city. It was clear that he was trained, moving with a purposeful yet nonchalant gait, frequently changing directions and occasionally pausing to feign interest in shop windows or public displays, all classic counter-surveillance techniques.

Despite Henrik's proficiency, David managed to keep up, blending seamlessly into the crowds and using every trick he knew to remain undetected. He maintained a safe distance, always mindful of the possibility that Henrik might suddenly double back or attempt to flush out a tail.

David watched Henrik head towards a hotel. The hotel was upscale, its lobby bustling with guests and staff. Henrik entered with the confidence of someone familiar with the place. David paused outside, considering his next move. Going in directly after Henrik would be too risky; he needed a subtler approach.

David decided to wait a few moments before entering the hotel. He casually strolled in, pretending to be just another guest. Inside, he scanned the lobby, looking for any sign of Henrik. The lobby was large, with several seating areas and a busy reception desk. Guests milled about, some checking in, others waiting for friends or business associates.

David casually walked over to a brochure stand, pretending to peruse the tourist pamphlets while keeping his peripheral vision trained on the area. He needed to spot Henrik without drawing attention to himself.

David's focus shifted as his phone vibrated with an incoming message. Glancing at the screen, he saw Becca's name and quickly opened the message. It read, "Turn around and walk into the hotel bar, back corner." His heart rate increased slightly, a mix of anticipation and caution. Becca's message meant she was nearby, watching, and had likely observed something he hadn't.

Without hesitation, David smoothly pivoted away from the reception desk, abandoning his initial plan. He walked towards the hotel bar, maintaining a casual demeanor. His senses heightened, he scanned the area subtly, trying to spot Becca or any potential threats.

The bar was dimly lit, creating an ambiance of relaxed sophistication. Patrons sat at tables and along the bar, engaged in quiet conversations over drinks. David's eyes adjusted to the dim light as he made his way to the back corner, as instructed.

As he approached the designated spot, he finally spotted Becca. She was seated at a small table, her back to the wall, giving her a clear view of the entire bar. She was dressed casually, blending in perfectly with the other patrons, but her posture and alert eyes betrayed her vigilance.

David and Becca sat across from each other, their conversation low and urgent amidst the ambient noise of the hotel bar. Becca's question hung in the air, "What are you doing here?"

David leaned in, his voice barely above a whisper. "I was tailing someone who was following me as I left a coffee shop," he explained. His eyes flickered around the room, still on high alert. "I had a meeting with Liz Sinclair. She's helping me dig into Twilight Technologies."

Becca's expression shifted, a mix of concern and realization dawning on her face. "Liz is burned, David. She has to be," she said with a certainty that sent a chill down David's spine. "There's no way Henrik could have gotten to you this quickly otherwise."

David felt a knot form in his stomach. The implications of Becca's words were clear and dangerous. He had walked into a trap without even realizing it.

Becca continued, her tone grave. "I think I got this all wrong. Henrik wasn't targeting me; he's here for you. This has to be connected to Twilight Technologies. They're trying to tie up loose ends."

David's mind raced. The pieces of the puzzle were falling into place, but the picture they formed was more sinister than he had anticipated. Twilight Technologies, a shadowy entity with unknown motives, was now a direct threat to his life.

"We need to act fast," David said, his voice firm despite the growing unease. "We can't let them get the upper hand."

Becca nodded in agreement, her eyes reflecting the same determination that David felt. "We'll need to be strategic and careful. They're playing a dangerous game, and we're right in the middle of it."

In the shadowed corner of the hotel bar, Becca's face was a mask of determination as she leaned in closer to David. "But I'm ready to act now, if you are," she whispered, her voice a blend of urgency and resolve. "I've got a plan, but I can't do it alone. I need you."

David's heart raced as he listened. The gravity of the situation was not lost on him. He felt a mix of apprehension and adrenaline, a familiar cocktail from his days in the field. "Tell me the plan," he said, his voice steady despite the turmoil inside.

Becca outlined her strategy with precision. "Henrik orders his dinner from the same place every night, delivered right to his hotel room. We're going to intercept that delivery."

David's mind raced as he processed the information. "Are you thinking of drugging him?" he asked, trying to anticipate her next move.

"Something along those lines," Becca replied, her eyes not leaving his. "I'll pose as the delivery person. Once he's vulnerable, we'll get the information we need and then turn him over to the FBI."

David felt a surge of protectiveness mixed with concern. The plan was bold, possibly too bold. But they were running out of options, and time. "It's risky," he said, his voice tinged with worry. "But if you think it can work, I'm in."

Becca's expression softened for a moment, acknowledging the risk. "I know it's dangerous, but we don't have much choice."

David nodded, his mind already racing through the logistics. "I'll be your backup. I'll keep an eye out while you make the delivery. We need a solid plan for getting out of there too, in case things don't go as planned."

Becca agreed, her face set in a determined line. "Once we have Henrik, we need to move quickly and quietly. We'll use the service exits to avoid drawing any attention."

David felt a familiar tension settle in his shoulders, the weight of responsibility and the thrill of action. They were stepping into dangerous territory, but he trusted Becca's judgment. They had been through so much together, and he knew they could rely on each other.

David watched with a mix of apprehension and admiration as Becca expertly maneuvered through their plan. The moment he called out to the delivery driver, his heart had skipped a beat, a part of him still questioning the audacity of their scheme. "For Henrik?" he called out.

The woman from MunchMobile handed David the food. "Thanks for the tip, man."

As David handed the food to Becca in the elevator, he couldn't help but feel a sense of camaraderie and thrill at their covert operation.

In the confined space of the elevator, Becca's actions were swift and precise. As she sprinkled the brown powder into the gyro, under the sandwich's contents, David raised an eyebrow. "Peanut butter powder?" he asked, a hint of disbelief in his voice.

Becca nodded, her expression serious yet focused. "He's allergic," she said simply, as if that explained everything. David couldn't help but chuckle at the irony of it all. "You're brutal. Risky move," he commented, though he couldn't hide the hint of respect in his tone.

Becca just patted her bag reassuringly, her eyes betraying a glimmer of determination. "I'm ready," she said, her voice steady.

As they stepped out onto the 10th floor, David felt a surge of adrenaline. He watched Becca approach room 1009, her movements confident yet cautious. When Henrik opened the door, David held his breath, but the exchange went smoothly.

Back in the hallway, the waiting was the hardest part. David's senses were heightened, every sound amplified in his mind. A couple of minutes passed. Then, the crash from inside the room jolted him back to reality.

Becca waited 30 seconds, then knocked on the door, "Hey man, sorry, forgot your drink? Ya want it?"

No answer.

David joined Becca at the door, watching as she pulled out the door lock scanner. The device whirred softly, a sound that seemed unnaturally loud in the tense silence of the hallway. The lock clicked open, and they entered the room.

The sight that greeted them was expected. Henrik lay on the floor, struggling for breath, his body contorted in an allergic reaction. David's training kicked in, and he quickly scanned the room for any threats or surprises. But it was just them and Henrik, vulnerable and incapacitated.

David looked at Becca, a silent question in his eyes. They had their target, now incapacitated and at their mercy. It was time to find out what Henrik knew, time to unravel the mysteries that had brought them to this moment. The weight of the situation settled on David's shoulders, a mix of responsibility and urgency. They needed answers, and they needed them now.

When David reached Henrik, he struggled to swing at him, but he couldn't muster the energy as he struggled to catch his breath. David flipped him over and zip tied Henrik's hands and ankles. He flipped Henrik back to face Becca.

Henrik continued to struggle to breathe.

Henrik's labored breathing filled the room, each gasp a desperate fight for air. Becca's tone was calm, almost conversational, as she explained the situation to Henrik. "Peanut butter in your gyro," she said, her voice laced with a hint of irony. "Must be tough, traveling so much with an allergy like that."

Henrik's eyes were wide with panic, his body writhing in discomfort and fear. Becca's gaze was steady, unflinching as she watched him struggle. "I have an epi-pen," she continued, her voice still calm. "I'm willing to let you use it. But first, I need some answers."

David stood silently, observing the scene. He could see the desperation in Henrik's eyes, the realization that his life hung in the balance. Becca's strategy was risky, but it was their best chance at getting the information they needed.

Henrik's struggle intensified, his breaths becoming more labored, more desperate. Becca glanced at David, her expression grim. "Looks like Henrik isn't going to get the help he needs," she said, her voice tinged with regret. "Just another unfortunate accident."

Henrik's eyes darted between Becca and David, the severity of his situation evident. Becca leaned in closer.

"Just a few simple questions, Henrik. Answer them, and you get the help you need."

David watched as Henrik's gaze fixed on him, a silent acknowledgment. "Me?" David asked, his voice a mix of surprise and realization. Henrik's nod was weak but clear.

"Twilight Technologies," Becca pressed on. "Did they hire you?" Henrik's response was a shake of the head, a clear 'no.'

David's mind raced. "Then who?" he asked, his voice urgent.

Henrik's struggle for breath was palpable, each gasp a battle. But he managed to utter a single word, a word that sent a chill down David's spine. "Stahl."

David's eyes widened. "Viktor Stahl?" he asked, seeking confirmation. Henrik's nod, weak but unmistakable, confirmed it.

The revelation crashed over David, sending ripples of shock and realization through him. Viktor Stahl—the name was not just another entry in the long list of criminals and operatives David had encountered in his career. This was a name that resonated with a deeper, more ominous tone. Viktor Stahl, known for his ruthless efficiency and unscrupulous methods, was a key figure in the underworld of international espionage and covert operations. His reputation was built on a foundation of fear and respect, a man who could make problems disappear as easily as he could make people vanish.

But it was more than just the name and the reputation that struck David. Viktor Stahl had been Lucien Morreau's right-hand man, a pivotal player in The Circle, an organization that had its fingers in a multitude of global machinations. Stahl was the shadow in the background, the executor of Morreau's darker designs, the man who carried out the tasks that required a certain moral flexibility. He was the architect of chaos, the silent orchestrator of events that had shaped the geopolitical landscape in ways that few could comprehend.

David's mind was a whirlwind of thoughts and connections, piecing together the fragments of information he had gathered over time. Stahl's involvement suggested a deeper, more sinister plot at play. The Circle, with its tendrils extending into the highest echelons of power, had been a force of immense influence and control. And now, with Lucien Morreau's fall from grace, it seemed that Stahl had stepped out of the shadows, moving pieces on a chessboard that few even knew existed.

The implications were staggering. If Stahl was targeting him, it meant that David was entangled in a web far more complex and dangerous than he had initially thought. It wasn't just about Twilight Technologies or the shadowy figures behind it; it was about a power struggle at the highest levels of global influence. In fact, Viktor Stahl could be the person behind Twilight Technologies.

David felt a chill run down his spine as he realized the gravity of the situation. He was not just a player in this game; he was a target, a pawn that someone wanted off the board. And the person moving the pieces was none other than Viktor Stahl, a master of the game whose next move was shrouded in mystery and menace.

Becca's gaze never left Henrik, her expression a mix of determination and urgency. They had their answer, a crucial piece of the puzzle.

Becca swiftly pulled out a set of zip ties from her bag, handing them to David. "Tie him to the boiler pipes," she instructed, her voice calm but firm. David, with practiced efficiency, secured Henrik's limp form to the sturdy pipes, ensuring the ties were tight enough to prevent any escape.

As David stepped back, Becca produced a syringe from her bag, its contents a mystery. She approached Henrik with a clinical detachment, injecting the syringe's contents into his arm. Almost immediately, Henrik's struggles ceased, his body going limp as he succumbed to unconsciousness. She then inserted the epi-pen to bringing him back from his allergic reaction.

Becca then pulled out her phone, dialing a number she knew by heart. As the call connected, she spoke with a tone of authority, "Room 1009. You'll find a gift that will get you a promotion. Thanks for taking care of this." She ended the call without waiting for a response, her expression unreadable.

David watched her, a mix of admiration and concern in his eyes. They had just incapacitated one of the world's most elusive assassins, a feat that few could boast of. Yet, the gravity of their actions and the potential repercussions were not lost on him.

Becca met David's gaze, a hint of weariness in her eyes. "Let's get out of here," she said, her voice betraying a hint of fatigue beneath her composed exterior.

They quickly gathered their belongings, ensuring they left no trace of their presence in the room. Moving with purpose, they exited the hotel room, closing the door behind them. The hotel's corridors were quiet, the hum of distant conversations the only sound accompanying their swift departure.

As they walked through the hotel lobby, David couldn't help but feel the weight of their actions. They had just set in motion a series of events that would undoubtedly have far-reaching consequences. Yet, in that moment, there was a sense of accomplishment, a feeling that they had taken a significant step in unraveling the tangled web of intrigue that surrounded them.

Exiting the hotel, the cool evening air hit them, a stark contrast to the tense atmosphere they had just left behind. They walked in silence, each lost in their thoughts, aware that the road ahead was fraught with danger and uncertainty. But for now, they had achieved a small victory, a step closer to uncovering the truth behind the shadows that threatened to engulf them.

Chapter 28

D avid sat silently in the passenger seat, his mind a tempest of thoughts and emotions as Becca skillfully navigated the car through the bustling streets of Washington D.C. The revelation that he had been the intended target of an assassination attempt orchestrated by Viktor Stahl sent shivers down his spine. The gravity of the situation was overwhelming; Henrik's failure was merely a temporary setback for Viktor, a man known for his relentless pursuit and ruthless tactics. David's heart raced with the realization that more assassins could be dispatched, ones who might not care about collateral damage. This put not only his life but also the lives of his friends in The Resistance in imminent danger.

As he glanced at Becca, a surge of guilt washed over him. He had inadvertently dragged her into this deadly game of cat and mouse. The thought of her being in harm's way because of his actions was unbearable. He admired her focus and determination, evident in her steady grip on the steering wheel and the resolute set of her jaw. Yet, beneath that facade, he could sense her concern, a subtle tension that mirrored his own.

In the midst of this turmoil, David's mind instinctively reverted to his training and experiences from his time in the FBI. He needed to work the problem, approach it with the methodical precision that had served him well in the past. There had been numerous occasions during his career when his life had been in jeopardy, when he had been the target of someone's vengeance or desperation. He began to mentally sift through those experiences, extracting lessons and strategies.

First and foremost, he knew the importance of staying one step ahead, of anticipating the enemy's moves. He needed to think like Viktor, predict his next steps. Would Viktor send another assassin? It was likely. Would he try the same method or adapt? David's mind raced through scenarios, each one a potential threat to their safety.

He also knew the value of intelligence, of gathering as much information as possible. Who were Viktor's associates? What resources did he have at his disposal? Understanding the enemy was crucial in crafting an effective defense. David remembered the countless hours he had spent poring over files and surveillance footage, piecing together the puzzles that criminals left behind. That same diligence was required now.

Another key aspect was protection. They needed a safe house, a secure location where they could regroup and plan their next move. It wasn't just about finding a place off the grid; it was about ensuring it was fortified, both physically and in terms of information security. The Resistance needed a haven, a place where they could breathe and think without the constant threat of being discovered.

Lastly, David knew the importance of allies. In the Bureau, he had always had a team, people he could trust with his life. The Resistance was his new team, but they were scattered and vulnerable. They needed to be brought together, united in their purpose and their defense. There was strength in numbers, and in the diverse skills each member brought to the table.

These thoughts swirled in David's mind, a whirlwind of strategy and planning, interspersed with the ever-present concern for Becca's safety. He realized that while the context had changed, the principles of his FBI training still applied. They were not just fighting for survival; they were fighting for a cause, for a future where they could live without the shadow of death looming over them.

Amidst the whirlwind of strategic thoughts and concerns for Becca's safety, David felt a profound need for spiritual guidance. He closed his eyes for a moment, seeking solace in prayer. "Lord," he whispered silently, his heart heavy with the weight of their predicament, "guide us through this darkness." He sought not just for physical protection but for wisdom and clarity. The challenges they faced were immense, and human intellect alone seemed insufficient. David yearned for divine insight, for that sense of peace and direction that he had often found in his faith. As he opened his eyes, there was a newfound determination in his gaze, a subtle shift that came from entrusting their plight to a power greater than themselves. With this prayer, David felt a sense of calm amidst the storm, a reminder that they were not navigating these treacherous waters alone.

Pulling into a parking garage, Becca drove up several levels before finding a secluded spot. The car came to a halt, and the engine's hum ceased, leaving them in a cocoon of silence. She turned to face David, her eyes reflecting a mix of resolve and vulnerability. "We'll get to the bottom of this," she declared, her voice firm. "We need to find a new safehouse in D.C., bring The Resistance back together, and keep working on this."

David felt a surge of emotion as he looked into Becca's eyes. The urgency of the situation, the depth of his feelings for her, everything he had been holding back, came rushing to the surface. He reached out, taking her hands in his, feeling the warmth and strength in her grip. "I love you, Becca," he confessed, his voice trembling with emotion. "I can't go another moment without you knowing that. We're in the Tribulation, the most challenging time in human history, and I don't want to spend another minute without you knowing my true feelings."

Becca's response was immediate and heartfelt. She reached up, her hands gently cradling his face, her eyes searching his soul. "I feel the same way, David," she whispered, her voice a blend of strength and tenderness. "I don't want to face this world without you by my side."

In that moment, in the dimly lit confines of the parking garage, with the chaos of the world just outside, they found a moment of profound connection and peace in each other's embrace. The challenges ahead were daunting, the path fraught with uncertainty, but in each other's arms, they found a strength and resolve they hadn't realized was missing. It was a small beacon of hope, a flicker of light in a world growing increasingly dark, a reminder that even in the midst of tribulation, love could provide a sanctuary, a source of courage to face whatever lay ahead.

Chapter 29

T he old textile mill, nestled in the southeast side of Washington D.C., stood as a relic of a bygone era. Its red brick facade, weathered by time, bore the marks of history, while the large, multi-paned windows were clouded with the dust of disuse. As Mark's car rolled into the expansive interior, the sound of tires on the concrete floor echoed through the cavernous space, giving the place an almost cathedral-like atmosphere.

Inside, the mill was a labyrinth of potential. The main floor, once filled with the hum of machinery, was now a vast, open area, punctuated by sturdy wooden pillars that supported the high ceilings. Exposed beams crisscrossed overhead, and the faint smell of oil and cotton lingered in the air.

David, Becca, and Dr. Goldman waited eagerly as Mark, Chaz, and Nadia stepped out of the car. Dr. Goldman's face lit up with a warm, welcoming smile as he embraced each of them. "My dear friends, it's so good to see you safe," he exclaimed, his voice echoing slightly in the large space.

Mark looked around, his eyes taking in the raw, industrial charm of the place. "Well, this is quite the hideout," he remarked, a hint of sarcasm in his voice. "It's got a certain... post-apocalyptic chic to it."

David chuckled, leading them further into the mill. "It's not just about appearances, Mark. This place is off the grid, hard to find, and even harder to infiltrate. We've got surveillance cameras covering every angle, and I've set up some traps just in case we have uninvited guests."

Nadia's eyes sparkled with curiosity as they approached what would be her domain. "Tell me more about this Internet backbone," she inquired, her mind already racing with the possibilities.

"It's a direct line, Nadia," David replied. "You'll have unparalleled access to the net, and I've sure you can create a few surprises in the system to keep our digital footprint invisible."

Chaz, who had been quietly assessing the security measures, nodded in approval. "Impressive work, David. This could be the fortress we need to plan our next move."

As they settled into the makeshift meeting room, the group gathered around a large, reclaimed wooden table, surrounded by mismatched chairs. The room was lit by a series of industrial lamps that cast a warm glow over the space.

Becca leaned forward, her eyes intense and focused. "We've all made sacrifices to be here. This mill is more than just our hideout; it's our command center. From here, we'll coordinate our efforts, share intelligence, and strike back against those who threaten our world."

David added, his voice steady and determined, "We're up against powerful enemies, but in this place, we're more than just a team. We're a family, united by a common cause. This is where we stand our ground."

The group exchanged looks of determination and solidarity, each one understanding the weight of their mission. In this old textile mill, they would forge their resistance, a beacon of hope in a world shrouded in darkness.

David and Becca stood at the head of the long, weathered table, their postures exuding a quiet authority. The rest of the group – Mark, Chaz, Nadia, and Dr. Goldman – were arrayed around them, their faces reflecting a spectrum of emotions from curiosity to concern.

David, his eyes scanning the attentive faces, cleared his throat to begin. "We've had a significant development," he said, his voice echoing slightly in the vast space. "Our encounter with Henrik Falk has shed new light on our situation."

Becca picked up where David left off, her tone underscored with a hint of urgency. "Henrik was here on a mission to eliminate David. But we managed to turn the tables on him." She paused, letting the gravity of her words sink in. "Our interrogation revealed that he was hired by Viktor Stahl. This means we're dealing with forces that have deep roots in global espionage."

The group absorbed this revelation in silence, each member processing the implications in their own way. Mark shifted uncomfortably in his chair, while Chaz rubbed his chin thoughtfully. Dr. Goldman's expression was one of grave concern, his eyes reflecting the seriousness of the situation.

It was Nadia who broke the contemplative silence. Her voice, usually light and playful, carried a weight of seriousness. "Have you guys seen the latest video from Gabriel Vale?" she asked, her gaze moving between David and Becca.

Both shook their heads in unison, their expressions curious. "No, we've been a bit preoccupied," David replied, a wry smile touching his lips despite the tension.

Nadia's demeanor grew more earnest, almost insistent. "You need to see it. It's different from his usual content. Important enough to warrant our full attention."

The group repositioned themselves around the table, a sense of collective anticipation building. Nadia reached for her laptop, her fingers moving deftly over the keyboard as she pulled up the video. The screen flickered to life, revealing the familiar face of Gabriel Vale, his presence as commanding as ever.

As the video began to play, the room fell into a hushed silence, each member of The Resistance intently focused on the screen.

Chapter 30

The stage was set with an air of palpable excitement, the kind that only a Gabriel Vale event could muster. Thousands of his followers filled the auditorium, their eyes fixed on the charismatic figure who stood confidently at the center, basking in the adulation of his audience. The atmosphere was electric, a mix of reverence and anticipation hanging thickly in the air.

Gabriel, ever the showman, knew how to play to his crowd. His voice, both soothing and authoritative, resonated through the hall. "I have something special to share with you today," he began, his words carefully chosen to stoke the curiosity of his followers. "Something that will truly blow your minds."

The crowd leaned in, hanging on every word. Gabriel paused for effect, letting the tension build before continuing. "First, let me share some incredible news. Virtual Gabriel has been used by over one billion people since its launch." He let the number sink in, watching as a wave of awe swept over the audience. "And many of you use it every day." The revelation was met with a thunderous standing ovation, a testament to the influence and reach of his creation.

As the applause died down, Gabriel motioned for silence, his charismatic presence commanding the room. "Now, I'm going to make your lives even better," he announced, his voice imbued with a hint of mystery. "Starting today, we are launching a new technology on our Vale Vision phones."

The crowd listened intently as Gabriel unveiled the details of his groundbreaking digital payment platform. "You can use your Vale Vision phones to pay for anything, anywhere," he explained. "It can act as a credit card for stores that haven't yet adopted our tech, and it can be used for peer-to-peer payments."

But it was his next announcement that truly captured the audience's imagination. "Even better," Gabriel continued, his voice rising with excitement, "this technology extends to a special, user-unique code that can be tattooed on your hand. Just pass your hand under a reader, and it scans your handprint and the special code to pay for your items."

A murmur of amazement rippled through the crowd, the concept of such convenience and technological advancement resonating deeply with them. Gabriel, sensing their excitement, added, "To increase adoption, we're offering 15% off for the next 90 days on anything purchased in Vale Vision's online store."

The announcement was met with another round of enthusiastic applause, the audience captivated by the vision of a future where technology and convenience merged seamlessly.

The atmosphere in the auditorium was electric, a palpable sense of excitement and anticipation filled the air as Gabriel Vale, the charismatic leader, prepared to introduce his special guest. The crowd, already buzzing from Gabriel's announcement of the groundbreaking payment technology, grew even more animated as Lucien Morreau stepped onto the stage.

A thunderous applause erupted as Lucien made his appearance, the audience rising to their feet in a standing ovation. The respect and admiration for Lucien were evident in every clap, every cheer that filled the room. Lucien, humbled by the warm reception, expressed his gratitude. "Thank you, Gabriel, for bringing me out here," he said, his voice resonating with sincerity.

Gabriel, with a smile of genuine affection, responded, "Lucien, it's been a blessing to work with you and witness the incredible transformation in your life." He then turned to the audience, his expression hinting at more exciting news to come. "Lucien may have something special to share with all of us," he teased.

Lucien, taking the cue, stepped forward, his presence commanding the room. "Yes, I do have something special to share," he began, his voice steady and confident. "I've been working tirelessly behind the scenes, and I'm thrilled to announce that our payment technology can now be used in 100% of countries across the world."

The crowd erupted in cheers, the significance of Lucien's announcement not lost on them. "We've been working around the clock, securing payment processing rights in every country," Lucien continued, his words fueling the excitement in the room. "And we've achieved this in record time."

The audience's response was overwhelming, a mixture of awe and admiration for what Gabriel and Lucien had accomplished. The two men stood side by side on the stage, basking in the adulation of the crowd, united in their vision of a world transformed by technology and cooperation.

In the green room backstage, the atmosphere was a stark contrast to the electrifying energy of the stage. Here, it was calm and collected, a space for reflection and strategic discussions. Lucien Morreau and Gabriel Vale sat comfortably, their conversation flowing seamlessly as they debriefed the successful announcement of the new payment technology.

The door opened, and Viktor Stahl stepped into the room, his presence commanding immediate attention. Lucien rose to greet him, a hint of surprise in his expression. "Viktor, welcome," he said warmly, extending a hand.

"Allow me to introduce you to Gabriel," Lucien began, but Gabriel interjected with a smile, "Actually, Lucien, Viktor and I are already acquainted. His security firm has been instrumental in some of my recent projects."

Lucien's surprise was evident, but he quickly masked it with a nod of understanding. Viktor's extensive international connections were no secret, and it made sense that he and Gabriel would cross paths.

Changing the subject, Lucien steered the conversation towards the payment platform launch. "This technology is a game changer," he said enthusiastically. "It's far more advanced than anything The Circle had in the works."

Gabriel nodded in agreement, his eyes reflecting the satisfaction of their accomplishment. "Indeed, it's a significant leap forward. And it seems we've caught Horizon off guard."

Lucien chuckled, a glint of triumph in his eyes. "Yes, the rumors are that Horizon was planning to announce their own platform, but we've completely undercut them. Their stock is plummeting as we speak."

Viktor, who had been quietly observing the exchange, finally spoke. "It's a strategic victory," he said, his voice low and measured. "Horizon's loss is our gain. This will reshape the market in our favor."

In the green room, a brief silence fell among the three men, each lost in their own thoughts about the future and the impact of their groundbreaking announcement. The air was thick with the sense of a turning point in history, a moment that would redefine the global financial landscape. As they sat there, Viktor's expression shifted subtly, a hint of concern replacing his previously composed demeanor. Breaking the silence, he turned to Gabriel, his voice carrying a weight of seriousness. "Gabriel, we may have a problem," he said, his eyes locking with Gabriel's. "And it could be a big one." The room's atmosphere, once filled with triumph and anticipation, suddenly took on a more somber tone, as the men braced themselves for the challenge Viktor was about to reveal.

Chapter 31

David sat in the car, parked inconspicuously down the street from Reedy's Bar, his eyes fixed on the entrance. The text message from Liz had been straightforward. *Reedy's Bar, 8pm, I have what you need.*

But nothing felt straightforward anymore.

His mind was a cyclone of thoughts and suspicions. Becca's theory that Liz had been compromised gnawed at him. He had trusted Liz for years, relied on her insights and connections. He had dated her for a few months and couldn't believe she'd betray him. The idea that she could be a part of this twisted game was unsettling.

He glanced over at Mark, who was focused on the task at hand, scanning the street for any signs of unusual activity. David admired Mark's ability to stay calm and collected in tense situations. It was a skill David had honed during his time with the FBI, but recent events had shaken his usual composure.

Nadia sat in the back seat monitoring communication channels in the area to ensure there were no surprises.

The plan seemed simple enough, but David knew better than to trust appearances. Every operation had its risks, its unforeseen complications. He couldn't shake the feeling that they were walking into something bigger, something more dangerous than they anticipated.

Becca was going to approach Liz in the bar and provide her a note with a new location. She was going to then exit the bar and move to the meeting point.

As he watched the bar, David's thoughts drifted to Becca. Her determination, her courage, it inspired him, but it also worried him. They were in this together, yet the stakes were personal for each of them. He couldn't bear the thought of anything happening to her. The weight of responsibility, of protecting not just himself but his team, pressed heavily on him.

He checked his watch. It was almost time. He took a deep breath, trying to steady his racing heart. This was it, another step into the unknown, another move in a deadly chess game. He prayed silently for wisdom, for protection, for the strength to face whatever lay ahead.

David watched Becca approach the bar. His instincts were on high alert, every movement, every sound seemed amplified. When her phone rang, he watched her closely, trying to gauge the nature of the call from her body language. Her frustration was evident, the way she ran her fingers through her hair, *the signal*. David's heart sank as he saw the signal to abort the operation, Becca caught a cab and disappeared into the bustling city.

He felt a surge of concern, his mind racing with questions about the call. The message on his phone, 'work called,' did little to ease his worries. He knew the implications all too well – the CIA had called her in, and that could mean a multitude of things, none of them good.

Turning to Mark and Nadia, he relayed the change in plans, his voice tinged with reluctance. Mark's abrupt suggestion that Nadia could take over caught him off guard. Nadia's eagerness to step in was admirable, but David's protective instincts kicked in. The operation was already compromised, and without Becca, the risks were too high.

Nadia's insistence, however, was firm. She argued her capability, her readiness, to take on the task. David's reluctance battled with the urgency of the situation. Reluctantly, he agreed, his gut churning with unease.

Inside Reedy's Bar, the atmosphere was a mix of dim lighting and the low hum of conversations. Nadia, with a determined stride, approached Liz Sinclair, who sat alone at a table, nursing a drink. Liz looked up, her expression one of mild curiosity as Nadia wordlessly slid the note across the table and turned on her heel to leave.

Nadia quickened her pace towards the back exit, her heart pounding with a mix of adrenaline and apprehension. As she pushed open the door, she was suddenly grabbed from behind. Two men, their grips firm and unyielding, dragged her outside.

"Hey! Let go of me!" Nadia protested, struggling against their hold. Her voice was muffled as one of the men clamped a hand over her mouth.

The two men zip tied her hands, taped her mouth, and threw her into the back seat of a waiting car. It drove out of the back alley and disappeared.

The night air was crisp as Liz Sinclair confidently strode out of Reedy's Bar, her heels clicking rhythmically against the pavement. She seemed unfazed by the bustling city nightlife, her focus solely on reaching the nightclub specified in the note. From their vantage point in the car, David and Mark watched her every move, their senses heightened.

Mark shifted restlessly in his seat, his gaze darting between Liz and the surrounding area. "Shouldn't we be moving?" he asked, his voice tinged with impatience.

David held up a hand, signaling for patience. "Just wait," he said, his eyes scanning the street. "There's more at play here." His trained eyes picked up the subtle signs of surveillance – two men discreetly trailing Liz, maintaining a careful distance, and a third positioned further back, his attention sweeping over the street.

"See that?" David pointed out the men to Mark. "Classic surveillance with a rear guard. They're tracking her, but they're also watching for anyone following them."

Mark nodded, understanding dawning on him. "So, what's the plan?"

"We know her destination. We'll take a longer route, avoid detection, and still get there in time to see what unfolds," David explained, his voice calm but firm.

He smoothly put the car into drive, skillfully navigating through the less frequented streets. The city lights blurred past them as they made their way to the nightclub, each lost in their thoughts about the unfolding situation. David's mind was a whirlwind of strategy and concern, especially for Nadia. He knew they had to tread carefully, for every move they made could have significant consequences.

The pulsating lights and thumping bass of the nightclub created an electric atmosphere as Liz Sinclair entered. She moved with an air of confidence, weaving through the crowd to the bar. The bartender acknowledged her with a nod as she ordered a drink, her eyes scanning the room casually.

Outside, the two men who had been tailing her were met with an unexpected obstacle. The nightclub's bouncers, imposing figures with stern expressions, blocked their entry. They tried to argue and bribe their way in, but the bouncers remained unmoved.

Chaz, standing a short distance away with the club owner, Bobby, watched the scene unfold. "Thanks, Bobby, appreciate your help with this," he said, grateful for the assistance. Before the rapture and before Chaz gave his life to the Lord and became a pastor, he was a club promoter. The nightclub was the perfect location to intercept Liz.

"Anything for you, Chaz," Bobby replied, his tone friendly. "Just give me the word when you want them in."

Back inside, Mark approached Liz at the bar, his approach casual but calculated. "Can I buy you a drink?" he asked, leaning slightly against the bar.

Liz glanced at him, a polite but firm "no thanks" on her lips.

Undeterred, Mark added, "It'd be a shame to finish the twilight tonight without a drink." He watched her closely.

Liz's demeanor shifted subtly, a nod indicating her understanding. Mark continued, "I have a friend of yours who would love to talk. He's had to take some precautions. Head to the stairs over there and down to the lower level."

Liz didn't hesitate. She set her drink down and made her way to the stairs, her movements smooth and purposeful. Mark followed discreetly, maintaining a safe distance as they descended to the lower level of the club, away from the prying eyes and ears of the main floor. The dimly lit staircase led them into a more secluded area, perfect for a private conversation.

In the dimly lit room, the tension was palpable as David and Liz faced each other. Liz's initial amusement at the clandestine nature of their meeting faded as she absorbed the gravity of David's words.

"Nice cloak and dagger moves," Liz remarked, trying to lighten the mood as she settled into the chair. Her attempt at humor fell flat in the charged atmosphere.

David remained standing, his gaze fixed on Liz. "I need to know that you can be trusted," he said, his voice steady but laced with an undercurrent of urgency.

Liz laughed, a sound that seemed out of place in the seriousness of the moment. "David, how long have you known me?" she asked, her smile fading as she saw the earnestness in his eyes.

"A long time, Liz," David replied. "But there's a lot at play here. Someone knew we were meeting for coffee the other day."

"Someone?" Liz echoed, her brow furrowing in confusion.

David nodded. "An assassin. Someone targeting me, Liz."

The shock on Liz's face was genuine. She fell silent, trying to process the enormity of what David was saying. The room was quiet, save for the distant hum of the nightclub above them.

"I must know where your loyalties lie," David continued, his voice firm.

Liz took a deep breath. "David, a lot has changed since 3/16," she began, her eyes drifting to the cross hanging around David's neck. She stood up and embraced him, a gesture of solidarity and understanding. "You too?" she whispered.

David was taken aback. "Me too, what?" he asked, confusion evident in his voice.

Liz pulled back slightly, looking into his eyes. "I can see it in your eyes. You're saved too?" she asked, her voice filled with a mix of surprise and relief.

David's expression softened. "Liz, you're a Christian? A Believer?" he asked, his surprise mirrored in his tone.

Liz nodded, a smile touching her lips. "3/16 gave me a lot to think about. I was depressed for some time, but eventually, I came to realize this was all part of God's plan."

The revelation created a new bond between them, a shared understanding that transcended their past professional relationship. In that moment, they were no longer just former colleagues; they were fellow believers navigating a world that had changed irrevocably.

Liz handed over the file to David. He took it, feeling its lightness, a sense of foreboding settling over him.

"Well, Liz, there doesn't seem to be much here," David remarked, his voice tinged with disappointment as he flipped through the sparse pages.

Liz nodded, her expression serious. "There isn't much because whoever set up Twilight Technologies was extremely meticulous," she explained. "They used seven layers of shell companies, each one more opaque than the last. And they're based in countries that don't digitize their business records, making it nearly impossible to trace anything back."

David's brows furrowed as he absorbed the information. "So, we're at a dead end?" he asked, the frustration evident in his voice.

"Not entirely," Liz replied, trying to offer a glimmer of hope. "I traced it all the way back to a shell company based in Dubai. But that's where the trail goes cold. I couldn't get any information about who owns that company. It's like they vanished into thin air."

David leaned back against the wall, the file hanging loosely in his hand. The complexity of the situation was daunting. Whoever was behind Twilight Technologies had gone to great lengths to cover their tracks, leaving them with more questions than answers.

"Thanks, Liz," David said, his voice low. "You've done more than I could have asked for. This isn't your fault. They're just... really good at hiding."

Liz gave a small, understanding smile. "I wish I could have found more, David. But I'll keep digging. Maybe something will turn up."

David nodded, appreciative of her efforts. "Keep me posted," he said, tucking the file under his arm. "And be careful, Liz. We clocked three people surveilling you tonight."

Liz's expression turned serious. "What should I do?"

David replied, "We'll get you out of here, but you might want to find some place to stay tonight that isn't your apartment."

Chapter 32

B ecca sat in the lobby of the CIA Director's office, her posture rigid, a mix of anger and determination etched on her face. She was not one to be easily intimidated, and today was no exception. The Director's assistant, Juliette, appeared at the door, beckoning her inside. "Director Dalton will see you now," she said, her voice neutral.

As Becca entered the office, she saw her former case officer, Martin, along with Director Marcus Dalton and the CIA's chief legal counsel, Meredith Vaughn. Dalton's gaze briefly met Becca's before he turned to Martin. "Martin, your presence isn't required for this discussion," he said, his tone dismissive.

Martin, looking slightly taken aback, nodded and quickly exited the room, leaving Becca alone with the Director and the legal counsel.

"Please, have a seat, Ms. Lawrence," Dalton said, gesturing towards the conference table. Becca moved to the table, her steps measured, her mind racing with thoughts of the injustice she felt was being done to her.

Dalton sat at the head of the table, with Vaughn to his right. He opened a file – Becca's file – and looked up at her. "You've gotten yourself into quite the pickle, eh Lawrence?" he remarked, his tone casual yet probing.

Becca's response was immediate and firm. "No, sir, I did my job, and I'd do everything again if I had to redo it. I was protecting then Majority Leader Hayes."

Dalton raised his hand, signaling her to stop. "Yes, yes, I understand. This is quite the mess, but you're not to blame," he said, his voice carrying a hint of frustration. "My predecessor was feckless and weak. She let rogue elements gain too much control and did nothing to stop them."

He pointed to the file in front of him. "This is what happens when you don't keep everyone on the reservation," he continued, his words sharp. "Another eyewitness came forward and corroborated your story. We tracked down the other two agents that were present. Former NSA. Well, now they're former. When the NSA found out what the two were up to, they dispatched them."

Vaughn winced at the mention of the agents' fate, her discomfort evident. Becca, however, remained stoic, her anger now mixed with a sense of vindication. She had known all along that she was in the right, and now, it seemed, the truth was finally coming to light.

Dalton closed the file and looked directly at Becca. "Ms. Lawrence, the CIA owes you an apology. You've been through a lot, and it's clear now that you acted with the best intentions and within the scope of your duty."

Becca nodded, her expression softening slightly. "Thank you, sir," she said, her voice steady. "I just did what I thought was right. What about Martin?"

Director Dalton leaned back in his chair, a hint of a smile playing on his lips as he observed Becca's reaction. "Case Officer Wilson? Oh, he's proven himself to not be up to the standards of the CIA. He's about to find out he's being reassigned to a diplomatic outpost in Uganda," he said casually.

Becca's face remained impassive, but internally, she felt a surge of satisfaction. Martin had caused her enough trouble, and it was gratifying to see him receive his comeuppance. However, she quickly refocused on the matter at hand, her professional demeanor unwavering.

Dalton's gaze shifted to a folder on the table. "Now, we're at a crossroads," he began, his tone serious. "You've earned the right to have your file cleared and to return to duty. Or," he paused, tapping the folder, "you could choose what's in this folder. A chance to make the biggest difference of your life in duty to the United States."

Becca's interest was piqued. She leaned forward slightly, her eyes fixed on the folder. The possibility of returning to duty was appealing, but the mystery of the folder's contents was intriguing.

Meredith Vaughn, the chief legal counsel, spoke up. "Agent Lawrence, this assignment is a once-in-a-lifetime opportunity, but it's one you should not take lightly."

Becca's curiosity was now fully aroused. "What exactly are you offering?" she asked, her voice steady but filled with anticipation.

Dalton opened the folder and slid it across the table towards Becca. "This is a special assignment, one that requires a unique set of skills and a deep commitment to our nation's security. It's highly classified, and the details are for your eyes only."

Becca reached for the folder, her fingers brushing against the cool surface of the paper. She opened it and began to read, her eyes scanning the pages quickly. As she absorbed the information, her expression shifted from curiosity to awe. The assignment was unlike anything she had encountered before, a challenge that would test her skills and determination to their limits.

She looked up from the folder, her decision clear in her eyes. "I'm in," she said firmly. "This is exactly the kind of challenge I've been looking for."

Vaughn's voice was firm, cutting through the air with a sense of urgency. "Not so fast, Agent Lawrence. Let's make sure you understand all the details of the assignment."

Becca, who had been ready to leap into action, paused and refocused her attention on Vaughn. She sensed the gravity of what was about to be disclosed and knew that every detail mattered.

"Officially, you'll resign from the CIA," Vaughn continued. "The rumor will be that you were cleared, but the details of the investigation were so muddy that you were upset with the outcome. This will be your cover story."

Becca nodded, absorbing the information. The idea of resigning and the cover story made sense for the kind of clandestine work they were proposing.

"You'll lose access to your normal contacts and colleagues at the CIA," Vaughn added, "but you won't lose access to the agency's resources. In fact, you'll have far more resources at your disposal than ever before, with minimal oversight."

The prospect of having extensive resources with little oversight was both exhilarating and daunting. Becca realized the level of trust and responsibility being placed on her shoulders.

"You will serve directly under the President's command," Vaughn explained, "taking on assignments that are too sensitive or complex for even the CIA to handle. This is beyond top secret, Becca. You'll be operating in the shadows, where even the shadows don't dare to tread."

Becca felt a thrill run through her. This was the kind of work she was made for – challenging, secretive, and crucial to national security.

"And finally," Vaughn said, pulling out a folder and sliding it across the table to Becca, "you will have a small team. We've taken the liberty of putting together a list of potential candidates. These are individuals with unique skills and backgrounds, each capable of contributing to the success of your missions."

Becca opened the folder and scanned the list. Each name was accompanied by a brief profile and a photo. She recognized all of the names – many she has worked with, each with a reputation for excellence and discretion.

"This is your team to shape and command," Vaughn said. "Choose wisely, and remember, the fate of many may rest on the decisions you make."

Becca closed the folder, her mind already racing with possibilities and strategies. She stood up, her resolve stronger than ever.

"I understand the assignment and the responsibilities that come with it," she said confidently. "I'm ready to take this on. Thank you for this opportunity."

Director Dalton and Vaughn exchanged a look of approval. Becca had accepted one of the most challenging and secretive roles in the intelligence community. She left the room, her steps firm and determined, ready to embark on a mission that would test her skills and resolve to their very limits.

Chapter 33

David and Mark's car rolled to a stop in the dimly lit garage bay of the old textile factory, the sound of the engine cutting through the silence. They exchanged a look of cautious satisfaction, pleased with the evening's progress, even if it hadn't yielded all the answers they sought about Twilight Technologies.

Stepping out of the car, they stretched their legs, the tension of the night's operation slowly unwinding from their muscles. The factory, with its vast, shadowy spaces and echoes of a bygone industrial era, felt like a fitting base for their clandestine activities.

"Good to be back," Mark muttered, his voice echoing slightly in the cavernous space.

David nodded in agreement, his mind still partially occupied with the night's events and the puzzle pieces they were trying to fit together.

They spotted Dr. Ephraim Goldman, a trusted ally and friend, working at a makeshift desk set up in one corner of the garage. The doctor looked up as they approached, his expression a mix of focus and fatigue.

"Hey, Doc," David greeted him, trying to keep his tone light. "How's everything here?"

Dr. Goldman offered a weary smile. "Quiet, mostly. Just keeping things running."

David's gaze swept the area, a nagging feeling of unease settling in his stomach. "Where's Nadia?" he asked, expecting her to be tinkering with some gadget or absorbed in her computer screens.

Dr. Goldman's expression shifted, a hint of concern creeping into his eyes. "Nadia? She hasn't returned yet. I thought she was with you."

David and Mark exchanged a quick, worried glance. Nadia should have been back by now. The plan had been simple enough, and her part in it was supposed to be quick and straightforward.

Mark's voice was tight with worry. "She was supposed to drop off a note at the bar and come straight back. That was hours ago."

David felt a surge of protectiveness and fear. Nadia, though capable and resourceful, could be in danger. They had all become targets in this high-stakes game, and every moment she was unaccounted for increased the risk.

"We need to find her," David said, his voice firm with resolve. "Something's not right."

Mark nodded, already pulling out his phone to start making calls. David could see the worry on Mark's face. David came over and squeezed Mark's shoulder, showing his support. Dr. Goldman stood up, ready to assist in any way he could.

The atmosphere in the garage shifted from one of cautious triumph to tense urgency. They had faced many challenges since the formation of their group, but the potential harm to one of their own brought a new level of seriousness to their mission.

As David coordinated with Mark and Dr. Goldman, his mind raced with possibilities and plans. They needed to act fast. Nadia's safety, and possibly much more, depended on it.

Chapter 34

Nadia's senses were overwhelmed, the disorienting combination of darkness and the relentless sound of screaming babies echoing in her ears. She shifted uncomfortably in the chair, her wrists chafing against the zip ties that bound her. Time had become a blurred concept, each passing moment indistinguishable from the last under the oppressive black bag that covered her head.

Despite the sensory assault, Nadia's mind raced, trying to piece together her situation. She remembered the bar, the note, the sudden, rough hands grabbing her, and then the jarring motion of being thrown into a car. Now, here she was, in an unknown location, subjected to psychological torment.

She forced herself to stay calm, to think strategically. Panic would be her enemy in this situation. Nadia knew the importance of mental resilience; she had trained for situations like this, though she never truly believed she'd find herself in one.

The sound of the screaming babies, a cruel and effective method of sensory overload, was designed to break her, to fray her nerves and make her vulnerable. But Nadia focused on her breathing, trying to find a rhythm amidst the chaos, a lifeline to cling to.

She mentally reviewed what Becca had told her about being held captive, recalling techniques to resist interrogation and maintain mental fortitude. She knew the first rule was to understand her captors' objectives. Were they after information? Intimidation? Both? She was scared but she focused on what she could control at this moment, her emotions.

Nadia's mind wandered to her friends, to David, Mark, and the rest of the team. They would be looking for her, she was sure of it. The thought gave her a flicker of hope, a small but significant spark in the overwhelming darkness.

She shifted again, testing the strength of the zip ties. They were tight, but not infallible. If she could just get her hands in front of her, she might have a chance to work on loosening them. It was a long shot, but in her current situation, any chance was worth taking.

As she strategized, the door to the room creaked open. The sound of footsteps approached, and Nadia steeled herself. She was about to face her captors, and she needed to be ready for whatever came next.

As the black bag was abruptly removed from Nadia's head, she blinked rapidly, her eyes struggling to adjust to the sudden influx of light. The room was stark and bare, with concrete walls and a single dim bulb hanging from the ceiling. Her captors stood before her, their faces obscured by masks, their eyes cold and calculating.

The relentless audio of screaming babies had ceased, leaving a ringing silence in its wake. Nadia's ears were still buzzing, but she focused on the men in front of her, trying to glean any information she could from their demeanor and attire.

One of the men, taller and seemingly the leader, leaned forward, his eyes boring into hers. "What were you doing at the bar? What did you hand to the woman?" he demanded, his voice gruff and menacing.

Nadia's mind raced, but she maintained a calm exterior. She knew that showing fear or hesitation could be perceived as a sign of guilt. "I didn't do anything," she replied steadily, her voice betraying none of the fear that churned inside her. "I saw a woman drop her receipt, and I simply handed it back to her. That's all."

The man's eyes narrowed, clearly skeptical of her explanation. "You expect us to believe that? You just happened to be at the wrong place at the wrong time?" he sneered.

Nadia met his gaze. "Yes, that's exactly what happened. I was just there for a drink. I don't know why you've brought me here or what you think I've done, but you've made a mistake." Tears began streaming down Nadia's face.

The captors exchanged glances, their expressions unreadable behind their masks. The tension in the room was palpable, and Nadia could feel the weight of their suspicion.

The taller man stepped back, his posture rigid. "If you're lying, we'll find out.

With that, the men turned and left the room, the door closing with a heavy thud behind them. Nadia was left alone once again, her heart pounding in her chest. She knew she had to find a way out, to escape and warn her friends. But first, she needed to free herself from these bindings. She began to work at the zip ties, her fingers moving deftly, fueled by a mix of fear and determination. She had to get out of here, and time was of the essence.

Chapter 35

T he atmosphere in the old textile mill was tense and somber as Becca arrived, her steps quick and purposeful. She swiftly made her way to where David and the others were gathered, her expression a mix of determination and concern. Moments later, the sound of another vehicle pulling up announced the arrival of Noah Thatcher.

David watched as Becca led Noah into the makeshift command center. He was tall, with a rugged demeanor that spoke of experience and resilience. As Becca introduced Noah to David, there was a sense of mutual respect between the two men, an unspoken understanding of the gravity of their situation.

Dr. Goldman, upon seeing Noah, broke into a warm smile and approached him with open arms. The embrace they shared was heartfelt, a testament to the bond forged in past missions and the relief of seeing a familiar, trusted face in these trying times.

Becca, taking control of the situation, addressed the group. "I've worked with Noah on several occasions," she began, her voice steady. "He's a skilled operative from the CIA's ground branch, and he's going to be a valuable asset to us. He'll also be joining me on some other assignments, but we'll discuss that later."

Noah nodded, his gaze scanning the room, taking in every detail. "Let's get to the point," he said, his voice calm but authoritative. "What do we know about Nadia's situation?"

David stepped forward, outlining the events leading up to Nadia's abduction. He spoke of the operation at the bar, the note passed to Liz, and how Nadia had stepped in when Becca was unexpectedly called away. He described how they lost contact with Nadia and their growing concern when she didn't return.

Noah listened intently, his expression grave. "We need to act fast," he said decisively. "Time is not on our side. Let's pool our resources, gather any surveillance we have, and start piecing together where they might have taken her."

In a quiet corner of the bustling textile mill, Noah pulled David and Becca aside, away from the flurry of activity. His expression was serious, his tone urgent.

"We need to bring Jack in on this," Noah stated firmly, his eyes meeting Becca's. "His expertise in digital and comms is unparalleled, and we need someone of his caliber right now."

Becca hesitated for a moment, her mind racing. Jack, a skilled operative known for his prowess in digital warfare and communications, was a valuable asset. However, he was unaware of her new role and the complexities it entailed.

"I've been considering involving Jack," Becca admitted, her voice tinged with uncertainty. "But he doesn't know about my new position yet."

Noah nodded, understanding the delicacy of the situation. "Regardless, we need his skills, Becca. Time is of the essence, and Jack's one of the best in the field."

Becca took a deep breath, her resolve hardening. "You're right, Noah. We need all the help we can get." She reached for her phone, scrolling through her contacts until she found Jack's number.

David watched silently, aware of the gravity of the decision. Bringing Jack into the fold meant expanding their circle of trust, a necessary but risky move.

Becca dialed the number, holding the phone to her ear. The line rang, and after a few tense moments, Jack's familiar voice answered.

"Jack, it's Becca," she began, her tone serious. "I need your help on something urgent. It's a matter of national security."

There was a brief pause on the other end of the line, a moment of silence that felt like an eternity.

"I'm in," Jack's voice came through, decisive and unwavering. "Tell me where and when."

Relief washed over Becca's face as she provided Jack with the details. She ended the call and turned back to Noah and David.

"Jack's on board," she announced, a hint of determination in her voice. "He'll be here as soon as possible."

Noah nodded in approval, and David let out a quiet sigh of relief. With Jack joining their efforts, their chances of finding Nadia and tackling the challenges ahead had just significantly improved.

In the dimly lit corner of the textile mill, Noah's expression was one of grim determination. He turned to Becca, his voice low but firm.

"We need to assemble a tactical team," he said. "Once we have Nadia's location, we need to move fast and hit hard. Any hesitation or half-measures could be fatal, not just for Nadia, but for the entire team."

Becca nodded, her face set in a mask of resolve. "Who do you have in mind?"

Noah began ticking off names on his fingers. "Mikey's a given. He's solid in the field. Then there's Carter and Rodriguez. Both top-notch. Ideally, we want a six-person team for this."

"I'm in," Becca stated without hesitation, her tone leaving no room for argument.

David, who had been listening intently, stepped forward. "I'm in too," he declared. "I've got experience with tactical operations. I can hold my own."

Noah regarded David for a moment, assessing his determination and resolve. He then nodded in agreement. "Alright, David. You're in."

Without wasting another second, Noah pulled out his cell phone and began making calls. His fingers moved swiftly over the screen, dialing numbers with practiced ease.

Becca and David watched as Noah spoke in hushed, urgent tones. With each call, their team was coming together, a group of skilled operatives ready to undertake a high-stakes rescue mission.

The atmosphere in the room was tense, charged with a mix of apprehension and readiness. They all knew the risks involved in what they were about to do. But the stakes were too high, and the life of one of their own hung in the balance.

As Noah ended his last call, he looked up at Becca and David. "Team's coming together," he said. "We'll be ready to move as soon as we have a location."

Becca nodded, her eyes reflecting a fierce determination. David clenched his fists, mentally preparing for the challenge ahead.

The atmosphere in the textile mill's makeshift operations room was electric with urgency as Jack, the latest addition to their team, set up his laptop. His fingers flew over the keyboard, connecting to various databases with the ease of a seasoned professional.

David, Dr. Goldman, Chaz, and Mark gathered around, watching Jack's every move with keen interest. Noah and Becca, already familiar with Jack's expertise, stood back, allowing him the space to work.

"Alright, let's see what we've got here," Jack muttered, his eyes scanning the screen. He quickly accessed the network, nodding in approval. "Nadia really outdid herself with this setup. Impressive."

As Jack settled into his task, the glow of the laptop screen illuminated his concentrated expression. He accessed a specialized software tool designed for signal intelligence, a program that allowed him to analyze and track cell phone signals with precision.

First, he input the coordinates of the bar where Nadia was last seen. The program immediately started scanning for all active cell phone signals in that area during the crucial time frame of Nadia's disappearance. The screen filled with a web of digital signals, each represented by a different color and pattern.

Jack's eyes moved rapidly as he sifted through the data, filtering out irrelevant signals. He was looking for anomalies – phones that appeared in the area suddenly and left just as quickly around the time of Nadia's abduction. These would likely belong to her abductors.

He adjusted the parameters, narrowing the search. Two signals stood out. They appeared in the vicinity shortly before Nadia's disappearance and left at high speeds immediately afterward. Jack tagged these signals for closer monitoring.

Next, he accessed a database that cross-referenced the unique identifiers of these cell phones with known databases, checking if they were linked to any individuals or organizations of interest. This process required careful navigation through layers of encrypted data, a task Jack handled with the expertise of a seasoned intelligence analyst.

As he worked, Jack maintained a running commentary, keeping the team informed. "These two signals are our best leads. They're behaving exactly how you'd expect from a snatch squad – in quickly, out quickly."

Finally, he initiated a real-time tracking protocol on these two signals. The software began to ping the cell phones, attempting to triangulate their current location based on signal strength and tower proximity. This was a delicate operation, as too frequent pinging could alert the phone's user, but Jack managed the balance expertly.

The room fell silent as they waited for the results, the tension mounting with each passing second. Then, the screen updated with a new location – a pinpoint on a map that could very well be where Nadia was being held. Jack's meticulous work had given them a tangible lead, a place to start their rescue mission.

"This is likely where Nadia's being held," he said, turning to face the team. His voice was calm but carried an undercurrent of urgency. "The signals lead to an industrial area on the outskirts of the city. Not the kind of place you'd expect to find anything legitimate happening."

David stepped forward, his expression grim. "We need to move fast. If they realize we're onto them, they might relocate her, or worse."

Noah nodded in agreement. "Jack, keep monitoring those signals. We need to know if they move. Everyone else, gear up. We're going in once the team arrives."

The arrival of Mikey, Carter, and Rodriguez brought a mix of tension and relief, a sense of seriousness tinged with the camaraderie of old friends reuniting under dire circumstances.

Carter, a burly man with a quick smile, was the first to approach Becca. He wrapped her in a bear hug, lifting her slightly off the ground. "Becca! It's been too long," he said, his voice booming in the large space.

Becca laughed, the sound mingling with relief and happiness. "Carter, put me down! We've got work to do," she replied, but her smile betrayed her gratitude for the familiar face.

Rodriguez, lean and sharp-eyed, followed suit. "Wish it was just for beers and catch-up," he said, his tone serious but his eyes warm. He gave Becca a firm, respectful hug.

Mikey, approached Dr. Goldman with a playful grin. "What's up, Doc?" he greeted, extending his hand for a handshake. "Seems like kidnappings are my new trend."

Dr. Goldman chuckled, shaking Mikey's hand. "Well, I certainly hope this trend ends soon," he replied, his voice tinged with a mix of humor and concern.

David watched the interactions, feeling a mix of emotions. Relief at the arrival of skilled reinforcements, anxiety about Nadia's situation, and a growing sense of urgency. These were professionals, each one capable and experienced in their own right. Their presence bolstered the team's chances of successfully rescuing Nadia.

As the initial greetings wound down, the group gathered around a large table littered with maps, laptops, and various pieces of equipment. The mood turned serious as they began to strategize their next move.

The atmosphere in the dimly lit room was thick with anticipation as Jack carefully laid out a detailed map of the building where Nadia was believed to be held captive. The team gathered around, their faces etched with focus and determination, as they studied the layout.

Noah, with a confident and authoritative demeanor, took the lead. He pointed to the north and south entrances on the map. "The south entrance is a no-go. It's got a reinforced steel door, practically impenetrable. We hit them from the north," he explained, his finger tracing a path on the map. "Drone recon shows two guards stationed here," he added, tapping the north entrance.

The team members leaned in, absorbing every detail. Mikey, with his usual straightforward approach, broke the silence. "What are the rules of engagement, Noah?"

Noah's eyes met each team member's in turn, his expression serious. "This operation is off the books, sanctioned only by God. Our primary objective is Nadia's safe return."

Becca, standing beside Noah, chimed in with a stern tone. "You see a threat, you take care of the threat. Stay sharp for any intel – cell phones, laptops, hard drives. Anything that can give us a lead on who's behind this."

Carter, unable to contain his excitement, grinned. "Man, oh man, I wouldn't want to be on the receiving end of this team tonight. Becca, you've got that fire in your eyes."

David, who had been quietly studying the map, finally spoke. His voice was calm but carried an undercurrent of resolve. "Our top priority is Nadia's safety. And dealing with the threat, once and for all."

Noah nodded, his gaze sweeping across the team. "Alright, team, let's gear up. We move in fast and silent. Nadia's counting on us."

As the team dispersed to prepare, the room buzzed with activity. They donned their tactical gear, each movement precise and practiced. Weapons were checked and rechecked, magazines loaded, and communication devices tested.

The team was almost ready to move out when Jack's voice cut through the focused hum of preparations. "Hey, guys, we might have a problem," he announced, his eyes not leaving the screen in front of him. The room fell silent as everyone's attention shifted to him.

"One of the cell phones we've been tracking is on the move," Jack continued, his fingers flying over the keyboard as he tracked the signal. "There's no indication that Nadia is moving with it, but it's a possibility we can't ignore."

"Nadia might be on the move."

Chapter 36

Noah turned to Becca, his expression asking the unspoken question. Becca, her face set in a mask of determination, didn't hesitate. "It doesn't change our involvement here. We proceed as planned."

David, standing beside Becca, nodded in agreement. "We should move on it now. Every second counts."

Noah, taking in the consensus, gave a firm nod. "Alright, let's do this. Time is of the essence."

The team quickly gathered their gear and headed towards the van parked outside. The atmosphere was tense but focused as they loaded up. Each member knew the stakes were high, and the uncertainty of Nadia's situation added an extra layer of urgency to their mission.

As the van doors closed and the vehicle rolled out of the garage, the team inside was a picture of readiness. Each member was mentally preparing for the operation ahead, running through scenarios and strategies in their minds. The drive to the target location was quiet, save for the occasional crackle of the radio and the low hum of the van's engine.

The van came to a discreet stop two blocks away from the target building, its engine humming softly in the quiet night. Inside, the team was a picture of quiet efficiency, each member double-checking their gear and weapons. Noah's voice cut through the silence, crisp and authoritative. "Comm check," he commanded.

One by one, the team members responded, their voices calm and clear over the comms. "Alpha 2, check," Mikey replied, followed by Carter, Rodriguez, and the rest, each confirming their readiness.

The final check came from Jack, back at the textile factory, his voice coming through the earpieces. "Overwatch hears you loud and clear, Alpha 1," he reported.

Noah nodded, satisfied. "Any updates? Over," he asked, his eyes scanning the darkened streets outside.

"Still two guards at the north entrance. No more movement in or out of the facility," Jack's voice crackled through the comms.

"Ok, we are charlie mike," Noah confirmed, using the military phonetic alphabet for 'continue mission'. He turned to Mikey, who was already poised and ready.

"Alpha 2, take us out," Noah instructed.

Mikey nodded, his expression focused. He opened the van door quietly, stepping out into the cool night air. The rest of the team followed, each moving with practiced stealth and precision. They quickly formed up, blending into the shadows as they moved towards the target building.

The streets were eerily quiet, the only sounds their soft footsteps and the distant hum of the city. Each team member was acutely aware of the importance of their mission, their senses heightened as they approached the danger zone.

As they neared the building, the two guards at the north entrance came into view, oblivious to the approaching threat. Noah signaled to the team, each member understanding their role without a word being spoken. They were a well-oiled machine, ready to execute their plan with lethal efficiency.

The operation was unfolding with military precision, each member of the team playing their part flawlessly. Mikey and Rodriguez had positioned themselves strategically, their rifles trained on the two guards at the north entrance. The rest of the team waited in the shadows, ready to move on Noah's command.

Noah's voice was calm and clear in their earpieces. "We pass 'Unforgiven,'" he said, using their pre-arranged code based on Clint Eastwood movies to indicate they were at a specific point in their mission plan. This system of codewords allowed them to communicate complex information quickly and without confusion.

"Good copy, Alpha team passes Unforgiven," Jack confirmed from his position back at the textile factory.

"Execute, execute," Noah ordered.

In perfect synchronization, Mikey and Rodriguez took their shots. The two guards dropped silently, neutralized with precision. The team wasted no time, swiftly moving to enter the building.

"Alpha 4, set up security at the entrance," Mikey ordered.

Once inside, Carter immediately took up a position to secure the entrance, his eyes scanning for any potential threats. The rest of the team, led by Mikey, moved quickly to the second floor.

Room by room, they cleared the second floor, their movements fluid and practiced. "Second floor clear, we pass Josey Wales," Noah reported, indicating the completion of another phase of their plan.

Without missing a beat, they descended to the first floor, methodically clearing each space. "First floor clear, we pass Heartbreak Ridge. Heading to the basement level," Noah communicated, his voice steady but tinged with urgency.

He turned to his team, his eyes conveying the gravity of the situation. "Alright team, keep your head on a swivel. If Nadia is here, it's on the next level. Let's bring her home."

The team felt the weight of his words, their resolve strengthening. This was more than just a mission; it was a rescue, a fight to bring back one of their own.

Noah gave Mikey a squeeze on the shoulder, signaling him to lead the way downstairs. The team followed, each member alert and ready for whatever they might face.

The basement air was thick with tension as Alpha team descended the stairs, their boots echoing softly against the concrete. Mikey, leading the way, peered around the corner with practiced caution. His eyes barely had time to register the figure holding an AR-15 before his training kicked in. A split-second decision, and he fired, dropping the armed man with precise shots.

But the fallen guard's rifle clattered to the ground, discharging a few rounds in its death throes. The sound was like a siren call to danger. Within moments, the quiet basement transformed into a battlefield.

"Contact front!" Rodriguez's voice cut through the chaos, his words sharp and clear. He was already in motion, finding cover behind a sturdy metal cabinet, his weapon trained down the hallway.

The team reacted with the synchronicity of a well-oiled machine. Each member instinctively sought cover, their movements fluid yet swift. The hallway erupted with the deafening roar of gunfire, muzzle flashes illuminating the dimly lit space.

David, his heart pounding in his ears, found himself crouched behind a stack of old crates. He exchanged a quick glance with Mikey, who nodded back, a silent communication forged in the heat of countless similar situations.

Rodriguez, his eyes scanning for targets, called out, "Two moving left, one right!"

The team responded in kind. Mikey and David focused their fire to the left, their shots precise and controlled. The rhythm of their gunfire was almost methodical, a deadly dance they had performed too many times before.

On the right, Rodriguez and Carter worked in tandem, their movements a testament to their training and experience. Each shot was a calculated decision, aimed to neutralize the threat with maximum efficiency.

The exchange was over in seconds, but to those involved, it felt like an eternity. The last of the guards fell, and for a moment, the basement was eerily silent, save for the ringing in their ears and the heavy breathing of the team.

Noah's voice cut through the stillness, authoritative yet calm. "Clear the basement. Check every room. We're here for Nadia."

The team moved with renewed purpose, their steps measured as they cleared each room methodically. The tension was palpable, a tangible force that drove them forward. They were close now, so close to completing their mission. The thought of finding Nadia, of bringing her back safely, was the fuel that kept them moving, kept them focused.

Becca picked up cell phones and hard drives along the way as they cleared each room, excited to figure out what intelligence they contained.

As they approached a locked door at the end of the hallway, the air seemed to thicken with anticipation. This was it. The moment of truth. The lock gave way under their expert handling, and the door swung open, revealing the room beyond.

There, in the dim light, tied to a chair with a black bag over her head, was Nadia. The sight of her, vulnerable yet unbroken, ignited a mix of relief and resolve in each team member. They had found her. Noah pressed his comms button, "Alpha 1 passes Mystic River, again, Mystic River. Alpha team, grab intelligence on the way out, consolidate on Alpha 4 and head to extraction point."

Now it was time to bring Nadia home.

Chapter 37

The stage was set with a modern, minimalist design, bathed in soft, ambient lighting that created an almost ethereal atmosphere. In the center stood Gabriel Vale, a charismatic figure, his presence magnified by the giant screens behind him displaying his image to the thousands in the auditorium and millions watching from home. Lucien Morreau, his demeanor calm and composed, stood slightly to the side, a silent yet powerful presence.

Gabriel, dressed in a sleek, tailored suit, paced the stage with a natural ease, his voice resonating through the microphone clipped to his lapel. "Today, my friends, we delve into a profound truth," he began, his tone warm and inviting. "A truth about truths. Each one of us, every person in this room, and watching from afar, has the power to define their own reality, their own truth."

The audience was captivated, hanging on his every word. Cameras panned over faces in the crowd, some nodding in agreement, others visibly moved by his words.

"In this world," Gabriel continued, "we are often told what to believe, what to think, what is right and what is wrong. But I say to you, each person's truth is unique, as unique as their fingerprint, their soul."

Lucien, standing tall and stoic, nodded slightly in agreement, his eyes scanning the crowd, absorbing their reactions.

Gabriel paused, allowing his words to sink in, then resumed, "Who are we to judge another's truth? Who are we to impose our beliefs, our values, on others? In the pursuit of true freedom, we must not only discover our own truths but also respect and accept the truths of others."

The audience erupted in applause, a wave of agreement and support washing over the auditorium. Gabriel raised his hands, signaling for quiet, his face a picture of humility and grace.

"Imagine a world," he said, his voice now a gentle, persuasive whisper, "where each person's truth is acknowledged, where we coexist not in spite of our differences, but because of them. This, my friends, is the path to true harmony, to a future where peace and understanding reign supreme."

Lucien stepped forward, his voice adding weight to Gabriel's message. "In this journey of self-discovery, let us be guided by love and acceptance. Let us build a world where every truth is celebrated, where every voice is heard."

The audience stood, a standing ovation that echoed through the auditorium.

The atmosphere in the auditorium shifted from excitement to a tense, anxious silence as the man in the tenth row collapsed into the aisle, his body limp and unresponsive. Panic rippled through the crowd as shouts for help echoed through the hall. Gabriel, from his position on the stage, quickly scanned the situation, his voice cutting through the chaos. "Is there a doctor here? Please, we need help!"

A man from the back rows dashed forward, his movements swift and purposeful. He knelt beside the fallen man, checking for signs of life before commencing CPR. The crowd huddled around, their faces etched with concern and fear. Despite the doctor's efforts, the man remained lifeless, his condition seemingly beyond help.

The man was dead.

Gabriel, his face a mask of concern, turned to Lucien and spoke in a low, urgent tone, "Lucien, the time is now. Use your gifts."

The audience, their attention now fixed on the unfolding drama, watched in a mix of confusion and anticipation. Gabriel and Lucien descended from the stage, moving with a solemn grace towards the scene. The doctor, recognizing the futility of his efforts, stepped back, allowing Lucien to take his place.

Lucien knelt beside the motionless man, his hands hovering just above him. He began to chant in a language unfamiliar to the audience, his voice steady and commanding. The crowd watched in stunned silence, their breaths held in suspense.

Suddenly, the man on the floor gasped, his chest heaving as life returned to his body. A collective gasp rose from the audience, followed by an outburst of bewildered murmurs. The man, now conscious, looked around in confusion, his eyes wide with disbelief.

Lucien stood, his posture commanding yet serene. He gestured for calm, and the audience slowly settled into a stunned silence. Gabriel, his face alight with awe and reverence, knelt before Lucien. He took Lucien's hand and kissed it, a gesture of deep respect and veneration.

Turning to the microphone, Gabriel addressed the audience, his voice resonating with profound emotion. "My friends, what you have witnessed here today is nothing short of a miracle. Lucien Morreau possesses a divine gift, a power to heal and even to raise the dead."

The audience, still reeling from the shock, erupted into a mix of applause, cries of amazement, and whispers of disbelief. The air was electric with a sense of wonder and awe, as they grappled with the reality of what they had just witnessed. Lucien, standing tall beside Gabriel, looked out over the crowd, his expression one of calm assurance, as if what had transpired was simply the natural order of things.

In the green room, the atmosphere was charged with an electric energy, a stark contrast to the solemnity of the stage they had just left. Lucien Morreau was practically vibrating with excitement, pacing back and forth like a caged animal, his eyes alight with the adrenaline of the performance they had just pulled off. Gabriel Vale, in contrast, sat calmly, a small, knowing smile playing on his lips as he watched Lucien relive every moment.

"Can you believe it, Gabriel? The crowd was absolutely in the palm of our hands! The shock, the awe –

it was unmistakable!" Lucien's voice was a mix of triumph and disbelief, his hands gesturing wildly as he spoke.

Gabriel nodded, his eyes following Lucien's restless movements. With a subtle gesture, he dismissed the remaining staff from the room, creating a bubble of privacy. He then stood up and walked over to a discreet side door, opening it with a sense of ceremony.

Two men entered the room, their demeanor a stark contrast to the theatricality of the staged miracle. The first, Damien, had played the role of the 'dead' man, and the second, Dr. Richard, had been the 'doctor' in the audience. Both men were greeted with a warm, heartfelt hug from Gabriel.

"Damien, you outdid yourself," Gabriel said with genuine admiration, clapping the man on the back. "That performance was nothing short of Oscar-worthy. And Dr. Richard, your acting was impeccable. You both sold it with such conviction. Thank you, gentlemen, for your dedication to the cause."

Damien, still catching his breath from the intensity of the act, grinned broadly. "It was an honor, Gabriel. To be a part of something this big, this influential... it's exhilarating."

Dr. Richard, more reserved but equally pleased, nodded in agreement. "The impact of what we did today... it's going to be monumental. We've set the stage for something truly transformative."

Lucien, who had stopped pacing, looked at the two men with a newfound respect. "You guys were amazing out there. You had me convinced, and I knew it was all a setup!"

The room was filled with a sense of camaraderie and shared purpose. They all knew they had participated in something that would ripple out far beyond the walls of the auditorium, something that would shape the narrative and beliefs of millions. Gabriel's eyes gleamed with the knowledge of the power they had just wielded, a power that went far beyond mere illusion.

Chapter 38

A week had passed since Nadia's harrowing experience, and the textile mill, now a makeshift headquarters for the team, was a hive of activity and recovery. The atmosphere was a blend of concern, determination, and a sense of purpose that bound everyone together.

Nadia, though physically unharmed, was grappling with the psychological aftermath of her ordeal. Night terrors haunted her sleep, leaving her exhausted during the day. Despite this, she showed a resilience that impressed everyone. Mark, in particular, had become a pillar of support for her. He spent hours listening to her, offering a comforting presence as she recounted her experiences and processed her emotions.

In one of the makeshift offices, Jack was hunched over a laptop, his fingers flying over the keyboard. He had seamlessly stepped into Nadia's role, managing the team's digital needs with a quiet efficiency. His screen was a flurry of code and data, a digital battleground where he fought to keep the team safe and informed.

In a larger room, converted into a briefing area, David and Becca were updating Noah and the other operators on the events of the past month. Maps, photographs, and documents were spread out on the table, each piece a part of the intricate puzzle they were trying to solve.

Noah listened intently, his expression serious as he absorbed the information. The other operators, Mikey, Carter, and Rodriguez, interjected occasionally with questions or comments, their faces a mix of concern and resolve. The air was thick with the weight of the situation, each person acutely aware of the stakes.

Becca, standing at the head of the table, spoke with a calm authority. "We've been dealing with a rapidly evolving threat. The situation with Twilight Technologies, the involvement of Viktor Stahl, and the recent incident with Nadia have shown us that we're up against a sophisticated and ruthless enemy."

David picked up where Becca left off. "Our priority remains to uncover the full extent of Twilight Technologies' operations and to dismantle their network. But we also need to be prepared for any further attempts against us. We've been reactive so far; it's time we take the initiative."

The team nodded in agreement, their faces set in determination. The room was filled with a sense of unity and purpose, each member ready to play their part in the dangerous game they were all a part of.

The atmosphere in the room shifted palpably as Dr. Ephraim Goldman entered. His presence always brought a sense of gravitas, but today there was an added urgency in his demeanor. The team, gathered in the dimly lit room, turned their attention towards him. Noah and his team, relatively new to the group's dynamics and the broader context of their mission, leaned in with a mix of curiosity and skepticism.

Dr. Goldman wasted no time. He motioned for the lights to be dimmed further and started a video. The footage showed Gabriel Vale and Lucien Morreau on a grand stage, the scene of Lucien's purported miracle. The team watched intently as Lucien seemingly raised a man from the dead, the crowd's reaction oscillating between shock and awe.

As the video ended, Dr. Goldman turned to face the team, his expression solemn. "What you've just witnessed is a pivotal moment in our current crisis. Gabriel is the false prophet, and Lucien, I still believe, is the Antichrist."

Carter, always the one to lighten the mood, chuckled and quipped, "What's next, locusts and rivers turning to blood?"

The room fell silent. David, Becca, and Dr. Goldman didn't share his amusement. Carter, sensing the seriousness, shifted uncomfortably in his seat.

"Oh, you're serious about this?" Carter finally asked, his tone now matching the gravity of the room.

Dr. Goldman, ignoring the question, continued. "We've already seen the peace deal, as foretold in Scripture. Now, we're entering a time of wars, famines. Expect prices to skyrocket."

Carter interjected again, disbelief lacing his words, "They want us to worship that Circle Belgium bastard?"

Noah shot Carter a stern 'shut up' look, signaling him to take this seriously.

Dr. Goldman nodded gravely. "Yes. They're going to push for global worship of Lucien. And there's more – they will enforce the mark of the beast. Without it, buying or selling will become impossible."

The room was silent, the weight of his words hanging heavily in the air.

Dr. Goldman's voice took on a prophetic tone. "Jehovah is about to unleash famine, disease, and wild animals, killing one-fourth of the world's population."

The team exchanged glances, the reality of their situation sinking in. This was no longer just a battle against a corrupt corporation or a dangerous individual. They were now in the midst of a biblical prophecy unfolding in real-time, a fight not just for their lives, but for the soul of humanity.

The room was hushed, the only sound the faint hum of the old textile mill's machinery in the background. Dr. Ephraim Goldman, standing at the front, opened an aged, well-worn Bible. The pages seemed to whisper as he turned them, each leaf carrying the weight of centuries of wisdom and prophecy.

He found the passage he was looking for and cleared his throat, his voice steady yet imbued with a deep reverence. "I looked, and there before me was a pale horse! Its rider was named Death, and Hades was following close behind him. They were given power over a fourth of the earth to kill by sword, famine and plague, and by the wild beasts of the earth." His eyes lifted from the page, meeting those of his audience.

"This," he began, "is Revelation 6:8. It speaks of the fourth seal being opened by the Lamb. This seal unleashes the fourth horseman of the Apocalypse, symbolizing death and the grave."

The team, gathered around, listened intently. Dr. Goldman's voice was not just recounting a passage; it was as if he was painting a picture of a reality that was becoming more tangible by the day.

"This horseman," he continued, "is not just a symbol of death in a general sense. It represents a culmination of catastrophes. The sword signifies war, the famine speaks for itself, and the plague represents widespread disease. The wild beasts, often less mentioned, could symbolize the darker side of human nature unleashed in times of desperation, or literal dangers from the natural world as humanity's footprint and balance with nature is disrupted."

He paused, allowing the gravity of the words to sink in. "We are witnessing these events unfold. The peace deal, the rise of Lucien and Gabriel, the societal upheavals – they are not isolated incidents. They are the unraveling of the seals, the progression of the end times."

David spoke up, his voice tinged with concern, "So, what you're saying is, we're not just fighting a physical battle against a corporation or a group of individuals. We're up against something much larger, something spiritual?"

Dr. Goldman nodded solemnly. "Exactly, David. This is a battle on two fronts – the physical and the spiritual. Our actions here, in the physical realm, are crucial, but we must also be prepared for the spiritual challenges that lie ahead."

"Hey guys, you should see this," Jack announced, his voice tinged with a mix of skepticism and concern. He held up his tablet for the group to see. The screen was a mosaic of faces, each telling a story of miraculous healing. "It's all over social media. People are claiming to be healed by Lucien. We're talking about everything from broken bones to cancer. Look at these videos; they're going viral as we speak."

The team crowded around Jack, their eyes scanning the rapidly updating feed. Each video showed a different person, some in tears, others in visible disbelief, narrating their experiences. A young woman with a leg brace held it up to the camera, claiming she could walk unaided for the first time in months after attending a Lucien Morreau event. Another showed an elderly man, his voice trembling with emotion, holding up what he claimed were medical reports confirming his cancer was gone.

The videos were diverse, but the message was the same: Lucien had healed them. The background of each video was filled with comments, a mix of awe, skepticism, and outright devotion.

David leaned closer, his eyes narrowing as he watched a video of a middle-aged man claiming his lifelong vision impairment had been cured. "This is insane," he murmured. "It's like a mass delusion... or something more orchestrated."

Becca, standing beside him, added, "It's not just the healings. Look at the language being used in the comments. 'Miracle worker', 'savior', 'prophet'. This is more than just a trend; it's a carefully crafted narrative."

Dr. Goldman, who had been quietly observing, spoke up. "It's a classic tactic. Win the hearts and minds of the people with miracles, real or staged, and you have a powerful tool for influence. This is not just about physical healings; it's about cementing Lucien's position as a figure of almost divine significance."

Noah, who had been scrolling through his own device, looked up. "There's a pattern to these posts. They're not random. They're geographically and demographically targeted. It's like they're trying to hit every demographic, every type of ailment, to maximize reach and impact."

The room fell into a contemplative silence, each member of the team processing the implications of what they were seeing. The battle they were engaged in was evolving rapidly, taking on dimensions that blurred the lines between reality and manipulation, physical and psychological warfare.

Chapter 39

R odriguez leaned forward, his hands clasped together, his gaze fixed on a spot on the worn wooden table. "I grew up Catholic," he began, his voice steady but tinged with a distant nostalgia.

Victor Rodriguez sat across from Pastor Chaz in a small, dimly lit room that served as a makeshift meeting space. The air was thick with the weight of unspoken thoughts, the kind that linger in the back of one's mind, surfacing only in moments of quiet reflection.

"My mom, she was devout. Took me and my siblings to mass every week, no matter what. It was... a constant in a life that wasn't always so steady."

He paused, lost momentarily in the memories of his childhood, of the echoing hymns and the scent of incense that filled the church. "Life was rough, you know? But it was all we knew. When I got out of high school, I needed something more, something to give me purpose. That's when I joined the Navy, ended up with the SEALs."

Pastor Chaz listened intently, his expression one of understanding and empathy. He had heard many stories, each unique yet woven with similar threads of searching and longing.

"In the SEALs, I found a kind of brotherhood, a sense of belonging. And after that, the CIA's Ground Branch. It was my life, my identity." Rodriguez's voice trailed off as he shifted in his seat, his gaze now meeting Pastor Chaz's.

"But then, 3/16 happened." He let out a slow breath, the weight of that day evident in his eyes. "At first, I didn't know what to believe. There were so many theories, so much chaos. But when I started hearing about the Rapture, it hit me. All those 'whacko' ideas I heard as a kid in church, the teachings about the end times... I never took them seriously. But now," he paused, searching for the right words, "now, it's like a missing piece of a puzzle has been put in place. It's all starting to make sense."

Pastor Chaz nodded, his expression one of gentle understanding. "It's a lot to take in," he said softly. "Realizing that what you once thought was distant or irrelevant is now unfolding before your eyes. It's a journey, Victor, one of faith and understanding. And you're not alone in it."

Rodriguez looked at Pastor Chaz, a sense of relief visible in his posture. "I guess that's why I'm here, Pastor. I'm trying to make sense of it all, trying to find my place in this new reality."

The air seemed to grow heavier as Victor Rodriguez's gaze turned distant, his mind traversing back through the years of service, through the myriad of experiences that had shaped him. His voice, once steady, now carried a tremor of vulnerability.

"I've done a lot of things, Chaz," he began, his eyes not meeting Pastor Chaz's but fixed on some unseen point in the past. "All in service to my country. I believed in what I was doing, believed it was right, just... in defense of Freedom."

His hands, which had been clasped firmly together, now unclasped and fidgeted slightly, betraying a restlessness within. "But I've seen things, Chaz," he continued, his voice dropping to almost a whisper. "Things that have shaken me to my core. Things that make you question... everything."

There was a pause, a moment where the silence seemed to echo with the weight of his unspoken memories. Then, Rodriguez let out a slow, measured breath, as if trying to expel some of the darkness that lingered within him.

"There have been too many nights to count," he confessed, his voice tinged with a weariness that seemed to seep into his very bones. "Nights where I've woken up drenched in sweat, heart pounding, trapped in nightmares that feel too real. Nightmares of faces and places, of decisions made and actions taken."

He finally turned to look at Pastor Chaz, his eyes reflecting a turmoil of emotions. "I've lived with these ghosts for so long, Chaz. They're a part of me, a part I can't seem to escape. I've fought for freedom, yes, but at what cost? At what cost to my soul?"

Pastor Chaz's expression was one of deep empathy, his eyes meeting Rodriguez's with a profound understanding. "Victor," he said gently, "the path of a warrior is a complex one. You've faced darkness and made choices in moments where most would falter. The burden you carry, the memories and the doubts, they're heavy. But they don't define you."

He leaned forward, his voice firm yet compassionate. "You're more than your past actions, more than the nightmares that haunt you. There's healing, Victor, and redemption. It's a journey, yes, but one that leads to peace.

A peace that surpasses all understanding, a peace that can heal even the deepest of wounds."

The air was thick with unspoken emotions, and in Rodriguez's eyes, tears shimmered, unshed but threatening to spill over.

He took a deep, shuddering breath, his voice barely above a whisper as he confessed his deepest fears. "I've been listening to you on CALEB, Chaz. I've seen the hundreds online, heard the stories of people finding hope, finding Jesus. But me?" His voice cracked, laden with a lifetime of burdens. "Is it too late for me? After everything I've done, everything I've seen... is there anything left of my soul?"

He paused, struggling to maintain his composure. "Does Jesus even want someone like me?"

Pastor Chaz's face was a picture of compassion and understanding. He leaned forward, his eyes locking with Rodriguez's in a gaze that seemed to reach into the very depths of his soul.

"Victor," he said softly, his voice steady and reassuring, "it's never too late. Jesus' grace is boundless, His love unconditional. He doesn't see us for our past actions; He sees us for who we are in Him. Your soul, no matter how battered or weary, is precious to Him."

He reached out, placing a comforting hand on Rodriguez's shoulder. "Jesus doesn't just want you, Victor. He longs for you. He longs to heal your wounds, to lift your burdens. He died for that very reason – so that no one, no matter their past, is beyond the reach of His love and redemption."

Rodriguez's eyes, filled with tears, met Chaz's. In them was a raw, aching vulnerability, a soul laid bare in its search for redemption.

"Jesus' arms are open to you, Victor. Always have been, always will be. All He asks is that you come to Him, just as you are. He will do the rest. He will restore what has been lost, heal what has been broken. In Him, you will find a new beginning, a new life."

The tears that Rodriguez had been holding back finally broke free, tracing silent paths down his cheeks. In that moment, something within him began to shift, a burden lifting, a heart beginning to heal. For the first time in what felt like an eternity, he felt a glimmer of hope, a sense of peace that he had long thought was lost to him.

In the presence of Pastor Chaz, under the gentle gaze of understanding and unconditional love, Victor Rodriguez began his journey towards redemption, towards a life transformed by the boundless grace of Jesus Christ.

Chapter 40

D avid Mitchell," Lucien Morreau's voice echoed with a mix of surprise and contemplation as he gazed out over the sprawling cityscape of Dubai from their high-rise vantage point. The room, perched sixty floors above the ground, was steeped in a tense silence, broken only by the distant hum of the city below.

Viktor Stahl, standing slightly apart, shifted uncomfortably under Lucien's scrutinizing gaze. "Yes, David Mitchell," he finally admitted, his voice steady but betraying a hint of defensiveness. "I thought he would be the right choice to steal the payment software code. He's skilled, and frankly, expendable. I never really trusted him at The Circle."

Lucien turned slowly from the window, his eyes narrowing as he fixed Viktor with a piercing stare. "You know, Viktor," he began, his tone measured but laced with a subtle rebuke, "sometimes you make decisions too hastily, labeling people as expendable who might not need to be. David... I always saw something of a son in him. Yes, he's a bit of a boy scout, but he's clever, resourceful."

Viktor, sensing the shift in Lucien's mood, hurried to explain the current predicament. "We have a problem now. The cleaner I sent to tie up loose ends has been captured by the NSA. David knows there was a hit ordered on him. I'm not sure if he knows who's behind it, but he's definitely aware that Twilight Technologies is a sham. He's got intel from someone he worked with in the past who dug into Twilight."

Gabriel Vale, who had been listening intently, interjected with a note of urgency. "We can't afford to let the payment technology fall into the wrong hands. Once we drive Horizon Holdings' stock below $4 a share, Vale Vision will acquire them and secure our hold on the tech. But as for David Mitchell..." His voice trailed off, leaving an unspoken threat hanging in the air.

Lucien, who had been deep in thought, suddenly spoke up with a decisive tone. "I think we should bring David in, offer him a position. He could be a valuable asset to us. Besides, his career options are limited now, thanks to The Circle's machinations. It's the perfect opportunity to turn a potential threat into an ally."

The suggestion hung in the air, a new strategy forming amidst the high-stakes game of corporate and technological espionage. Lucien's gaze returned to the window, overlooking the city as if envisioning the vast web of possibilities and plans that lay ahead.

Viktor Stahl leaned forward, his expression serious as he broached the next critical issue on their agenda. "Well, if that's settled regarding David Mitchell, we need to address another pressing matter. Israel is becoming a potential obstacle in our path. With Gabriel's influence steadily guiding his followers towards placing their trust in you, Lucien, there's still the issue of Israel. They're close to completing the Temple, and once that's done, the Jewish people will turn towards their traditional worship, which could significantly hinder our plans."

Lucien Morreau raised a hand, signaling for patience. "I understand the concerns, Viktor," he said calmly, his eyes reflecting a deep, strategic thought. "But I don't foresee it as a problem. Our focus should be on the global adoption of UnityCoin. Once that's in place, even the Israelis will have no choice but to align with our agenda."

Gabriel Vale, always thinking a step ahead, proposed a proactive approach. "Perhaps we should consider organizing some major events at the Temple itself, featuring Lucien as the keynote speaker. It would be a strategic move to directly engage with the Israeli populace and sway them towards our vision."

Lucien's eyes lit up at the suggestion, a spark of excitement in his voice as he began to brainstorm. "That's an excellent idea, Gabriel. We could use these events not just for speeches, but for demonstrations of our technological advancements, perhaps even showcasing some 'miracles' to captivate their hearts and minds. We need to present a vision so compelling that it draws their attention away from their traditional beliefs."

The three men leaned in, their conversation growing more animated as they discussed potential strategies and tactics. Lucien, in particular, seemed invigorated by the challenge, his mind racing with possibilities on how to weave his influence into the very fabric of Israel's cultural and religious identity.

As they plotted, the room was filled with a sense of foreboding ambition, each man aware of the profound impact their decisions could have on the global stage. The stakes were high, and the game they were playing was one that could reshape the world's geopolitical and spiritual landscape.

Chapter 41

In a spacious, well-lit room adjacent to the Prime Minister's office, a large-scale model of the new Jewish Temple stood majestically on a central table. Prime Minister Daniel Roth and Chief Rabbi Yosef Mendel gathered around as Moshe Feinstein, his eyes alight with passion and pride, began to explain the intricate details of the Temple's design.

"As you can see," Moshe began, gesturing towards the model, "we've meticulously recreated the layout of the Second Temple, while incorporating modern necessities. This is more than a building; it's a bridge between our past and our future."

He pointed to the model's outer court, the Court of the Gentiles. "This expansive area is open to all, symbolizing our commitment to inclusivity and dialogue with the world." The court was vast, surrounded by colonnades, and paved with large, smooth stones, replicating the historic design.

Next, Moshe's finger moved to the Women's Court. "Here, we've maintained the traditional separation of spaces, but with a modern sensibility. The area is elevated, offering unobstructed views of the Temple activities, ensuring everyone feels part of the ceremonies."

The model's attention to detail was breathtaking. Miniature olive trees dotted the landscape, and the gates, especially the Beautiful Gate, were intricately designed, with golden accents that glinted even in the scaled-down version.

Moshe then guided them to the inner sanctuary, the Holy Place. "This is the heart of our Temple," he said reverently. The Holy Place was a long room, its walls lined with gold, and at the far end stood the golden altar of incense, the table for showbread, and the menorah.

"Beyond this, separated by a richly embroidered curtain, is the Holy of Holies," Moshe continued, his voice lowering in reverence. The Holy of Holies was a perfect cube, its walls and floors lined with gold, representing the most sacred space in Jewish tradition.

"Underneath the Temple, we've constructed a series of mikvahs for ritual purification," Moshe added, pointing to the lower part of the model. These baths were designed with modern filtration systems, yet they retained the traditional essence.

Finally, Moshe highlighted the integration of modern technology. "We've discreetly incorporated advanced security systems, climate control, and even augmented reality features for educational purposes, ensuring that our Temple is not only a beacon of our faith but also a testament to our progress as a people."

Prime Minister Roth and Chief Rabbi Mendel looked on, visibly moved.

"Let's move into my office," Prime Minister Roth said.

In the ornate office of the Israeli Prime Minister, Daniel Roth sat across from Chief Rabbi Yosef Mendel and Moshe Feinstein, the head of the Temple Project. The atmosphere was one of solemnity mixed with anticipation, as they discussed the final details of the opening day ceremony for the newly completed Temple.

Moshe Feinstein, his voice filled with a blend of pride and responsibility, outlined the day's proceedings. "We're expecting over a million people to visit throughout the day. It's a historic moment, not just for our nation, but for Jews worldwide," he said, his eyes gleaming with the significance of the event.

Prime Minister Roth nodded thoughtfully before introducing a delicate subject. "Gentlemen, I have received a request from Lucien Morreau. He wishes to play a role in the opening day ceremonies."

The reaction was immediate. Moshe Feinstein's face flushed with indignation. "Lucien Morreau? That's preposterous! This is a sacred event for our people. His presence in any official capacity would be wholly inappropriate!"

Chief Rabbi Mendel, always the voice of calm and reason, interjected with a more measured tone. "Prime Minister, while I understand the diplomatic sensitivities, I must concur with Moshe. The Temple's opening is a deeply religious occasion. It would be improper for someone who does not share our faith, especially someone as controversial as Mr. Morreau, to have a prominent role. However, we could extend an invitation for him to visit on a subsequent day, or perhaps he could join in the celebrations from Dubai."

Prime Minister Roth listened intently, weighing their counsel. "I appreciate your insights," he said finally. "I will convey to Mr. Morreau that while we respect his interest in our nation's historic moment, the nature of the opening day ceremonies requires us to limit participation to those within our faith. We will, however, extend an invitation for him to join us at a later date."

The three men continued their discussion, focusing on the logistics and security arrangements for the day. Despite the potential diplomatic ripples, they were united in their commitment to preserving the sanctity of the Temple's opening, a day that was to be a celebration of faith, history, and the enduring spirit of the Jewish people.

Chapter 42

The atmosphere in the room was thick with tension and focus as David, Becca, Jack, and Mark huddled around a cluttered table, strewn with papers and digital devices. The air was charged with a sense of urgency, each team member keenly aware of the stakes at hand.

Jack, his eyes flickering across the screens in front of him, broke the silence. "So, we've been digging through the intel from the warehouse, and it's led us to Mirage Capital Group in Dubai. It's a labyrinth of shell companies, but Mirage Capital seems to be the real deal."

Becca leaned in, her expression serious. "Mirage Capital, huh? Any direct links to Twilight Technologies?"

Jack nodded, scrolling through a complex web of data. "Yeah, it's like peeling an onion. Two dozen shell companies later, and here we are. Mirage Capital has legitimate holdings, including a security firm that's pretty active locally."

David, who had been listening intently, interjected with a hint of concern in his voice. "Do we think Viktor is involved in this?"

Jack sighed, his frustration evident. "It's murky. I hit a wall. My contact in Dubai just went dark."

At that moment, Nadia entered the room, her determination masking the lingering shadows of her recent ordeal. "I want to help. I don't want to be left in the dark. I can be useful."

Mark, ever the protector, looked at her with a mix of concern and admiration. "Nadia, we don't want to stress you out more than necessary."

Nadia's response was firm, yet tinged with vulnerability. "I need to be involved. I can't just sit back."

Becca nodded in agreement. "You're welcome to join us, Nadia."

The conversation shifted as Mark turned to David. "What about Liz? Could she help us dig deeper into Mirage Capital?"

Becca shot David a look that spoke volumes, a silent warning against involving outsiders. David hesitated, caught in a moment of indecision. "I... could ask her," he said, his voice betraying his uncertainty.

Before they could delve deeper, Becca's phone buzzed. She glanced at the message and stood up. "Looks like this meeting is on pause. Jack, we've got an assignment."

David rose and embraced Becca, his concern for her safety evident in his embrace. "Be safe out there," he whispered.

Becca pulled back, meeting his gaze with a mix of affection and resolve. "I will. And David, be careful with involving anyone outside of this team."

With that, she and Jack left the room, leaving the rest of the team in a contemplative silence, each lost in their thoughts about the complex web they were beginning to unravel.

"Guys, I think I've got something here," Nadia announced, her eyes not leaving the computer screen in front of her.

David and Mark immediately turned their attention towards her, their expressions shifting from contemplation to keen interest. They moved closer to Nadia's workstation, peering over her shoulder at the data displayed on her screen.

"What did you find?" David asked, his tone a mix of curiosity and hope.

Nadia pointed at a list of phone numbers on the screen, her finger tracing the lines of data. "I've been cross-referencing the numbers dialed from the cell phone we found. Several of these numbers are dead ends, but three of them are interesting."

Mark leaned in closer, his eyes narrowing as he studied the information. "Interesting how?"

Nadia clicked on one of the numbers, bringing up a detailed call history. "This number," she began, "has made repeated calls to a known associate of Viktor. And the other one," she clicked on the second number, "is registered to a company that's a front for Mirage Capital Group."

David's expression hardened as the pieces started to fit together. "So, we're potentially looking at direct communication between our kidnappers and Viktor's network."

Nadia nodded, her face a mask of determination. "Exactly. And if we can trace these calls further, we might be able to uncover more about their operations and possibly their next moves."

Mark let out a low whistle, impressed. "Nadia, that's incredible work. This could be the lead we've been looking for."

David placed a hand on Nadia's shoulder, a gesture of gratitude and respect. "Well done, Nadia. This is a big step forward. What about the third number that you said was interesting?"

Nadia replied, "I was just double-checking to make sure what I found was correct."

"Yes?" Mark inquired.

"It's the CIA. The third number is someone at the CIA."

Chapter 43

T he room was dimly lit, the air thick with a sense of gravitas as Becca stepped into her first briefing with Kilo Team. The walls were adorned with maps and screens displaying various data points, creating an atmosphere that was both intense and secretive. At the center of the room stood a man with a commanding presence, his demeanor exuding both authority and experience. This was Alexander "Xander" Stone, a former Lieutenant Commander of the Navy SEALS, now the leader of this enigmatic unit.

Becca, ever the professional, extended her hand with a formal greeting. "Lieutenant Commander Stone, it's an honor to meet you."

Xander shook her hand firmly, a hint of a smile on his face. "Please, call me Xander. We're not in the US military here. And since we technically don't exist, rank is a bit of an afterthought. Though, do keep in mind, I report directly to the President."

Becca nodded, absorbing the weight of his words. The room felt like a world apart, a place where the usual rules didn't apply.

Xander motioned for her to take a seat at the briefing table. "You might have gotten a glimpse of what this command is about when you signed up, Becca. But that was just scratching the surface."

He paused, his gaze meeting hers with an intensity that conveyed the seriousness of their operations. "Officially, Kilo Team doesn't exist. We operate in the shadows, the blackest of black ops. We have our own research staff, support network, and ground operations teams. While we can call on military support if needed, we generally handle things in-house."

Becca listened intently, her mind racing with the implications of his words. This was a level of autonomy and secrecy she hadn't experienced before.

Xander continued, "Our operations are too volatile for the regular military or clandestine services. That's where we come in. Kilo Team has the authority to craft our own plans, to read between the lines, and to execute operations that best serve the interests of the United States and its allies."

He leaned forward, his voice lowering to a grave tone. "If you're caught, Becca, retrieval will be an internal matter. And if it's not possible..." He paused, letting the reality of their work sink in. "You'll be left behind. So, don't get caught."

Becca felt a chill run down her spine. The stakes were clear, and the risks were immense. Yet, there was a part of her that thrived in such environments – where the line between success and failure was razor-thin.

"I understand, Xander," she replied, her voice steady despite the adrenaline coursing through her veins. "I'm ready for whatever comes our way."

Xander nodded, a look of respect in his eyes. "I thought you might say that. Welcome to Kilo Team, Becca. Let's get to work."

The briefing room, already charged with a palpable sense of purpose, grew even more intense as Xander called for the rest of the team to enter. The door swung open, and in walked Noah, Carter, Rodriguez, Jack, and Mikey. Each of them carried an air of confidence and readiness, the kind honed through years of experience in the field.

Xander's gaze swept over the group, a hint of pride in his eyes. "Becca, you've picked a solid support team here.

You've practically decimated the CIA's ranks," he said with a wry smile.

He turned to Noah's team. "Gentlemen, your reputation precedes you. The CIA is going to miss you, but you're going to be an invaluable asset to Kilo Team."

Then, his attention shifted to Jack. "Welcome to the team, Jack. Your skills in digital intelligence are going to be crucial."

Becca watched as Xander acknowledged each member of her team, feeling a sense of camaraderie and anticipation building within the room.

Xander then introduced Tyler Johnson, a seasoned Delta Force operator who had been with Kilo Team for four years. "Tyler will be joining your team for the first year," Xander explained. "His experience and insights will be vital in helping you achieve your objectives."

Becca extended her hand to Tyler, welcoming him to the team. She could see the wealth of experience in his eyes, the kind that only comes from years in the field.

Xander caught Becca's gaze and clarified, "Let me be clear, Tyler is not here to babysit. He's an operator, and he reports to you. He's not here to report back to me. You're the one I'll be speaking with, Becca. I trust you'll be transparent, as always."

He paused, his tone becoming more serious. "In Kilo Team, you'll have a level of autonomy you never had at the CIA. There, you had to call home for permission. Here, you have objectives and targets, and if the situation expands, it's up to you to adapt and make the necessary decisions in the field."

Becca nodded, absorbing Xander's words. The responsibility was immense, but so was the opportunity. She looked around at her team, feeling a surge of determination.

"Thank you, Xander," she said confidently. "We're ready for whatever comes our way."

The team members exchanged glances, a silent agreement passing between them. They were a unit now, a team bound by a common purpose and a shared resolve to face whatever challenges lay ahead.

"Alright, we got all the squishy feely rah-rah crap out of the way, now let's get down to brass tacks," Xander began, his voice carrying a sense of urgency.

"We have a situation brewing in the Middle East. As you know, Israel is set to open the Temple in 10 days. It's quite a security challenge, but we're leaving that up to our friends in Israel. What we're looking at is a terror cell forming in Egypt. They are planning to send in 20-30 men into Israel, during the opening of the Temple, all infected with a highly contagious form of smallpox."

The team members exchanged worried glances. The implications of what Xander was saying were clear and dire.

"They know there's no way they would get suicide vests into that secure of an event, but a little biological terrorism? Right up their alley," Xander continued. "They plan on using some of the old smuggling tunnels that Hamas built to make their way in undetected and then blend into the crowd. With enough of them, they think they'll have quite the impact on the event. With so many international visitors coming, this could spread far faster internationally than can be contained."

Jack, who had been quietly working on his laptop, connected it to the main screen, pulling up a map of the Sinai desert. "This is an overhead shot from 7 hours ago of a makeshift camp," he explained, pointing to various parts of the image. "You can see here, here, and here. These are housing units for the men. Here is the building we believe is holding the smallpox."

The team leaned in, studying the map intently as Jack continued. "They have heavy support here, here, and here. They have trucks with technicals. They have shoulder-mounted rockets. They have heavy munitions and a lot of small arms on site."

The room was silent for a moment as the gravity of the situation sank in. Each team member understood the stakes were high, and the mission was critical.

Xander looked around the room, meeting each team member's eyes. "This is where we come in. We need to neutralize this threat before it reaches Israel. It's going to be dangerous, and it's going to be tough, but I know this team can handle it."

Noah raised a valid question, his brow furrowed in confusion. "Why doesn't the military just bomb the place, or why isn't Mossad taking them out?" he asked, looking around the room for answers.

Xander, leaning against the table with his arms crossed, replied with a calm yet firm tone. "Mossad has thousands of tips and is only acting on the ones they consider highest value. They believe this one has a low likelihood of happening. No military wants to drop a bomb on the highly volatile Egypt. It could trigger a war, and the peace deal with Israel is already fragile."

He paused for a moment, letting his words sink in before continuing. "But we can send you in, clean up this mess in a low-impact way. Egypt doesn't have to acknowledge they ever had a terrorist camp. Israel can play nice with their neighbor. The US doesn't have to get involved. Clean for all parties involved."

Xander then began to lay out the plan in more detail. "Ok, so here's what we got. Get in, clear out all of the terrorist elements, get a sample of the smallpox, blow the whole place and get out."

Becca, who had been listening intently, interjected with a note of concern in her voice. "Get a sample of the smallpox? Isn't that dangerous?"

Noah, standing beside her, nodded reassuringly. "We've got this, Becca," he said confidently. "Mikey's a trained doctor. He has experience getting samples like this, and we'll have the appropriate gear."

Mikey, who had been quietly observing the conversation, gave a nod of agreement. "I've done this kind of thing before. We'll take every precaution to ensure it's done safely and securely."

The briefing room was charged with a focused intensity as Xander addressed the team. His voice was firm, his gaze steady as he delivered the final instructions. "Wheels up in three hours," he announced, his tone leaving no room for doubt about the urgency of their mission.

"We have a contact on the ground in Egypt who has acquired us a location to operate out of. When you're on the ground, Becca, you and the team can finalize operational details." Xander's eyes briefly met Becca's, conveying a silent message of trust and responsibility.

He continued, "We have helicopters available for an air insert or extraction, as well as trucks for a ground assault. Once you get in-country, the details are up to you." There was a weight to his words, an acknowledgment of the autonomy and the gravity of the task at hand.

The team members exchanged quick, determined glances. They were professionals, each well-versed in the art of covert operations, and they understood the stakes.

"Good luck and come back safe," Xander concluded, his voice a mix of command and genuine concern.

As the team began to disperse to prepare for the mission, Becca lingered for a moment, her mind already racing through potential strategies and contingencies. Noah approached her, a look of resolve on his face. "We've got this, Becca. We'll make it work, whatever it takes," he said, his voice low but full of conviction.

Becca nodded, her expression resolute. "Let's do this," she replied, her voice steady. The team was a well-oiled machine, each member an integral part of a greater whole, and she had every confidence in their abilities.

Chapter 44

R odriguez, leaning over the table with a determined look, insisted, "A helicopter insertion is the only way this will work. It's fast, direct, and gives us the element of surprise."

Mikey, equally adamant, countered, "Driving in is safer. If we come in with a helo, the enemy will hear us coming into the valley. We'll be sitting ducks."

The old tobacco warehouse stood in Cairo, Egypt like a forgotten relic of a bygone era, its weathered exterior bearing the marks of time and neglect. The once vibrant red bricks had faded to a dull, earthen hue, and the large wooden doors hung slightly ajar, creaking softly with every gust of wind. Moss and ivy crept up the walls, adding a touch of green to the otherwise monochromatic structure.

Inside, the stagnant open space was a stark contrast to the bustling activity of the team. The air was thick with the scent of aged wood and a faint, lingering aroma of tobacco that had long since been stored and processed here. Dust motes danced in the shafts of light that filtered through the dirty, paneled windows, casting long shadows across the concrete floor.

In the center of the room, a makeshift operations command had been set up. The space was a blend of old and new: the rustic charm of the warehouse intertwined with the sleek, modern technology of their equipment. Laptops hummed softly on a series of folding tables, their screens filled with charts, maps, and satellite photos. A couple of TV monitors were mounted on stands, displaying live feeds from a drone currently hovering over the terrorist camp.

The walls around them were adorned with large maps and photos, each marked with annotations and colored pins. Cables snaked across the floor, connecting the various pieces of equipment and creating a web of technology in the heart of the old building.

The operational planning had been going on for hours, and Becca could feel her frustration mounting. She was about to interject when Noah stepped in, his voice calm but firm. "Let's take a ten-minute break, get some air, and then we'll get back at it."

As the team dispersed, Noah pulled Becca aside. "This is normal," he reassured her. "The guys always get heated during operational planning. It's how we make sure nothing gets missed. Once the plan comes together, everyone will be on board."

He pointed to a map spread out on the table. "Rodriguez is right, though. Helo insertion is the best bet. We can't pull off a HALO jump with this short notice." He indicated where the enemy had their technicals parked. "They have too much field of fire."

Becca, deep in thought, suggested, "What if we split into A and B teams and insert just on the side of each of these hills, then hoof it in on foot? Each team's sniper takes out the technical and the guards on these two sides of the camp. The guards on the other side won't see it happening because their view is blocked. We'll have a clear entrance into the camp."

Noah considered her plan. "If the two teams engage at the same time, we enjoy a tactical advantage and can clear half the camp before the guard element on the opposite side can make it back into camp. We just need to neutralize heavy artillery coming with that guard element."

"What if we drop a small payload from a drone onto that truck?" Becca suggested. "That will neutralize it. We can do that when we hit the camp. Then we're only dealing with clearing the incoming force on foot. Force on force."

Noah nodded, impressed with her strategic thinking. "That could work."

He called the team back together. "Break is over, we have a plan." The team gathered around the table, their previous disagreements set aside as they focused on the new strategy. Becca outlined the plan with confidence, each member listening intently, their expressions shifting from skepticism to agreement as she spoke.

Jack interjected, "New intelligence you guys should see."

The team, gathered around the large monitor, watched intently as the drone's live feed displayed the layout of the terrorist camp. Jack's finger traced the screen, highlighting key areas.

"Here's the camp over here," he pointed to the top right corner of the screen, his voice steady and focused. He then maneuvered the drone's camera to reveal another critical piece of information. "And over here," he continued, shifting the view, "looks like a Quick Reaction Force (QRF) for the camp. About 25 minutes away on these roads."

Rodriguez, usually composed, put his head into his hands, the weight of the situation pressing down on him. "So once they call for help, we only have 25 minutes to clear the camp, get a sample of smallpox, and extract?" His voice was tinged with a mix of concern and disbelief.

Carter, known for his boisterous nature and unshakeable confidence, let out a chuckle that cut through the tension. "Get your big boy pants on," he said with a grin, trying to lighten the mood. "Remember Kandahar? Never seen you move so fast. 25 minutes is a lifetime when you have Big Nelly."

He reached over and affectionately patted his machine gun, which he had nicknamed 'Big Nelly.' The weapon, known for its reliability and firepower, had been Carter's companion in many tight situations.

The team members exchanged glances, each processing the information in their own way. The revelation of the QRF's proximity added a new layer of complexity to their mission. Time was now an even more critical factor, and the margin for error had significantly narrowed.

Noah addressed the team, his tone a mix of frustration and determination. "How did we miss this?" he asked, his eyes scanning the faces of his team members.

Jack, who had been meticulously analyzing the drone footage, responded without hesitation. "The intelligence analysts thought it was just a farm, but a few more overhead passes with the drone show a large number of military-aged males on site. There have been at least two supply runs from this farm to the camp. They're definitely connected."

The revelation added another layer of complexity to their mission. The farm, previously dismissed as inconsequential, was now a significant piece of the puzzle. It was a reminder of the ever-evolving nature of field intelligence and the need for constant vigilance.

Noah nodded, absorbing the information. "Okay, 25 minutes," he said, his voice steady but with an edge that conveyed the seriousness of the situation. He glanced around the room, making eye contact with each team member. "Let's run through the plan details a few more times. We go in tonight. Get jacked."

The team members leaned in, their focus intensifying as they began to review the operation plan once again. Each detail was scrutinized, every contingency considered. The plan had to be flawless; there was no room for error.

Chapter 45

The helicopter ride was a blend of tension and focus, slicing through the Egyptian night sky at 2:00 am. The aircraft, a stealthy Black Hawk, hummed with a low, rhythmic throb, its blades cutting through the air with precision. Inside, the team sat in silence, each member lost in their thoughts, mentally preparing for the mission ahead. The only light came from the dim glow of the instrument panels, casting eerie shadows across their faces.

Becca, her mind a whirlwind of strategy and anticipation, was running through the plan in her head. Every detail, every contingency, she reviewed them all, ensuring nothing was overlooked. The helicopter's constant vibration was a subtle reminder of the reality of their situation, the imminent danger that awaited them on the ground.

The pilot's voice, crisp and clear, broke through her concentration. "2 mikes out, Alpha team." The announcement was a jolt back to the present, a reminder that the time for planning was over. Action was imminent.

Noah led Alpha team consisting of himself, Becca, and Rodriguez. Mikey led Bravo team with himself, Carter and Tyler.

The helicopter descended rapidly, hugging the contours of the landscape to avoid detection. They reached their destination, the southwest side of a large hill. On the other side of this hill lay the terrorist camp. With practiced efficiency, the helicopter quickly dropped Alpha team and then veered off towards the other side of the valley to drop Bravo team.

Alpha team's movements were silent and precise as they hiked up to the top of the hill. The only sounds were the soft crunch of boots on the rocky terrain and the occasional rustle of gear. They moved like shadows, each step carefully placed to avoid making any noise.

Noah's voice, calm and steady, broke the silence in their earpieces. "Viper, Alpha team passes Metallica." The codenames, based on 80s bands for Alpha team and 80s movies for Bravo, added a layer of security to their communications.

"Bravo, this is Alpha, comms check," Noah continued.

Mikey's voice came through, clear and confident. "Bravo hears you 5 by 5, two mikes from first checkpoint."

Noah used hand signals to tell Alpha team to hold. They crouched in the darkness, their bodies tense with anticipation. The night air was cool, the sky a tapestry of stars above them.

After two minutes, Mikey's voice again filled their earpieces. "Bravo team passes Gremlins."

Jack's response was immediate. "Good copy, Alpha, and Bravo. Alpha passes Metallica, Bravo passes Gremlins. No change in camp movements. Looks quiet down there. I count 3 guards on each side near you with 4 additional guards on the north side. QRF is quiet. You're clear to move."

"Charlie Mike, Viper," Noah replied, his voice a whisper in the night.

He lifted his hands, signaling Alpha team to move out. Becca felt a surge of adrenaline as they advanced. Her heart pounded in her chest, a rhythmic drumbeat that matched the urgency of their mission. This was it, the moment they had trained for, planned for. Every sense was heightened, every muscle tensed for action. She was ready, they all were. The mission was underway, and they were the tip of the spear, moving silently into the heart of danger.

The rocky terrain underfoot was treacherous, a labyrinth of jagged stones and uneven ground that required careful navigation. The moonlight cast long, dark shadows across the landscape, turning each rock and crevice into a potential hazard. Becca and the Alpha team moved with deliberate caution, their boots finding purchase on the solid ground amidst the loose stones.

Fifteen minutes into their trek, Mikey's voice crackled through the headset, "Bravo passes Dead Poets Society." Becca estimated they were trailing Bravo team by about three to four minutes. The terrain was challenging, but they were making good time.

Noah's voice followed, "Alpha passes Van Halen."

"Why did you get the cool mission names?" Mikey quipped over the comms.

"It's good to be king," Noah replied with a hint of humor.

Turning to Becca, Noah asked, "Are we good to proceed?"

"Charlie Mike," Becca responded, her voice steady and focused.

"Becca, set rear security," Noah instructed.

Rodriguez, positioned with his sniper rifle, carefully aimed at the guards closest to them, prioritizing the one manning the heavy machine gun. Noah, acting as his spotter, relayed the necessary adjustments for wind and distance.

"Noah speaks into his mic, "Bravo team, status?"

"Ready," came Mikey's prompt reply.

"3... 2... 1... Execute," Noah commanded.

Three shots rang out in quick succession, each finding its mark. The guards closest to Alpha team were down before they knew what hit them.

"Clean shots, southeast side neutralized," Mikey reported.

"Limo Charlie. Proceed," Noah responded, confirming the message was loud and clear.

He lifted his hands, signaling Alpha team to advance. They moved closer to the camp, their steps quickening as they closed the distance.

In a fluid motion, Noah launched a handheld drone, a small device equipped with an explosive payload. He expertly set the destination, and the drone buzzed away, swiftly crossing the camp to hover directly above the truck on the north side. The drone was a silent harbinger of destruction, poised to neutralize a significant threat.

Alpha and Bravo teams continued their approach, converging on the camp from their respective positions. The night was alive with the sound of their movement, the tension unmistakable in the air. They were moments away from engagement, the culmination of their meticulous planning and stealthy approach. The mission was in full swing, and each team member was acutely aware of the stakes. They moved as one, a cohesive unit ready to face whatever lay ahead in the terrorist camp.

As they edged closer to the camp, Noah abruptly raised his hand, signaling Rodriguez and Becca to halt. Becca's heart raced as she scanned the area, trying to discern the cause of their sudden stop. Then she saw him—a lone figure emerging from one of the tents, his movements casual as he headed towards the latrine area. Instinctively, Noah, Rodriguez, and Becca dropped into a squat, their bodies tensing as they sought to merge with the rugged terrain around them. The night was eerily silent, save for the soft crunch of the man's footsteps on the gravel. They remained motionless, barely breathing, as the man passed by, oblivious to their presence.

But then, the man stopped.

Chapter 46

The tense silence of the night was shattered in an instant. The man, who had turned his gaze directly towards Noah, barely had time to register the threat before a single, silenced shot from Noah's AR sent him collapsing to the ground. Noah's eyes darted across the camp, scanning for any sign that their cover was blown. For a moment, it seemed they were safe, and he signaled for the team to advance.

But then, the stillness was broken by the one sound they dreaded most in their stealth operation—a dog's bark. It pierced the night, a clarion call to the camp. Becca's heart pounded in her chest, her mind racing as she braced for what was to come. Armed men, roused from their slumber, poured out of the tents, disoriented but dangerous.

Alpha and Bravo teams sprang into action, their training taking over. Gunfire erupted, a cacophony of chaos as Becca found herself in the thick of it. Each shot she fired was a blend of fear and focus, her training guiding her actions even as the fog of war clouded her thoughts. Noah's commands cut through the noise — "Contact front!" then "Push right!" — as they sought cover.

Rodriguez's voice rang out, "Frag out!" followed by the muffled thud of a grenade, its explosion engulfing a tent and its occupants in a deadly embrace. Noah, with precise timing, signaled the drone to eliminate the threat of the heavy artillery truck, its explosion lighting up the night.

As the gunfight raged, Becca's mind was a whirlwind of adrenaline and determination. Each fallen enemy was a reminder of the stakes at hand. Jack's voice over the comms brought a new urgency, "Enemy QRF twenty mikes out." Time was running out.

After a harrowing few minutes, every terrorist in the camp was dead.

Noah's leadership was unwavering as he directed the team. Carter and Tyler set up security, while Mikey hurried to collect the crucial smallpox samples. Becca, tasked with gathering intel, moved through the camp, collecting phones and laptops from the fallen terrorists.

Entering a tent, she found a laptop mid-operation, its screen flickering as it deleted vital data. Her fingers flew over the keyboard in a futile attempt to halt the process. That's when she saw it - a file linking Lucien Morreau to the camp. Her mind raced, piecing together the implications. Could Lucien Morreau be funding a terrorist camp? The thought was chilling.

But her efforts were in vain; the data slipped away, leaving only questions and suspicions. She relayed her findings to Noah, who responded with a mix of surprise and pragmatism, "Well isn't that a thing."

Noah's voice, steady yet infused with a sense of urgency, cut through the night. "We have 12 minutes, team. Finish up, let's get out of here," he commanded, his eyes scanning the chaotic aftermath of their assault.

Rodriguez, knee-deep in the task of setting the charges, grunted in acknowledgment. His hands moved with practiced precision, but a frown creased his brow as he encountered an unexpected snag. Wires and detonators lay spread out before him, a puzzle that demanded a swift solution.

Noah, noticing Rodriguez's hesitation, moved closer, his voice low and controlled. "Alpha 3, talk to me. What's the situation?"

Rodriguez didn't look up, his focus unwavering on the task at hand. "Hit a bit of a snag, Alpha 1," he replied, his tone betraying a hint of frustration. "The detonator's acting up. Give me 2 mikes to bypass this."

Noah, ever the leader, offered his assistance while keeping an eye on their surroundings. "Need a hand with that?" he asked, ready to dive in.

Rodriguez shook his head, his hands deftly working on the wires. "I'm working the problem Alpha 1."

Noah nodded, understanding the delicacy of the situation. "Alright, keep me posted. We're on the clock here."

Rodriguez's fingers moved with increased urgency, stripping wires and reconfiguring connections. "Almost there..." he muttered under his breath.

After a tense moment, Rodriguez let out a small sigh of relief. "Got it! Charges are set and ready to blow. We're good to go, Alpha 1."

In those final moments, as the team prepared to withdraw, Becca's mind was a storm of emotions and thoughts. The potential link to Lucien Morreau added a new, disturbing layer to their mission, one that would undoubtedly have far-reaching consequences.

As the team moved swiftly through the dark, rugged terrain, their exfiltration from the terrorist camp was marked by a tense silence, punctuated only by the occasional crackle of loose stones underfoot. Becca's mind, however, was far from silent. It was a whirlwind of thoughts, trying to piece together the complex puzzle that had just unfolded before her.

The revelation that Lucien Morreau, a man of immense influence and power, was potentially funding a terrorist group to unleash a smallpox attack at a globally significant event was both shocking and deeply troubling. The implications were vast and sinister, painting a picture of a man willing to use chaos and fear to manipulate global events to his advantage.

As she moved, Becca replayed the scene in the tent. The laptop screen, the file linking Morreau to the camp, the frantic attempt to stop the data wipe—it all pointed to a meticulously planned operation. But why would Morreau, a man with seemingly limitless resources and connections, resort to such a barbaric and desperate measure? Was it a power play, an attempt to destabilize the region, or something even more nefarious?

Her thoughts were interrupted by the sound of Noah's voice over the comms, "Stay sharp, team. We're not clear yet." Becca refocused, her training taking over. But in the back of her mind, the questions continued to swirl.

As they neared the extraction point, Becca considered the broader implications. A biological attack of this scale would not just be a tragedy; it would be a geopolitical earthquake. It could shift the balance of power in the region, create global panic, and potentially lead to widespread conflict. And if Morreau was indeed behind it, what was his endgame? Was this part of a larger strategy, a chess move in a game only he understood?

The more she thought about it, the more Becca realized the depth of the rabbit hole they were peering into. This was no longer just a matter of counterterrorism; it was a matter of global security, involving players who operated in the shadows, manipulating events to suit their obscure agendas.

As the helicopter's blades began to whir in the distance, signaling their imminent extraction, Becca knew that this mission was just the beginning. Unraveling the tangled web woven by Lucien Morreau would require all her skills and resources.

Chapter 47

David sat alone in the dimly lit room, the soft glow of a single lamp casting long shadows across the walls. His mind was a whirlwind of thoughts and emotions, a tumultuous sea that refused to be calmed. He gazed at the empty space beside him, where Becca would usually be, her presence a comforting constant in his life. But now, she was out there, somewhere, doing what she believed in, fighting for a cause greater than themselves.

He understood the nature of her work, the unpredictability, the danger. It was part of who she was, and he loved her all the more for it. Her passion, her commitment to making a difference, it was one of the many things that drew him to her. But in these moments of solitude, the weight of her absence pressed heavily upon him.

David thought about the discovery that someone at the CIA may be involved with Nadia's kidnappers made him concerned for Becca. Though he knew she didn't work directly for the CIA anymore, who knew what a bad actor on the inside could do.

David's thoughts drifted to the larger picture, the world in turmoil, the Tribulation. It was a time of chaos and uncertainty, a period that tested the faith and resolve of many. He pondered the significance of their actions in such a time. Did it matter? Could they truly make a difference in a world seemingly spiraling towards its prophesied destiny?

Yet, as he sat there, lost in contemplation, a sense of resolve began to take root within him. He knew that giving up was not an option. Like Becca, he couldn't abandon the fight for what was right, for justice and freedom. It was more than a duty; it was a calling.

David's faith was a beacon in the darkness, a guiding light that shone unwaveringly. He believed that every life saved was a victory, every soul given a chance to find redemption and grace. In these troubled times, this belief was more important than ever. God, he knew, didn't call them to be successful by worldly standards but to be faithful to the cause of righteousness and truth.

As he sat there, a sense of peace began to settle over him. The challenges ahead were daunting, but they were not insurmountable. With faith as his shield and love as his guiding star, David knew he could face whatever the future held. He would continue to fight, to stand for what he believed in, and to support Becca in her mission. Together, they were a force for good, a small light in the darkness, but a light nonetheless.

And so, David waited, his heart filled with love, faith, and a quiet determination. The fight for freedom, for justice, for the chance to bring others to the saving grace of Jesus Christ, would go on. And he would be there, standing firm, until the very end.

David sat in the quiet of his room, his tablet casting a soft glow in the dim light. The world outside was in chaos, a stark contrast to the stillness around him. He wasn't one to obsess over the news, but these days, it was hard to look away. The scenes unfolding across the globe were like something out of a dystopian novel, yet they were all too real.

On the screen, images flickered of riots and unrest in various countries. The adoption of Gabriel Vale's UnityCoin had sparked an economic turmoil that seemed to mirror the dark prophecies of the scriptures Dr. Goldman had shared with them. David watched, a sense of surreal disbelief washing over him. Bread, a basic staple, now cost a day's wages. The world was spiraling into a crisis of scarcity and inflation, with people scrambling for the most basic of needs.

His thoughts drifted to the upcoming opening of the Temple in Israel. It was a historic event, one that he had a personal connection to, albeit a complicated one. David remembered the days he spent with Lucien Morreau and The Circle, negotiating the peace treaty that had paved the way for this moment. It was a bittersweet memory. On one hand, the treaty had brought about a significant change, a moment of peace in a region long torn by conflict. On the other hand, knowing what he now knew about Lucien, the memory was tainted.

David couldn't help but feel a mix of awe and resentment. Awe, for the monumental impact the treaty had on the world stage, and resentment for the man who orchestrated it all, Lucien Morreau. The man he once admired and worked closely with was now the source of much of the pain and suffering he saw in the world.

As he watched the news, David's mind wrestled with a whirlwind of emotions. There was fear for what the future held, anger at those who were causing such widespread suffering, and a deep sense of sorrow for the innocent lives caught in the crossfire. Yet, amidst all these tumultuous feelings, there was also a glimmer of hope.

The alignment of current events with the scriptures was undeniable. It was as if the ancient words were coming to life before his very eyes. This realization brought a sense of clarity and purpose. David knew that these were not just random events; they were part of a larger plan, a divine narrative unfolding in real time.

With a deep breath, David set the tablet aside. He knew that the road ahead would be fraught with challenges and uncertainties. But he also knew that he was not alone in this journey. His faith, his friends, and his unwavering commitment to stand against the darkness gave him strength.

In the quiet of his room, David closed his eyes and whispered a prayer. A prayer for guidance, for strength, and for the wisdom to navigate the turbulent times ahead. The world outside might be in chaos, but inside, David found a peace that surpassed all understanding, a peace that anchored him in the midst of the storm.

"Arnie's books on Fifth Ave. 6pm. Don't be late. 😌"

The text message David has been waiting for. He grabbed his coat and set out into the city.

Chapter 48

David's heart pounded as he navigated through the maze of bookshelves, the familiar scent of paper and ink filling his senses. He spotted Liz in the distance, her presence a beacon in the crowded bookstore. As he approached, her face lit up with recognition, and she enveloped him in a warm, sincere hug. "I've missed you," she said, her voice tinged with genuine affection.

David returned the embrace, but his mind was a whirlwind of conflicting emotions. Trusting Liz was a gamble. Their last encounter had left him with more questions than answers, and her sudden profession of faith had seemed almost too convenient. Yet, there was something in her demeanor, a certain earnestness, that made him want to believe her.

As they pulled away from the hug, Liz's eyes held a seriousness that immediately caught David's attention. She handed him a piece of paper, her fingers brushing his as she did so. "I found something on Mirage Capital," she said, her voice low and urgent.

David's eyes scanned the list she had given him, and his heart sank. Among the names of shareholders in Mirage Capital, one stood out like a sore thumb, sending a jolt of shock through his system. Noah Thatcher. The name echoed in his mind, each syllable a hammer strike to his trust and beliefs.

"How confident are you about this list?" David asked, his voice barely above a whisper. The bookstore around them faded into a blur, the rows of books and murmurs of patrons becoming distant and inconsequential.

Liz's eyes met his, steady and unwavering. "I have highly placed sources in Dubai's business registration and taxation department," she explained. "They keep immaculate records. Dubai might let you hide your assets from your home country, but they make sure to keep track for their own purposes. Do you recognize any of the names?"

David felt a knot form in his stomach. Noah Thatcher, a name he had come to associate with integrity and leadership, was now linked to Mirage Capital, a company shrouded in mystery and dubious dealings. The revelation sent his mind reeling, a torrent of questions flooding his thoughts.

"No," David said matter-of-factly. "I just wanted to make sure this was solid before we dug deeper. I appreciate your help with this." David maintained a straight face, not showing any emotion. But inside, David was angry.

Was Noah involved in something sinister? Was this a mistake, or was there a deeper, more troubling explanation? David struggled to reconcile the image of the man he knew with the name on the list in front of him.

Liz's voice brought him back to the present. "I'm glad I could help. Let me know if you need any help digging up info on any of these people."

David looked into Liz's eyes, searching for any hint of deceit, but found none. In that moment, he chose to trust her, to lean on the hope that her intentions were pure. The path ahead was uncertain, and the stakes were higher than ever. But with Liz's help, perhaps they could unravel the truth behind Mirage Capital and the enigmatic involvement of Noah Thatcher.

As they stepped out of the bookstore, the bustling city noise enveloped them, a stark contrast to the quiet, contemplative atmosphere they had just left behind. The air was crisp, carrying the promise of an approaching evening. People hurried past, lost in their own worlds, as the city lights began to flicker to life.

Liz turned to David, her expression softening. "It's been really good seeing you, David," she said, a hint of vulnerability in her voice. "If you're up for it, I'd be open to grabbing dinner sometime."

David paused, the weight of the day's revelations still heavy on his mind. He appreciated Liz's offer, her attempt to bridge the gap that had formed between them. Yet, his mind was a tumult of emotions and unanswered questions, making it difficult to focus on anything else.

He offered her a small, somewhat strained smile. "Thanks, Liz. That's kind of you," he replied, his voice tinged with a non-committal tone. "I just have a lot on my plate right now."

Liz nodded, understanding flickering in her eyes. "I get it, David. You've been through a lot," she said gently. "Just know that I'm here if you need someone to talk to, or if you just need a break from all this craziness."

David appreciated her understanding and the sincerity behind her words. "I'll keep that in mind. Thank you, Liz," he said, feeling a sense of gratitude for her support.

With a final nod, David turned and walked away, his steps echoing on the city pavement. As he disappeared into the crowd, Liz watched him go, a mix of concern and hope in her eyes. The evening air carried away their conversation, leaving behind a silent understanding and an unspoken promise of support in the days to come.

Chapter 49

G reat mission."

Becca and Noah sat across from Xander, the air thick with the residue of their recent operation in Egypt. The walls, adorned with maps and screens, seemed to close in as they recounted the events, the tension palpable.

Xander, leaning back in his chair, interlaced his fingers, his gaze shifting between Becca and Noah. "Your after-action reports are impressive," he began, his voice steady and authoritative. "It shows excellent leadership and execution on your part. Well done."

Becca nodded, a flicker of satisfaction in her eyes. "Thank you, Xander," she said, her voice firm. "But I need to discuss the intel regarding Lucien Morreau. It's critical and could change our understanding of the entire operation."

Xander's expression remained unreadable. "I've read your report, Becca," he replied calmly. "However, the other intel gathered on-site didn't corroborate your findings about Morreau. Without additional evidence, I'm hesitant to pursue this lead."

Becca's frustration was evident. "But the evidence was right there on the laptop. It linked Morreau to the funding of the terrorist camp. We can't just ignore this."

Xander turned to Noah, seeking his input. "Noah, what are your thoughts on this?"

Noah shifted uncomfortably in his seat. "I didn't see the evidence Becca is referring to," he admitted. "And if it's not backed by other intel, it might be a dead end. Maybe we should pass this information to the CIA. Let them handle it."

Becca's brow furrowed, her sense of urgency growing. "We can't just hand this off and hope someone else will follow through. This could be a major piece of the puzzle in understanding Morreau's operations."

Xander regarded her for a moment, his expression thoughtful. "Becca, I understand your concern, but we operate on concrete evidence. Speculations, no matter how compelling, aren't enough. We need more to go on."

Becca leaned forward, her determination unwavering. "Then let's find that evidence. We can't let this slide. Morreau's involvement could have global implications."

Xander sighed, the weight of command evident in his demeanor. "I'll consider your request, Becca. But for now, we stick to the facts we have. Keep this on your radar, but don't let it distract from our primary objectives."

Becca's jaw set in resolve, even as disappointment flickered in her eyes. She knew this was not the end of it. The meeting adjourned with a sense of unfinished business hanging in the air, a silent acknowledgment that the truth was still out there, waiting to be uncovered.

Outside the briefing room, the corridor was quiet, the tension from the meeting with Xander still lingering in the air. Noah glanced at Becca, noticing the anger simmering just beneath her composed exterior.

"I know you're convinced Lucien Morreau is behind this, stirring global strife like he did at The Circle," Noah began, his voice low and steady. "But without concrete evidence, Xander won't escalate it to the President. And without that, Kilo Team won't act against Lucien."

Becca's fists clenched at her sides, her frustration palpable. "It's like hitting a brick wall," she muttered, her voice laced with irritation. "Morreau is out there, possibly funding terrorism, and we're just standing by."

Noah stopped, turning to face her. "Listen, Becca, I understand your frustration. I'll help you gather more evidence, but we need to stay focused on the bigger picture."

Becca's eyes met his, a storm of emotions swirling within. "I just hate feeling so powerless," she admitted.

Noah placed a reassuring hand on her shoulder. "We're not powerless. We just need to be strategic. Let's head back to The Resistance. They might have uncovered something while we were away. We need to see if they've been sitting on their hands or actually making progress."

Becca took a deep breath, the fire in her eyes dimming slightly but not extinguished. "Alright," she conceded. "Let's see what The Resistance has been up to. Maybe they've dug up something we can use."

Together, they walked down the corridor, their steps echoing softly. Despite the setback, there was a sense of determination between them, a shared resolve to uncover the truth, no matter how deep it was buried.

Chapter 50

David's expression was grave as he leaned against the wall of their makeshift headquarters, his gaze fixed on Nadia. "I've received some information," he began, his voice low and serious. "It's disturbing, unverified, and if true, it could put our entire team at risk. I need to verify it, but I can't do it alone."

Nadia, sensing the urgency in his tone, leaned in closer. "You can trust me, David. What is it? Who's involved?"

David hesitated, weighing his words carefully. "Before I tell you, I need to know something. Can you tap the phone of a former CIA ground operator?"

Nadia's eyebrows shot up in surprise. "That's... complex," she said slowly. "You're talking about layers of encryption, security protocols, not to mention the legal and ethical implications."

David nodded, understanding the magnitude of what he was asking. "I know it's a big ask, but can you do it?"

Nadia sighed, her mind racing through the technical challenges such a task would entail. "In a TV show, this would be the part where the hacker says 'yes' after listing all the impossible hurdles," she said with a wry smile. "But this is the real world, David. Hacking into a phone with that level of protection? It's highly unlikely, if not impossible."

David's shoulders slumped slightly, but he nodded in understanding. "I had to ask," he said quietly.

Nadia's curiosity was piqued. "What's going on, David? Who are we talking about here?"

David took a deep breath, the weight of his dilemma evident in his eyes. "It's someone close to us, someone we've worked with. I can't say more until I have solid proof. But if this is true, it changes everything."

Nadia studied David's troubled expression, her mind racing with possibilities. "Okay, David. I may not be able to hack the phone, but maybe there's another way to get the information you need. Let's think outside the box. We're a team, and we'll figure this out together."

David gave her a grateful nod, the burden of his secret slightly eased by her support. "Thank you, Nadia. I knew I could count on you."

David sat alone in the dimly lit room of their makeshift headquarters, the only sound the faint hum of a distant generator. The room, once bustling with activity, now felt eerily silent, amplifying the turmoil in his mind. He leaned back in his chair, his gaze lost in the shadows that danced across the walls, illuminated only by the soft glow of his laptop screen.

His thoughts were a whirlwind, each possibility more unsettling than the last. If Liz was indeed the traitor, the implications were dire. She could be planting evidence, a masterstroke to remove a key player from their resistance and seed discord within their ranks. The thought of such deceit made his stomach churn. He had trusted Liz, believed in her, and the possibility of her betrayal felt like a personal affront.

But then there was Noah. The idea of Noah being a wolf in their midst was almost too painful to consider. Becca's trust in Noah was unwavering, her respect for him deep-rooted. The revelation of his betrayal would not just be a strategic blow; it would shatter her, perhaps irreparably. David could almost feel the weight of her potential heartbreak, and it filled him with a profound sense of dread.

And yet, there was a third, equally troubling possibility. What if Liz was being fed false information? It would render her an unwitting pawn in a larger game, her intelligence reports tainted and unreliable. This scenario, while absolving her of malicious intent, presented its own set of challenges. It meant that their enemy was always one step ahead, manipulating them through a web of lies and half-truths.

David rubbed his temples, feeling the onset of a headache. Each scenario was a labyrinth of uncertainties and potential traps. The stakes were incredibly high, and the wrong decision could spell disaster for their entire operation.

He let out a long, weary sigh. The burden of leadership weighed heavily on him, the responsibility of making the right call a constant pressure. In this shadowy game of espionage and counterintelligence, trust was their most valuable asset and their greatest vulnerability.

David knew he needed more information, more evidence. But time was not on their side, and every moment of indecision was an opportunity for their adversaries to gain ground. He leaned forward, his eyes narrowing with determination. One thing was clear: they needed to act, and soon. The path forward was fraught with danger, but they had come too far to falter now.

His phone buzzed with a new secure message: "I'm back."

Chapter 51

The new Temple on the Temple Mount in Jerusalem stood as a breathtaking testament to both ancient tradition and modern innovation. As the morning sun cast its first golden rays upon the city, the Temple's white limestone walls glowed with a warm, ethereal light, creating a stark contrast against the deep blue of the sky.

Approaching the Temple complex, one was immediately struck by the harmonious blend of old and new. The main structure, inspired by descriptions of Solomon's Temple, rose majestically, its facade adorned with intricate carvings depicting scenes from Jewish history and scripture. The entrance was flanked by two towering bronze pillars, their surfaces etched with delicate Hebrew inscriptions, shimmering in the sunlight.

The outer courtyard was expansive, paved with smooth, polished stone that reflected the sky above. Olive trees, symbols of peace and prosperity, were strategically planted around the perimeter, their silvery leaves rustling gently in the breeze. In the center of the courtyard stood a large, ornate bronze basin, supported by twelve oxen statues, representing the twelve tribes of Israel. Water flowed from their mouths, creating a serene, burbling sound that added to the sacred atmosphere.

Beyond the courtyard, the Temple itself was a marvel of architectural prowess. The building was crowned with a gilded roof that shone brilliantly, visible from great distances across Jerusalem. Tall, narrow windows with intricately designed stained glass allowed natural light to filter into the interior, casting colorful patterns on the smooth stone floor.

Inside, the main hall was awe-inspiring. The walls were lined with polished cedar, imported from distant lands, giving off a subtle, pleasant fragrance. The Ark of the Covenant, a replica of the original, was placed in the Holy of Holies, shielded from view by a richly embroidered curtain, woven with gold thread and images of cherubim.

To the side of the main hall, smaller chambers served various purposes, including study rooms and areas for prayer and meditation. Each room was meticulously designed, with handcrafted wooden furnishings and ornate silver and gold decorations, reflecting the sanctity of the space.

Throughout the complex, modern technology was seamlessly integrated. State-of-the-art security systems were discreetly placed, ensuring the safety of the worshippers and the sacred artifacts. Advanced lighting and climate control systems provided comfort while remaining unobtrusive, preserving the ancient ambiance of the Temple.

As visitors walked through the Temple complex, there was a palpable sense of history being both preserved and renewed. It was a place where the past and present converged, a physical embodiment of the enduring spirit and resilience of the Jewish people. The Temple on the Temple Mount stood not only as a house of worship but as a symbol of hope, unity, and the unbreakable bond between a people and their heritage.

Dr. Ephraim Goldman's heart was heavy with a profound sense of history and spirituality as he walked through the newly constructed Temple on the Temple Mount. His old friend, Moshe Feinstein, head of The Temple Project, guided him through the complex, his voice filled with a mix of pride and reverence.

As they entered the main hall, the morning light filtered through the stained-glass windows, casting a kaleidoscope of colors on the polished stone floor. Dr. Goldman's eyes were drawn upwards to the gilded roof, shimmering in the light, a symbol of divine presence and human aspiration.

"This is incredible, Moshe," Dr. Goldman murmured, his voice barely above a whisper, as if afraid to disturb the sanctity of the space. "The blend of tradition and modernity... it's breathtaking."

Moshe nodded, his eyes reflecting the same awe. "We wanted to honor our past while embracing the future. This Temple is not just a building; it's a testament to our enduring faith and resilience."

As they moved through the Temple, Dr. Goldman's thoughts were a whirlwind of emotion and memory. He recalled the ancient texts he had studied for decades, the historical accounts of the First and Second Temples, and the long, tumultuous journey of the Jewish people. This new Temple, standing majestically on the Temple Mount, was a powerful symbol of their unbroken spirit.

In the Holy of Holies, where the replica of the Ark of the Covenant was housed, Dr. Goldman felt a profound connection to his ancestors. He imagined the High Priest of ancient times, entering this most sacred space, and he felt a deep sense of continuity with his heritage.

"The craftsmanship is extraordinary," he commented, admiring the intricate carvings on the cedar walls. "Every detail is a reflection of devotion and meticulous care."

Moshe led him to a small chamber off the main hall, designed for study and prayer. "This room," Moshe explained, "is dedicated to scholars and thinkers, to continue the tradition of learning and interpretation that is so central to our faith."

Dr. Goldman felt a lump form in his throat. This room symbolized his life's work, the intersection of faith and intellect, tradition and inquiry. He ran his fingers over the smooth wooden tables, each etched with quotations from the Torah and Talmud.

As they concluded the tour, workers bustled around them, making final preparations for the grand opening. Dr. Goldman felt a surge of hope and responsibility. This Temple was not just a monument to the past; it was a living, breathing center for worship, learning, and community.

"Thank you, Moshe," he said, his voice steady but filled with emotion. "This is more than I could have ever imagined. It's a beacon of light for our people and for the world."

Moshe clasped his hand, his eyes shining with unshed tears. "Ephraim, my friend, this is just the beginning. The journey of our people continues, and this Temple will be a guiding star on that journey."

As they stepped out into the bright Jerusalem sun, Dr. Goldman took one last look at the Temple. He felt a profound sense of gratitude and purpose. This was a new chapter in a story that spanned millennia, and he was privileged to witness it.

Chapter 52

A s the doors of the Temple opened, the crowd surged forward, eager to witness the grandeur of the newly constructed sanctuary. Among them, two men in sackcloth, with long, unkempt hair and beards, each carrying a wooden staff, moved with a purposeful grace, almost unnoticed in the throng of visitors. They positioned themselves near the entrance, where they could be heard by many, and began to preach with a fervor that quickly drew attention.

In unison, their voices rose above the murmur of the crowd, "Holy, holy, holy, is the Lord God Almighty," their words resonating with a deep reverence.

Then, taking turns, they began their impassioned sermon, their voices harmonizing and contrasting in a captivating rhythm.

One of the men, his eyes alight with a fervent glow, spoke first. "Behold, the Lamb of God, who takes away the sin of the world!" he proclaimed. "In Him is life, and that life is the light of all mankind."

His companion continued, his voice rich and resonant. "He was despised and rejected by mankind, a man of suffering, and familiar with pain. Like one from whom people hide their faces, he was despised, and we held him in low esteem."

The first speaker took up the thread again, his words flowing like a river. "But He was pierced for our transgressions, He was crushed for our iniquities; the punishment that brought us peace was on Him, and by His wounds, we are healed."

The second man's voice rose in a crescendo, "For God so loved the world that He gave His one and only Son, that whoever believes in Him shall not perish but have eternal life."

The first man's voice softened, inviting and warm. "Come to me, all you who are weary and burdened, and I will give you rest. Take my yoke upon you and learn from me, for I am gentle and humble in heart, and you will find rest for your souls."

His companion added, "For there is one God and one mediator between God and mankind, the man Christ Jesus, who gave himself as a ransom for all people."

The first man's voice took on a prophetic tone. "He is coming with the clouds, and every eye will see Him, even those who pierced Him; and all peoples on earth will mourn because of Him."

The second man concluded with a call to action, "Repent, for the kingdom of heaven has come near. The time is fulfilled, and the kingdom of God is at hand; repent and believe in the gospel."

In the heart of the Temple, the atmosphere shifted palpably as the two witnesses continued their impassioned preaching about Jesus Christ. The crowd, initially curious, began to bristle with discomfort and then outright indignation. The sacred grounds of the Temple, they felt, were no place for such declarations, especially not on this momentous day of its opening.

A murmur of discontent rippled through the crowd, growing louder and more agitated. Groups of people started chanting traditional Jewish prayers and songs, attempting to drown out the voices of the two men in sackcloth. Their chants swelled, a collective effort to reclaim the sanctity of their space.

But something extraordinary happened. Despite the volume and fervor of the crowd, the voices of the two witnesses carried with an uncanny clarity. It was as if their words were being amplified, reaching every corner of the Temple grounds. The chants of the crowd, in stark contrast, seemed to lose their force, becoming strangely muted as if absorbed by an unseen barrier.

The witnesses' message of repentance and belief in Jesus Christ penetrated the air, unimpeded by the disharmony around them. Their voices, imbued with a supernatural resonance, reached every ear, undiluted and clear. Men, women, and children, regardless of their intention to ignore or oppose, found themselves involuntarily listening to the call for repentance.

"Turn to the Lord Jesus Christ," one of the witnesses implored, his voice ringing with a compelling urgency. "He is the way, the truth, and the life. No one comes to the Father except through Him."

"Repent, for the Kingdom of Heaven is at hand," the other continued, his tone both stern and compassionate. "In Him is the forgiveness of sins and the promise of eternal life."

The crowd, despite their efforts to resist, found themselves enveloped in a profound moment of spiritual confrontation. The words of the witnesses, unyielding and powerful, stirred a range of emotions - from anger to awe, from denial to deep, introspective contemplation.

The Temple grounds, once filled with a sense of celebration and reverence, descended into chaos as Moshe Feinstein's frustration boiled over. He watched, his face a mask of indignation, as the two witnesses continued their unwavering proclamation. Turning to his security team, he issued a terse command, his voice laced with authority and a hint of desperation, "Remove them, by force if necessary."

Dr. Ephraim Goldman, his expression etched with concern, approached Feinstein. "Moshe, these men, they are not ordinary preachers. They are the ones spoken of in the Christian scriptures, in Revelation. They are God's witnesses, and I fear they cannot be removed by human means."

Feinstein, his mind clouded by the urgency to restore order, dismissed Goldman's warnings with a wave of his hand. "Scriptures or not, this is our Temple, and they have no right to disrupt it."

The security guards, trained and stern, made their way through the agitated crowd. They approached the witnesses with a professional calm, but their request for the men to leave was met with a serene yet unyielding refusal. "We are here by God's command and will leave only when our purpose is fulfilled," one of the witnesses stated, his voice resonating with an otherworldly conviction.

As a guard reached out to physically remove one of the witnesses, the other struck his staff into the ground. In an instant, a swirling cloud of locusts came down from the heavens, enveloping the guards in a buzzing, disorienting swarm. The security guards, caught off guard, retreated, swatting away the relentless insects.

The crowd's anger reached a fever pitch. A man, his face twisted in rage, picked up a loose brick and hurled it at the witnesses. But with a swift movement, the first witness raised his staff, deflecting the brick effortlessly. Then, in a moment that would be etched into the memories of all present, he opened his mouth and breathed fire. The flames consumed the brick thrower, leaving the crowd in stunned silence.

Panic ensued as people scrambled in all directions, their previous anger replaced by fear and awe. The Temple grounds, meant to be a place of peace and worship, had become a scene of supernatural confrontation.

Feinstein stood frozen, witnessing the undeniable power of these two enigmatic figures. Dr. Goldman's earlier words echoed in his mind, a chilling reminder of the ancient prophecies that spoke of such events. The two witnesses, unharmed and undeterred, continued their preaching, their voices now carrying an even greater weight of authority and mystery.

As the crowd dispersed in fear, a deep sense of uncertainty settled over the Temple. The day that was meant to be a historic celebration had turned into a moment of profound spiritual reckoning, leaving all who witnessed it to grapple with the reality of a power far beyond their understanding.

Chapter 53

In the bustling makeshift headquarters of The Resistance, the atmosphere was electric with a sense of purpose and urgency. Nadia, her fingers dancing across the keyboard, was deep in concentration, orchestrating a new project that could change the course of their mission. Around her, the screens of CALEB, their secure communications network, were alive with videos of the two witnesses, their words echoing in a multitude of languages.

Chaz and Mark huddled close, watching in awe as the videos played. "It's incredible," Chaz whispered, "they're speaking in every language. Everyone, everywhere, can understand them."

Mark nodded, his eyes wide with wonder. "It's like the day of Pentecost, but on a global scale. This is a game-changer."

Nadia paused her typing, looking up at the screens. "We need to capitalize on this momentum," she said, her voice tinged with excitement. "There's a hunger for truth out there, and we have the means to feed it."

Her idea was simple yet revolutionary. A daily show on CALEB, featuring an animated character delivering messages of hope and truth. The voices of Chaz and Mark, disguised and unrecognizable, would bring the teachings of the Bible to life, offering guidance and wisdom to the newfound believers scattered across the globe.

Dr. Goldman's message buzzed through on the network, his words infused with an infectious enthusiasm. "I've witnessed something extraordinary here. The world is changing, and we must be ready to lead the way."

Nadia turned to her colleagues, her eyes shining with determination. "We're not just going to react anymore. We're going to set the narrative. We're going to teach, inspire, and lead. This is our chance to push back against the darkness."

Chaz clapped his hands together, a grin spreading across his face. "Let's do it. Let's bring the light to every corner of this world."

Mark nodded in agreement, his voice steady and resolute. "And let's not forget, we're countering Vale's lies. Every word of truth we spread is a strike against his deception."

The team set to work, their energy and creativity fueling the project. The animated character, a friendly and engaging figure, took shape on the screens, ready to deliver its first message of hope.

As the first episode was broadcast, the response was immediate and overwhelming. Messages of gratitude and curiosity flooded CALEB's channels, with viewers from all corners of the earth tuning in to hear the teachings of Jesus Christ.

In their secure headquarters, The Resistance watched as their new offensive took root. They were no longer just defenders; they were now leaders in a movement of truth and light, guiding countless souls through the tumultuous times of the Tribulation. With each broadcast, they were not just countering Vale's falsehoods; they were building a community of faith, strong and resilient, ready to face whatever challenges lay ahead.

Chapter 54

David sat quietly in the driver's seat, his gaze fixed on the majestic Abraham Lincoln Memorial in the distance, a symbol of strength and resilience. The weight of the situation pressed heavily on him, casting a shadow over the serene setting. He turned to look at Becca, her face illuminated by the soft glow of the streetlights, as she shook her head in disbelief at the list of names he had handed her.

"There's no way Noah is involved," Becca insisted, her voice tinged with a mix of disbelief and conviction. "I've known him for years."

David nodded slowly, understanding her reluctance to suspect a trusted colleague. "I felt the same way about Liz," he admitted, his voice low. "But one of them is lying or otherwise compromised."

The air in the car felt thick with tension and unspoken fears. Becca's question hung in the air, "What do you want to do?"

David's mind raced with plans and contingencies, but his heart was heavy with concern for Becca. He knew the dangers she faced in her role, the kind of assignments that would test her limits. He prayed silently for her safety, wishing he could shield her from the perils of their reality.

"I've got something in mind, but it's not going to be easy," he finally said, his voice steady despite the turmoil inside.

As he spoke, David's thoughts drifted to a life that could have been – a life untouched by the chaos of the Tribulation. He wished they had met in simpler times, before the world had been thrown into turmoil. In his heart, he knew their time on Earth would be fleeting, but he clung to the promise of eternity in heaven. That promise was a beacon of hope in the darkness, a reminder that their struggles were not in vain.

He glanced at Becca again, her profile etched with determination and strength. In her, he saw a kindred spirit, a fellow warrior in the fight for what was right. Despite the uncertainty of their path, he felt a deep connection to her, forged in the fires of shared trials and a common purpose.

As they sat in silence, the Lincoln Memorial standing tall in the distance, David made a silent vow to stand by

Becca, to support her in every way he could. Their journey was fraught with danger, but together, they would navigate the treacherous waters of the Tribulation, holding fast to their faith and to each other.

David sat at a secluded table in a quiet café, the hum of distant conversations creating a veil of privacy. He watched as Liz approached, her steps confident yet graceful. She greeted him with a warm, familiar smile, one that stirred memories of a past that seemed like another lifetime.

"David, it's good to see you," Liz said as she took a seat across from him. Her eyes held a hint of nostalgia, a reflection of shared history.

David returned the smile, though his was tinged with a sense of purpose. "Thanks for meeting me, Liz. I appreciate your help with this."

David's phone buzzed on the table. He and Liz both glanced at it, the message read, "9 pm, behind Jackie's Diner on Missouri Ave." David quickly swiped away the message.

He proceeded to feed her false information about two names on the list she had given him. His voice was steady, his gaze direct, as he wove a convincing narrative. "I need your help tracking down any other corporations in Dubai these two are involved with," he said, watching her reaction closely.

Liz nodded, her expression serious. "I'll see what I can find out. I'm worried about you, what's going on?"

David's voice dropped to the level of a whisper. "I shouldn't be telling you this, I don't want any trouble to come your way," he shared. "But, I have a source who has devastating information about Lucien Morreau. I think we'll finally have the upper hand to take him down."

"I'll keep it our secret, David. Let me know what I can do to help."

"I know I can count on you, Liz. You've always been there for me."

The conversation shifted as Liz touched David's arm gently. "I miss the days when we used to date," she confessed softly. "I've been praying for you, you know."

David felt a pang of something undefinable – a mix of nostalgia, regret, and gratitude. "Liz, I'm involved with someone right now," he said gently, meeting her gaze. "But I still care deeply for you as a friend."

They exchanged small talk, reminiscing briefly about simpler times, yet David's mind was elsewhere, calculating the next move in their intricate game of chess.

As they parted ways, Liz promised to get back to him with information in a couple of days. David watched her leave, a complex mix of emotions swirling within him. He knew he was playing a dangerous game, one that required deception and trust in equal measure. Yet, in the grand scheme of their mission, every move was critical, every piece vital.

As he sat alone at the table, David's thoughts turned to Becca and the path they were walking together. He felt a renewed sense of determination, a resolve to protect not only their mission but also the bond they shared. In a world where trust was a rare commodity, he knew that the connections they forged were their greatest strength.

With a deep breath, David stood up, ready to face the next challenge. The game was in motion, and he was a key player. The stakes were high, but he was not alone.

Chapter 55

The alley behind Jackie's Diner was a narrow, forgotten stretch of urban decay, a stark contrast to the warm, inviting glow of the diner's neon sign. The walls, a patchwork of faded graffiti and peeling paint, whispered stories of a neighborhood that had seen better days. Puddles from a recent rain shimmered under the sparse light from flickering street lamps, casting eerie reflections on the damp ground.

David sat motionless in the dark room of the abandoned apartment building, his eyes fixed on the scene below through night vision goggles. The room was a relic of a bygone era, with peeling wallpaper and a musty smell that spoke of years of neglect. A faint draft whistled through the cracked windows, but David barely noticed, his entire being focused on the alley.

Back at the Resistance's headquarters, Nadia and Becca huddled around monitors, watching the live feed from the webcams David had strategically installed. The cameras, hidden among the debris and shadows, offered multiple angles of the alley, turning it into a stage where a dangerous play was about to unfold.

The car, an old sedan, sat idling in the alley, its exhaust fumes mingling with the damp night air. It was a lure, a carefully placed piece in a larger game of deception and intrigue.

At precisely 9:12 pm, two men entered the alley. Their movements were cautious, deliberate, as they scanned their surroundings with the practiced ease of predators. The faint glow of their silenced pistols was just visible under their coats as they approached the car.

David's heart pounded in his chest, a silent drumbeat in the stillness of the room. He watched, breath held, as the men peered into the car. The moment stretched, taut as a wire, before snapping as the men realized the trap.

With a fluidity born of urgency, they retreated, disappearing into the night as quickly as they had appeared. David's heart sank, a heavy weight of disappointment and frustration settling in his chest.

In the headquarters, Nadia and Becca exchanged a look of grim understanding. The plan was successful, but they knew David would be heartbroken knowing an old friend turned on him.

David remained in the dark room, the night vision goggles now a green window to a scene of desolation. The alley, a place of revelation, lay empty, its secrets carried away into the night.

He felt a profound sense of heartbreak, not just for the former friend who betrayed him, but for the path that had led him here, to this moment of solitude amidst the shadows of a world that was unraveling at the seams.

David's phone rang, piercing the silence of the room. He glanced at the screen – it was Liz. With a sense of foreboding, he answered.

"David," Liz's voice came through, tinged with a mocking sweetness. "When did you figure it out?"

David remained silent, his mind racing. Instead of answering, he asked, "What are you doing, Liz?"

Her tone shifted, adopting a mocking meekness. "Oh, David, I've missed you so much. God placed you back in my life for a reason." Then, just as quickly, her voice hardened. "David, for someone who can read liars as a profession, you really fell hard for my Christian convert schtick. You're just as gullible as you were when we dated years ago."

David's jaw tightened, but he kept his emotions in check. "What are you up to, Liz?" he asked again, more firmly.

There was a brief pause before she replied, her voice now cold and matter-of-fact. "I got an offer I couldn't refuse. I'll be seeing you again, David."

Before he could respond, the line went dead. David sat in stunned silence, the phone still pressed to his ear. He quickly dialed Becca.

"Becca, Liz just called me," he said urgently as soon as she answered.

Becca's voice was tense. "We couldn't trace the call. We had DC Metro Police on standby outside her apartment. When we confirmed she was behind it, they went in, but she gave them the slip. She's in the wind, David. We don't know where she is or where she's going."

David felt a chill run down his spine. Liz, someone he had once trusted, was now a threat – a dangerous unknown in a world already teetering on the edge of chaos. He knew the stakes were high, and Liz's betrayal added a personal dimension to the already complex web of global intrigue they were navigating.

"Keep me updated, Becca," David said, his voice steady despite the turmoil inside. "We need to stay one step ahead."

He ended the call and looked out the window at the darkened alley below, a symbolic reflection of the shadowy path that lay ahead. David knew that the road to uncovering the truth would be fraught with danger and deception. But he also knew that the fight for what was right, for the light in the midst of darkness, was a fight worth pursuing, no matter the cost.

Chapter 56

T he makeshift headquarters of the Resistance, a nondescript building in a forgotten part of the city, had one redeeming feature – a flat roof that offered a panoramic view of the urban landscape. Here, under a sky streaked with the colors of dawn, Becca and Victor Rodriguez sat side by side, each holding a steaming cup of coffee.

The air was cool and crisp, a gentle breeze carrying the faint sounds of the waking city. Becca turned to Rodriguez, her eyes reflecting the soft light of the morning sun. She had always admired his strength and resilience, but today, there was a new softness in her gaze, a warmth that spoke of shared understanding and camaraderie.

Rodriguez took a sip of his coffee, savoring the rich, bold flavor before speaking. "I had a talk with Chaz," he began, his voice carrying a note of something new, something akin to wonder. "It was... life-changing, Becca."

Becca leaned in, her interest piqued. "Tell me about it," she encouraged, her tone gentle.

He looked out over the city, his eyes distant yet bright. "I've been carrying this weight, you know? All the things I've done, seen... I thought they had broken me beyond repair." He paused, collecting his thoughts. "But Chaz, he showed me something else, something I never thought was possible for me."

"And what's that?" Becca asked, her voice soft.

"Hope. Redemption. A new beginning." Rodriguez's voice was thick with emotion. "He talked to me about Jesus, about His grace and love. How it's never too late for anyone, no matter what they've done."

Becca's face lit up with a radiant smile, her heart swelling with joy for her friend. "That's incredible, Victor. I'm so happy for you."

Rodriguez turned to her, a genuine smile breaking through. "I feel like I've been given a second chance, Becca. A chance to start over, to find peace. I've decided to follow this path, to see where this faith takes me."

Becca reached out, placing a supportive hand on his shoulder. "This is a new journey, Victor. And it's a beautiful one. You're not alone in this. We're here for you, every step of the way."

"What about you, Becca? How are you doing?"

Becca sat still, her gaze distant, as she spoke softly about the heart-wrenching challenge of leaving her daughter behind for missions.

"Every time I gear up, there's this heavy feeling in my chest, knowing I'm leaving her," she confessed, her voice tinged with a mix of determination and sorrow. "She's my world, and the thought of not being there for her, of missing even a moment of her life, it tears at me. But I also know that what I'm doing is for the Lord. It's just ... it's hard."

She paused, her eyes reflecting the inner turmoil of a mother torn between duty and the deep, instinctual need to be with her child. "It's a constant battle within me, balancing the love for my daughter with the responsibility I feel towards this mission. Each goodbye is a reminder of the stakes we're facing, and the hope that one day, she'll understand the sacrifices made for a greater good."

"That's a lot to carry, Becca. God has placed a lot on your shoulders, your daughter will understand."

The two sat in comfortable silence for a moment, each lost in their thoughts, the city slowly coming to life below them. The sun climbed higher, casting a golden glow over the rooftops.

Rodriguez took another sip of his coffee, a sense of calm washing over him. "Thanks, Becca. It means a lot, having you and the team's support."

Becca nodded, her smile unwavering. "We're a family, Victor. We stick together, through everything."

The peaceful moment on the rooftop was abruptly interrupted by the simultaneous pinging of their cell phones. Becca and Rodriguez exchanged a glance, each instinctively reaching for their devices. The screen of Becca's phone displayed a new message notification, its contents briefly illuminated in the soft morning light.

"It looks like the family is getting together for a little meeting," Becca remarked, her tone shifting from the contemplative mood of their rooftop conversation to one of professional readiness.

Rodriguez nodded, his expression turning serious as he read the message on his own phone. "Xander's calling us in. Must be something important."

They both stood up, the tranquility of the morning momentarily set aside as they prepared to re-enter the world of strategic planning and covert operations.

Chapter 57

T he atmosphere in the Kilo Team headquarters was charged with a mix of tension and anticipation as Becca and Rodriguez entered. The room, usually buzzing with the low hum of activity and conversation, fell into a respectful silence as Xander, Noah, and the rest of the team turned their attention to the newcomers.

Xander, standing at the front with a commanding presence, greeted them with a nod. "Welcome back," he said, his voice firm yet carrying an undercurrent of warmth. "First off, congratulations on the success in Egypt. Your efforts were exemplary."

The team exchanged brief, knowing glances, acknowledging the compliment but aware that such meetings were rarely just for commendation. They were right. Xander's expression turned grave as he continued.

"However, we've received new intel. Five high-value targets escaped the camp before our strike. They're currently en route to the United States, aboard a vessel nearing Virginia Beach. Their intent is alarming – they're planning to disperse a highly contagious variant of smallpox at various populous locations across the country."

A ripple of concern passed through the team. The stakes were clear and urgent.

Xander clicked a remote, and the screen behind him lit up with a satellite image of the Atlantic Ocean, a red dot indicating the vessel's last known position. "Your mission is a boat interdiction, approximately 200 miles offshore. Time is of the essence. We're going to team up with SEAL Team 4. Your job is to handle the terrorists. Team 4 will help clear and provide security. We need to stop these terrorists before they make landfall."

Noah stepped forward, his eyes scanning the team. "This is a high-risk operation. We'll need to be swift, precise, and prepared for heavy resistance. We can't let this virus reach the mainland."

Becca felt a surge of determination. The mission resonated with her deeply, knowing the potential catastrophe they were racing to prevent. She exchanged a look with Rodriguez, a silent agreement that they were in this together, ready to face whatever challenges lay ahead.

The room was abuzz with the energy of imminent action as Xander concluded his briefing. "I'll leave it to you for operational planning. Time is tight, so figure it out quickly," he said, his tone underscoring the urgency of the situation.

Noah immediately took charge, his demeanor focused and authoritative. "Jack, pull up the live satellite feed," he commanded. The large screen at the front of the room flickered to life, displaying a detailed image of the ocean with a red dot steadily moving towards the coast.

"Alright, team," Noah began, pointing to the screen. "We're joining forces with SEAL Team 4 for this operation. We'll use high-speed boats to intercept the ship. Our approach will be from the rear to minimize detection."

The team leaned in, their eyes fixed on the screen as Noah outlined the plan. "Once on deck, we have three key areas to secure. First, we take the bridge. Control of the ship is our top priority. Second, we sweep the crew quarters. Our primary objective is to locate and neutralize the terrorists. Finally, we disable the ship and leave it for the Navy to handle."

He turned to Becca, "You have operational control. The SEALs will assist in clearing the ship and provide security. Once our mission is complete, they'll take over."

Mikey, always keen on details, asked, "Who's leading SEAL Team 4?"

Noah's lips curled into a half-smile. "Shane Wolf."

Carter let out a laugh, a mix of surprise and excitement. "Wolf? Oh, this is going to be fun."

Becca, intrigued by Carter's reaction, asked, "Fun good?"

Carter nodded enthusiastically. "Oh yeah. Wolf is a top-notch operator. He's the kind of guy you want on your side in a fight like this."

The team's mood shifted from focused intensity to a more confident, almost eager anticipation. The presence of a respected figure like Shane Wolf added an extra layer of assurance to the mission.

Noah continued, "We'll rendezvous with SEAL Team 4 at these coordinates." He pointed to a spot on the map. "From there, we move in fast and hard. This operation requires precision and speed. We can't afford any mistakes."

The team members nodded in agreement, their faces a blend of determination and readiness. They understood the stakes and the need for flawless execution.

As the meeting wrapped up, the team dispersed to finalize preparations. Becca took a moment to review the satellite images and the ship's layout. Her mind was already racing through scenarios, planning each move with meticulous care.

Chapter 58

The RHIB cut through the dark waters, its engine a low growl against the quiet of the night. Becca sat, her gaze fixed on the horizon, her mind a whirlwind of strategy and anticipation. The weight of responsibility pressed heavily on her shoulders, each decision she made carrying the potential for life or death.

Her hands, clad in tactical gloves, gripped her weapon with a practiced ease, yet her heart raced with the adrenaline of the impending operation. This was more than just another mission; it was a test of her leadership under the most extreme conditions.

Shane Wolf's voice crackled through the headset, breaking the silence. "Alpha, this is Bravo, what's your status?"

Noah, ever the calm and collected leader, responded promptly. "We're 15 mikes from you. How copy?"

"Lima Charlie, copy 15 mikes," Shane replied. "Satellite imagery shows three roving patrols on deck.

When we hit the boat, we'll take starboard, you take port. Have Mikey take out the rear patrol and we'll take the patrols on the bow. See you in 15 mikes."

Becca's mind raced, visualizing the ship's layout and the positions of the patrols. The plan was clear, but the sea was unpredictable, and so were the terrorists. She knew that timing and stealth were crucial.

As the two RHIBs converged, Becca felt a surge of confidence. They were a formidable team, each member an expert in their field. She glanced at her teammates – Noah, Mikey, Rodriguez, Carter, and Tyler – each one focused and ready for action.

The sea spray hit her face, a stark reminder of the reality of their situation. They were about to storm a ship in the dead of night, facing an unknown number of hostiles. The risk was high, but so was the necessity of their mission.

Becca's thoughts turned to the terrorists on board the ship. They were planning an attack that could cost countless lives. Stopping them was not just a mission; it was a moral imperative. She felt the weight of that responsibility, but also the resolve to see it through.

As the RHIBs neared the target, Becca's senses heightened. Every training scenario she had ever been through played in her mind, preparing her for the task ahead. She checked her gear one last time, ensuring everything was in place.

The night was dark, the sea was rough, but their determination was unwavering. Becca knew that the next few minutes would be critical. She took a deep breath, steadying herself. This was it. The moment of truth.

The RHIBs slowed as they approached the ship, the darkness their ally. Becca's heart pounded in her chest, not with fear, but with the fierce determination of a warrior ready for battle. This was her element, and she was ready to lead her team to victory.

The night air was thick with tension as Mikey, call sign Alpha 2, scaled the ladder with the agility and silence of a seasoned operative. Reaching the top, he quickly surveyed the deck, his trained eyes spotting the rear roving patrol almost instantly. His voice, calm and controlled, broke the silence over the comms. "Alpha 2 in position."

From the other side of the ship, two SEAL operators, Bravo 4 and Bravo 6, confirmed their readiness. "Bravo 4 in position." "Bravo 6 in position."

Noah's voice, authoritative and clear, came through the headset. "Execute, execute, execute."

In a synchronized ballet of precision and lethality, three silenced gunshots rang out, almost imperceptible against the backdrop of the ocean's gentle hum. Each shot found its mark, neutralizing the deck patrols with clinical efficiency. The radio crackled with three succinct confirmations. "All clear."

With the deck secured, the rest of Alpha and Bravo teams made their ascent. The climb was swift, each member moving with a purpose, their bodies honed instruments of warfare.

Bravo 1, Shane Wolf, took command of the situation. "Bravo 6, Bravo 8, provide security." His voice was firm, leaving no room for doubt or hesitation. The designated SEALs moved into position, their eyes scanning the surroundings, alert to any potential threat.

The remaining members of Alpha and Bravo teams converged on the bridge. Their movements were a well-rehearsed choreography, each step and turn executed with practiced precision. They entered the bridge with a burst of controlled energy, weapons at the ready, prepared for any resistance.

The bridge was dimly lit, the only illumination coming from the array of screens and control panels. The team fanned out, covering every angle, securing the area with a professional calmness that spoke of countless similar operations.

Noah and Wolf, the leaders of their respective teams, exchanged a brief nod, an unspoken acknowledgment of the mission's progress. The atmosphere was charged, each team member acutely aware of the stakes. They were deep in enemy territory, on a ship carrying terrorists intent on unleashing a deadly virus. Failure was not an option.

The bridge, now under their control, was the first critical step in neutralizing the threat. But the mission was far from over. The ship was large, and the terrorists could be anywhere. Time was of the essence, and every second counted.

The tension in the air was palpable as Noah, call sign Alpha 1, quickly assigned roles. "Bravo 5, Alpha 6, you have the bridge," he commanded, his voice steady but urgent. Tyler, known as Alpha 6, nodded in acknowledgment, his eyes scanning the room for potential threats.

"Bravo 1, take your team and start clearing below decks. Alpha will handle the crew quarters," Noah continued, his mind racing through the layout of the ship and potential hotspots for enemy engagement.

Bravo team moved with purpose, descending into the bowels of the ship. Their footsteps were muffled, their movements a blend of stealth and speed. The ship's interior was a labyrinth of corridors and compartments, each corner a potential ambush point.

Meanwhile, Alpha team began their methodical clearing of the crew quarters. The quarters were cramped and dimly lit, a maze of narrow hallways and small rooms. Every door they approached was a new risk, every room a potential trap.

Rodriguez and Becca, moving in tandem, turned a corner and were met with the unexpected. A guard, armed with an AK47, stood ready. The encounter was sudden, the distance between them minimal. Rodriguez reacted instinctively, his training taking over as he fired two shots towards the guard.

But the guard was quick too. His weapon roared in the confined space, a slug tearing through the air and finding its mark. Rodriguez was hit, the impact knocking him to the ground. The slug had entered his side at a bad angle, blood beginning to seep through his clothing.

Becca's voice was a mix of urgency and fear as she shouted into her headset, "Alpha 4 is down, I repeat, Alpha 4 is down. Took a shot, he's bleeding."

Noah's response was immediate. "Mikey, go assist now!" His voice was a commanding force amidst the chaos. He then radioed Bravo 1, "We need two of your guys up here to assist with clearing the crew quarters."

Bravo team, ever efficient, quickly sent two of their members to aid Alpha team. The two Bravo operatives moved with speed, their weapons at the ready, as they joined the effort to secure the crew quarters.

The ship's narrow corridors echoed with the sounds of their movement, a symphony of tactical precision. Each room they cleared added to the tension, the knowledge that the terrorists could be holed up anywhere, waiting to strike.

Rodriguez lay on the ground, his breathing labored, pain etched on his face. Becca was by his side, her battle medic training kicking in as she applied pressure to the wound, trying to stem the flow of blood. Her hands were steady, but her eyes betrayed her concern for her teammate.

Mikey arrived, his presence a reassurance in the midst of the crisis. He knelt beside Rodriguez, quickly assessing the situation. "Hang in there, Rodriguez," he said, his voice calm but firm. "We've got you."

Chapter 59

The atmosphere in the cramped hallway of the ship was heavy with grief and shock. Becca knelt beside Rodriguez, her hands still pressed against his wound, though she knew it was futile. His final words echoed in her mind, a bittersweet mix of humor and faith even in his last moments. "Thank you for your friendship... I'll see you in Heaven... Don't be jealous I get to meet Jesus first." His voice, once filled with strength and camaraderie, faded into silence.

Rodriguez's eyes, once alert and full of life, now stared emptily at the ceiling. Becca felt a surge of sorrow, her heart heavy with the loss of not just a teammate, but a friend. She gently closed his eyes, a silent farewell to a brave soul.

Mikey returned, his expression one of determination, unaware of the tragic turn. "We're going to get you home, buddy," he said, moving towards Rodriguez. His words halted as he saw the scene before him. The realization hit him hard, his face contorting with grief.

Becca looked up at Mikey, her eyes filled with tears. "It's too late, Mikey. He's gone," she said, her voice barely above a whisper. The finality of her words hung heavily in the air.

Noah's voice crackled over the comms, breaking the somber silence. "This is an empty hole. They're not here. Alpha 6 went through the papers on the bridge, and their guests never showed up. We have to assume they're in the wind. Bravo 1, the ship is yours. Good score on the weapons shipment in the hull, your bosses are going to be happy about that. Alpha team, consolidate on me. Bring Alpha 4 with you, we're exfilling."

The team moved into action, their training overriding the shock and grief. They worked together to carefully move Rodriguez's body, ensuring they treated their fallen comrade with the respect and dignity he deserved. The weight of his loss was not just physical as they carried him; it was a profound emotional burden, each step a reminder of the harsh realities of their mission.

As they moved through the ship, the silence was a stark contrast to the earlier chaos of gunfire and commands. Each team member was lost in their own thoughts, reflecting on the risks they faced, the sacrifices made, and the unpredictable nature of their duty.

The exfiltration was methodical, each member of the team supporting the others as they made their way back to their extraction point. The sea air was a cold slap against their faces, a harsh reminder of the reality they were returning to.

The atmosphere at the Kilo Team headquarters was somber as Alpha team returned, each member carrying the weight of loss in their silence. The usually bustling base felt unusually still, as if in respect for the gravity of their loss. Rodriguez's absence was a gaping void, felt by everyone who knew him.

Xander, their commanding officer, stood waiting for them. His usual stern demeanor softened by the shared grief. As the team disembarked, he approached them with a solemnity that spoke volumes. His eyes, usually sharp and assessing, now held a depth of empathy and understanding.

"Team," Xander began, his voice steady but tinged with emotion. "I know there's nothing I can say that will make this easier. Rodriguez was more than a teammate;

he was a brother to us all. His sacrifice will not be forgotten."

The team, so disciplined and stoic, allowed their guard to drop in this moment of collective mourning. Some nodded in silent agreement, others looked away, their eyes glistening with unshed tears. The loss of Rodriguez was a stark reminder of the risks they faced every day, the price of the path they had chosen.

Xander continued, "We'll debrief tomorrow. For now, take the time you need. Remember Rodriguez as he was - a brave and dedicated soldier, a man who stood by us all, unwavering in his commitment."

As Xander spoke, memories of Rodriguez flashed through Becca's mind - his laughter echoing through the barracks, his unwavering support during missions, and his unshakeable faith even in the face of danger. It was these memories that brought a small, sad smile to her face amidst the grief.

Becca sat alone in the dimly lit corner of the common room, her gaze fixed on the flickering flame of a solitary candle set upon a small table. The room was quiet, save for the occasional murmur of conversation and the soft clinking of utensils as her teammates tried to find solace in a late-night meal. But for Becca, the world seemed to have come to a standstill, the loss of Rodriguez creating a void that felt both vast and intensely personal.

She wrapped her arms around herself, as if trying to hold together the pieces of her shattered composure. Rodriguez's death had hit her harder than she had anticipated. They had been through so much together, had shared moments of triumph and despair, had saved each other's lives more times than she could count. And now, he was gone.

In her heart, Becca knew Rodriguez was in a better place. His faith had been unwavering, a beacon of hope in the darkest of times. She remembered their conversations about heaven, about the peace and joy that awaited them after their earthly struggles. But that knowledge did little to ease the ache in her heart.

She had lost comrades before, each loss leaving its own scar. But Rodriguez's death felt different. Maybe it was the suddenness of it, the brutal finality that had snatched him away without warning. Or perhaps it was the realization that with each loss, a part of her own spirit seemed to erode, leaving her feeling more isolated, more vulnerable.

Becca's thoughts drifted to the mission, replaying the events over and over in her mind. Could she have done something differently? Was there a moment, a decision, that might have changed the outcome? The rational part of her knew that in their line of work, the margin between life and death was often razor-thin, dictated by chance as much as by skill or planning. But that knowledge did little to quell the rising tide of guilt and what-ifs.

A gentle hand on her shoulder brought her back to the present. She looked up to find Noah standing beside her, his expression a mirror of her own grief and confusion. Without a word, he sat down beside her, offering silent companionship in the face of their shared loss.

As the night wore on, Becca found a measure of comfort in the presence of her team. They were a family, bound together by a shared purpose and the trials they had endured. Together, they would mourn Rodriguez, honor his memory, and continue the fight he had given his life for.

But in the quiet moments, when she was alone with her thoughts, Becca couldn't shake the feeling of emptiness, the sense that a part of her had been irretrievably lost. She knew the pain would ease with time, that she would find a way to move forward. But for now, she allowed herself to grieve, to feel the full weight of the loss that had forever changed her world.

Xander called everyone to the briefing room. The team members, still grappling with the aftermath of their last mission, gathered around the central briefing table, their expressions a mix of fatigue and determination.

Xander stood at the head of the table, his face etched with lines of concern. He cleared his throat, drawing the attention of the room. "I've called you all here for an update on our ongoing situation," he began, his voice steady despite the gravity of the news he was about to deliver.

"The terrorists we believed were on that ship carrying the smallpox virus... they weren't there. We now have new intelligence suggesting they've changed their route and are attempting to cross the border from Mexico into the United States."

A murmur of frustration and concern rippled through the team. The thought of such a deadly threat slipping through their fingers was a hard pill to swallow, especially on the heels of their recent loss.

Xander continued, "Homeland Security is taking the lead on this. They're mobilizing teams along the border and coordinating with Mexican authorities to intercept these terrorists before they can enter the country."

Becca felt a knot of tension in her stomach. The stakes were incredibly high, and the thought of a biological attack on U.S. soil was chilling. She glanced around the room, seeing her own apprehension reflected in the faces of her teammates.

Jack, standing beside Xander, added, "We're on standby to assist if needed, but for now, our role is to support Homeland Security's efforts from here."

The room fell silent, each team member lost in their own thoughts. The threat of a smallpox outbreak was a grim reminder of the dangerous world they lived in, a world where the line between safety and chaos was perilously thin.

Xander's voice broke the silence. "I know this is a lot to take in, especially after what we've just been through."

As the meeting concluded, the team dispersed, each member carrying the weight of the mission ahead. Becca lingered for a moment, her mind racing with the possible scenarios they might face. The threat was real and imminent, and she knew that they would need to be at their best to face what was coming.

Chapter 60

The screen flickered to life, revealing the unmistakable figure of Rex Savage, the iconic rock n' roll star known for his rebellious spirit and larger-than-life persona. He was seated in a dimly lit room, the buzz of a tattoo machine audible in the background. His face, always so animated and full of life, was now etched with a sense of solemnity and conviction.

"Hey, world," Rex began, his voice carrying that familiar rasp of rockstar charisma. "You know me, I've always lived on the edge, always done things my way. But today, I'm taking it a step further." He gestured towards his forehead, where a tattoo artist was meticulously inking a design. "This isn't just any tattoo. This is my UnityCoin mark, right here where everyone can see it."

The camera zoomed in, capturing the intricate details of the UnityCoin symbol as it took shape on Rex's forehead. "Lucien Morreau, man, he's the real deal," Rex continued, a hint of reverence in his tone. "This mark, it's not just for transactions. It's a statement, a declaration that I stand with Lucien and his vision."

As the video streamed across the internet, it sparked a wildfire of reactions. Influencers and celebrities, each with their own unique following, began uploading their videos. They flaunted their new UnityCoin tattoos, some on their hands, others daringly on their foreheads, echoing Rex's sentiment of allegiance and rebellion.

The trend caught on like a fever. Across major cities, long lines formed in front of sleek, futuristic machines branded with the UnityCoin logo. These machines, appearing almost overnight, offered the promise of being part of something bigger, something revolutionary. People from all walks of life, driven by a mix of curiosity, conviction, and the allure of being part of a global movement, eagerly inserted their hands into the machine. The buzz of the tattoo mechanism became a symbol of unity and rebellion, a physical mark of belonging to a new world order.

As the tattoos were etched into skin, the UnityCoin symbol became more than just a mark. It became a symbol of a rapidly changing world, a world where allegiance to Lucien Morreau and his vision was worn not just in the heart, but visibly on the body. The phenomenon spread, capturing millions in its wake, each person proudly displaying their mark, a testament to the influence and reach of Lucien Morreau's charismatic pull.

In a small, dimly-lit living room, a group of people gathered around an old television, the flickering images casting shadows on their worried faces. The news anchor's voice filled the room, discussing the latest developments in the UnityCoin saga.

"Reports are coming in from all over the globe," the anchor said, his tone a mix of disbelief and subtle coercion. "People who refuse to get the UnityCoin mark are finding themselves increasingly isolated. As more businesses adopt UnityCoin as their exclusive transaction method, those without the mark are unable to purchase basic necessities."

On the screen, footage showed long lines outside stores, with marked individuals being ushered through while those without the mark were turned away, their faces a mix of defiance and despair. The camera panned to a woman holding a small child, her eyes brimming with tears as she pleaded with a store manager, only to be coldly dismissed.

The scene shifted to a panel discussion where a well-dressed commentator spoke with an air of condescension. "It's a simple choice, really. Get the mark and participate in society, or don't and face the consequences. Why should the rest of us suffer because of a few people's stubbornness?"

Back in the living room, a middle-aged man turned off the television, his expression grim. "They're making it sound like we're the problem," he said, his voice tinged with frustration. "As if not wanting that mark is some kind of selfish act."

A young woman, her face drawn and tired, added, "It's everywhere on social media too. People are calling us selfish, saying we're endangering the economy. They don't understand, it's not just a mark. It's about our beliefs, our freedom to choose."

An elderly man, sitting quietly in the corner, spoke up, his voice steady but filled with sadness. "It's getting harder every day. They're turning society against us, making it seem like we're the enemy for holding on to our principles."

The group fell into a somber silence, each lost in their thoughts about the rapidly changing world. Outside, the streets were quiet, a stark contrast to the bustling activity

414

of those bearing the UnityCoin mark. Inside, the group felt the weight of their decision, a choice made from conviction but fraught with increasing hardship and isolation.

Chapter 61

T he situation in Israel had escalated beyond anyone's expectations. The two witnesses, steadfast in their mission, continued to preach with an unyielding fervor that both fascinated and infuriated the masses. Israel, initially attempting to ignore the duo, found itself grappling with a situation that defied all logic and understanding.

Vigilantes, fueled by frustration and disbelief, had tried to forcibly remove the witnesses. Each attempt ended in failure, with aggressors consumed by a mysterious fire that seemed to emanate from the mouths of the witnesses themselves. The pair appeared almost otherworldly, their needs for sustenance minimal, and when they did require food, it materialized at their feet as if by divine provision.

Their preaching was relentless. When one rested, the other took up the mantle, their voices echoing through the Temple Mount, reaching every ear with messages of repentance and salvation through Jesus Christ. The government's efforts to erect barriers to silence or contain them proved futile, as each obstruction was supernaturally demolished.

Chief Rabbi Yosef Mendel, a respected figure in the Jewish community, viewed the presence of the witnesses as a direct challenge to the foundations of Judaism. The claim that Jesus was the Son of God was intolerable in his eyes, and he demanded their immediate removal.

In a desperate move, Israel deployed its elite special forces to the Temple Mount, hoping that a show of military strength would intimidate the witnesses into leaving. However, the witnesses responded by calling down a fierce storm, the winds and rain driving the soldiers back, leaving them drenched and demoralized.

In the dimly lit confines of his office, Prime Minister Daniel Roth sat behind his desk, his face a canvas of worry and contemplation. The phone on his desk rang, piercing the silence. He glanced at the caller ID and hesitated for a moment before answering. It was Lucien Morreau.

"Prime Minister Roth, this is Lucien Morreau," came the confident, almost charismatic voice from the other end.

"Mr. Morreau," Roth replied, his tone guarded. "I assume you're calling about the situation at the Temple Mount."

"Indeed, I am," Morreau said smoothly. "I've been following the events closely. It's quite the spectacle, isn't it? Two men, claiming to be divine messengers, causing such a stir."

Roth's grip tightened on the receiver. "It's more than a spectacle, Mr. Morreau. It's a crisis. They're disrupting the peace and challenging our authority."

"That's precisely why I'm calling, Prime Minister. I believe I can be of assistance," Morreau offered.

Roth raised an eyebrow. "And how do you propose to help, Mr. Morreau? We've tried everything – negotiations, force, even special operations. Nothing has worked."

Morreau's voice was laced with confidence. "I have... unique abilities, Prime Minister. Abilities that can resolve this situation without further chaos. I've dealt with extraordinary events before, as you well know."

Roth was skeptical. Morreau's reputation preceded him – a man of influence and power, yes, but also of mystery and unverified claims. "And what do you want in return, Mr. Morreau?"

"Nothing but goodwill, Prime Minister. Consider it a gesture of support to your government and the people of Israel," Morreau replied.

Roth pondered for a moment. The situation was desperate, and conventional methods had failed. Morreau was controversial, but the public was growing restless, and the international spotlight was increasingly uncomfortable.

"Alright, Mr. Morreau. If you believe you can help, come to Israel. But I must warn you, the situation here is unlike anything we've faced before."

"I understand, Prime Minister. I'll make the arrangements to arrive as soon as possible. You won't regret this decision," Morreau assured him.

As Roth hung up the phone, he couldn't shake off a sense of unease. He had just made a deal with a man shrouded in mystery, a man who claimed powers no one could verify. Roth looked out the window at the Jerusalem skyline, wondering if he had invited a solution or a greater problem to his nation's capital.

Chapter 62

The scene outside the Temple Mount was a tableau of anticipation and unease. Lucien Morreau's motorcade, sleek and imposing, pulled up with a quiet authority, drawing the eyes of the throngs of people who had gathered. They were an eclectic mix, some driven by faith, others by curiosity, all waiting to witness what felt like a confrontation ripped from the pages of ancient scripture.

Morreau emerged from his vehicle, his demeanor exuding a calculated confidence. He was flanked by Chief Rabbi Yosef Mendel and Prime Minister Daniel Roth, both of whom wore expressions of deep concern. As they made their way towards the Temple grounds, the crowd parted, a sea of faces marked by a blend of reverence and skepticism.

The two witnesses, standing in stark contrast with their simple sackcloth garments, turned to face Morreau as he approached. Their preaching, which had been fervent and unyielding, intensified in both volume and passion.

The first witness, his gaze locked onto Morreau with an intensity that seemed to transcend the physical space between them, raised his voice. It boomed across the Temple Mount, clear and resonant, carrying the weight of ages. "Hear, O people of Israel and all who dwell on the earth! This man who approaches, clothed in pride and deceit, is the harbinger of darkness. He is the beast spoken of in the sacred texts, but his time of reckoning has not yet come."

The second witness, his demeanor equally commanding, continued the proclamation, his voice harmonizing with his companion's. "This ground upon which we stand is hallowed, consecrated by the Most High. It is not a place for falsehood and manipulation. You, Lucien Morreau, are not welcome here. Your presence defiles the sanctity of this place."

Together, they spoke, their words intertwining like a sacred chant. "We stand here not by our own authority but by the will of the One who sent us. We are the voices crying out in the wilderness, preparing the way for the return of the King of Kings. We are the heralds of truth in an age of deception."

The first witness, his voice rising in fervor, declared, "The time is near when all shall see the true nature of this world. The veil of illusion will be lifted, and the hearts of many will be revealed. Those who walk in darkness, like this man before us, will be exposed by the light of truth."

The second witness added, "We call upon all who hear our voices to repent, to turn away from the deceptions of this world and seek the face of the Almighty. For in Him alone is salvation, in Him alone is hope."

Morreau, unfazed by the accusation, responded with a smooth, almost rehearsed calmness. "No, my friends, it is you who are not welcome. The people of Israel seek peace in their worship, and you are disturbing that peace. It's time for you to leave."

The air around the witnesses seemed to shimmer as they grew in presence, their figures almost transcending their human forms. They spoke in unison, their voices resonating across the Temple grounds, "There is but one true God – the Father, the Son, and the Holy Spirit. Beware of this man of evil, Lucien Morreau."

Morreau, attempting to assert his control, raised his hands and commanded, "I order you to leave these sacred grounds immediately."

The first witness, his voice booming like thunder, countered, "You have no power here, Morreau. Your very existence hangs by the thread of the Almighty's mercy."

The second witness then raised his hands skyward, his voice taking on a prophetic edge as he pronounced a chilling prophecy, "For the next ninety days, no rain shall fall upon the earth. The Mediterranean Sea shall turn to blood, its creatures perishing. Israel will suffer until it renounces the deceiver and repents."

As the second witness's words echoed across the Temple Mount, a hush fell over the crowd. Prime Minister Daniel Roth and Chief Rabbi Yosef Mendel, standing beside Lucien Morreau, exchanged glances filled with a mix of fear and disbelief. The gravity of the witnesses' prophecy was not lost on them; it was a declaration that threatened to shake the very foundations of their nation and the world.

Roth, a man usually composed and confident in the public eye, felt a cold shiver run down his spine. The words of the witnesses, delivered with such conviction and authority, seemed to cut through the air, leaving an indelible mark on all who heard them. He glanced at the sky involuntarily, half-expecting to see the first signs of the prophesied drought.

Beside him, Chief Rabbi Mendel's expression was one of deep concern, his eyes reflecting the turmoil within. As a religious leader, he was acutely aware of the significance of such prophecies. The idea that Israel would suffer for its association with Morreau, a man he had initially supported, was deeply troubling. The witnesses' message was clear: Israel had strayed from its spiritual path, and the consequences would be dire.

The Rabbi's mind raced with the implications of the prophecy. The turning of the Mediterranean Sea into blood, a plague reminiscent of the biblical exodus, was a terrifying prospect. It symbolized not just a physical calamity but a spiritual crisis for the nation of Israel. The thought that their suffering would continue until they collectively renounced Morreau and repented was a call to action that could not be ignored.

Roth, trying to maintain a semblance of control, whispered to Mendel, "What do we do?"

Mendel, his eyes still fixed on the two witnesses, responded in a low, troubled tone, "We must consult with our advisors, both spiritual and political. These are not ordinary men; their power is evident. We need wisdom beyond our own to navigate this."

As they stood there, the weight of the situation bearing down on them, both men realized that the challenge posed by the two witnesses was unlike any other.

Morreau, his face twisted in a mix of anger and disbelief, shouted back defiantly. But before he could finish, the first witness interrupted him, "You are not welcome on these holy grounds."

With a dramatic and forceful strike of his staff on the ground, the witness caused boils to erupt on the skin of Morreau and his companions. The sight was grotesque and terrifying, instantly turning the crowd's awe into fear.

Prime Minister Daniel Roth, standing just a few steps away, felt an excruciating pain erupt across his skin. Within moments, his flesh was marred by angry, oozing boils that seemed to appear out of nowhere.

Roth, a man accustomed to the pressures of leadership and the rigors of public life, was utterly unprepared for this physical affliction. The pain was intense, searing through his body like fire. He looked down at his hands, horror-stricken, as the boils swelled and burst, each one a small eruption of agony.

The shock on his face was palpable, a mixture of pain, disbelief, and fear. He had witnessed the supernatural power of the two witnesses, but never had he imagined that he would be a direct recipient of their divine retribution.

Morreau, now in visible pain and humiliation, turned and retreated hastily from the Temple grounds. The crowd, which had gathered to witness what they thought would be Morreau's triumphant confrontation, was now in a state of shock and confusion. Murmurs and gasps rippled through the masses as they watched these powerful men brought low by an unseen, divine force. The crowd, which had been silent in anticipation, now erupted in a cacophony of boos and jeers, their disillusionment with Morreau manifesting in vocal disapproval.

As the motorcade disappeared into the distance, the witnesses resumed their preaching, their message of repentance and divine warning echoing through the air. The crowd, still processing the surreal and terrifying events they had just witnessed, dispersed in a whirlwind of emotions, their minds racing with the implications of what had just unfolded on this extraordinary day.

<u>Epilogue</u>

I n the opulent confines of Lucien Morreau's Dubai residence, the atmosphere was thick with tension and frustration. Morreau, his face partially obscured by cold compresses, sat brooding in a luxurious armchair. The boils that marred his skin were a constant, painful reminder of his recent humiliation at the Temple in Jerusalem.

Gabriel Vale and Viktor Stahl stood before him, their expressions a mix of concern and anticipation. The room, usually a place of grandeur and power, felt stifling, charged with Morreau's barely contained rage.

Gabriel, with a hint of concern lacing his voice, turned to Lucien. "Lucien, the people are starting to question your abilities. The incident with the boils... it's causing doubts about your power to heal. We need you back on the program to reaffirm their faith in you. Your absence is fueling skepticism."

Lucien's expression darkened, his frustration evident. "I can't just make these boils disappear," he snapped, the pain and irritation from his affliction seeping into his tone. "I have to let them heal naturally. I'll return to the program when I'm ready, not a moment sooner."

Sensing Lucien's growing irritation, Gabriel quickly proposed a solution. "We can work around this. Let's shoot a video and use an AI filter to remove the boils digitally. It'll look like you've healed yourself. It's imperative we maintain the narrative of your powers."

Lucien's eyes narrowed as he considered Gabriel's suggestion. After a moment, he gave a curt nod, the wheels in his mind already turning on how to spin this setback to his advantage. "Fine," he conceded. "Set it up. We'll give them their miracle."

Viktor, ever the pragmatist, interjected, "Lucien, as much as I understand your desire for revenge, we must be realistic. The two witnesses... they're beyond our reach. Our efforts might be better spent on Vale Vision. We can use the platform to counteract their message, sway public opinion in our favor."

Gabriel, always the pragmatist, added. "Lucien, we can't ignore the facts. The Mediterranean turning to blood and the absence of rain since your encounter with the witnesses... it's causing a global uproar. People are scared, and they're starting to question your powers."

Before Morreau could respond, the door opened, and Liz Sinclair entered the room. Her presence was like a fresh breeze, momentarily easing the tension.

"Lucien, it's good to be back," Liz said with a confident smile. "I wish I could've stayed under cover longer, but David was getting too close."

Morreau's expression softened slightly at the sight of Liz. "You did well, Liz. It's unfortunate about David, but now we know where his loyalties lie."

Viktor glanced at Morreau, a silent acknowledgment of his earlier suspicion about David. Liz, sensing the shift in the room, quickly added, "I bring good news from China. We've managed to gather enough leverage over the Premier. With a little push, we can get UnityCoin approved there."

The news seemed to invigorate Morreau, a spark of his old ambition returning to his eyes. "Excellent, Liz. With China on board, our reach will be truly global. We'll have the world in the palm of our hand."

Liz added, her voice steady, "Reports are coming in of smallpox infections breaking out across the United States, and it's beginning to spread internationally."

Gabriel leaned forward, a glint of satisfaction in his eyes. "Excellent. This chaos is the perfect breeding ground for furthering our agenda. The more unstable the world becomes, the more they'll need our UnityCoin system."

Viktor, usually more reserved, allowed a thin smile to cross his lips. "It's working then. The fear and confusion will drive people to seek stability, and we will provide it. This is a crucial step in consolidating our power."

Lucien, who had been listening intently, nodded in agreement. "Yes, this is good. But we must be cautious. We don't want this to backfire on us. Liz, ensure that our media channels are prepared to spin this in our favor. We need to be seen as the solution, not the cause."

As the group began to discuss their next moves, the room's atmosphere shifted from one of defeat to one of plotting and scheming. The setback at the Temple was just that - a setback. For Lucien Morreau and his associates, the game was far from over.

Rise of the False Prophet is book 2 in the Final Revelation book series. Get the best-selling first book in the series, *Raptured Souls,* at your favorite bookseller!

Made in United States
Orlando, FL
12 March 2024

44691922R00264